W9-CMU-295

INDIAN RIVER CO. MAIN LIBRARY

3 2901 00383 4208

LP
F
KEN

Kenyon, Sherrilyn,
1965-
BAD attitude /
Sherrilyn Kenyon.

IRC Main Library
1600 21st Street
Vero Beach, Florida 32960

BAD
ATTITUDE

This Large Print Book carries the
Seal of Approval of N.A.V.H.

BAD ATTITUDE

Sherrilyn Kenyon

WHEELER PUBLISHING

Copyright © 2005 by Sherrilyn Kenyon

All rights reserved.

This book is a work of fiction. Names, characters, places and incidents are products of the author's imagination or are used fictitiously. Any resemblance to actual events or locales or persons, living or dead, is entirely coincidental.

Published in 2006 by arrangement with Pocket Books, a division of Simon & Schuster, Inc.

Wheeler Large Print Romance.

The text of this Large Print edition is unabridged. Other aspects of the book may vary from the original edition.

Set in 16 pt. Plantin by Christina S. Huff.

Printed in the United States on permanent paper.

Library of Congress Cataloging-in-Publication Data

Kenyon, Sherrilyn, 1965–
    BAD attitude / by Sherrilyn Kenyon.
      p. cm. — (Wheeler Publishing large print romance)
    ISBN 1-59722-161-9 (lg. print : hc : alk. paper)
    1. Americans — Iraq — Fiction. 2. Iraq — Fiction.
  3. Large type books. I. Title. II. Wheeler large print romance series.
    PS3563.A311145B33 2006
    813′.54—dc22
                                   2005034009

3 2901 00383 4208

For my mother,
who meant the entire world to me.

National Association for Visually Handicapped
------------------------- *serving the partially seeing*

As the Founder/CEO of NAVH, the only national health agency solely devoted to those who, although not totally blind, have an eye disease which could lead to serious visual impairment, I am pleased to recognize Thorndike Press* as one of the leading publishers in the large print field.

Founded in 1954 in San Francisco to prepare large print textbooks for partially seeing children, NAVH became the pioneer and standard setting agency in the preparation of large type.

Today, those publishers who meet our standards carry the prestigious "Seal of Approval" indicating high quality large print. We are delighted that Thorndike Press is one of the publishers whose titles meet these standards. We are also pleased to recognize the significant contribution Thorndike Press is making in this important and growing field.

Lorraine H. Marchi, L.H.D.
Founder/CEO
NAVH

* Thorndike Press encompasses the following imprints: Thorndike, Wheeler, Walker and Large Print Press.

Acknowledgments

My husband, brother, and sons, for being the center of my universe. For my friends, who are always, always there no matter what: Lo, Janet, Bryn, Loretta, Donna, Jennifer, and my wonderful posse: Alethea, Dee, and Nicole.

For all the fans and members of my groups, who are so generous with their support and laughs. And in particular for the RBLs and DH groups. You guys really rock!

For Lauren, Louise, and Maggie, for giving me the chance to do something off the beaten path and for believing in the idea so strongly. To Lauren (again), Nancy, and Megan for all the hard work you guys do on my behalf. It's always appreciated more than any of you will ever know.

For my father-in-law and husband, for all the Army information and the inner workings of government agencies. Lo, for all her Navy knowledge. And to Janet, for all the hours of research you do.

But most of all, for my mother, without

whom I would never have dreamed the impossible. You gave me the greatest gifts of all: life, sarcastic humor, love, and the ability to imagine other worlds. I miss you, Mom. I always will.

Prologue

Iraq, 2003

There wasn't anything on earth much hotter than the desert in August. Steele lay in the hole he'd dug in the sand under his tent to keep him sheltered in case of a mortar attack, trying to remember the cool, honeysuckle-scented breezes that used to ease the hot summers of his childhood.

If he lay here long enough, he could almost block out the sounds of army operations in the background. The sound of trucks moving, soldiers calling out to each other. The smell of blood, sweat, and fear. The feel of the hard, hot rifle biting into his side as he kept it tucked in beside him.

God, he just wanted to go home again.

His thoughts turned to Brian, who up until two days ago had shared this tent with him, and winced.

Maybe he didn't want to go home after all.

He could still feel the sting of Teresa's words after he'd called her to see how she was doing.

How do you think I'm doing, asshole? I just had to go tell my six-year-old son that his father is dead. I hate you, you worthless bastard! You swore to me that you'd keep him alive. You're the one who should be dead, not him. No one would even care if it were you.

The worst part was, he knew she was right. Brian wouldn't have even been here if Steele hadn't talked him into enlisting with him after college. They'd been childhood friends together, and Brian had worshipped him. Teresa had wanted Brian to go into the corporate world, but stupid him, he'd talked Brian out of it.

"C'mon, Brian, I'll take care of you. It'll be just like it was when we were kids. Remember how we'd play pretend soldier with our BB guns? It'll be great. Just the two of us, watching each other's backs. No one can touch us."

Now he was paying for that arrogance.

It should have been him who'd died — no one would give two shits if it had been. Teresa's hatred was irrational, but then a lot of army wives went through that when their spouses died. Even though they knew the risks, the reality of it was hard to swallow and even harder to live with.

Maybe in time she'd forgive him.

He let out a slow, tired breath, which was halted as two men came into his tent, carrying army footlockers.

"Sergeant." The two privates saluted him.

Steele had to force himself not to roll his eyes at the gesture, which, given their current surroundings, could get someone shot. But their CO had determined that even if it meant a bullet in the head from a sniper, military protocol must be followed. . . .

Unless it was the good captain. Then "proper channels" took on a whole new meaning.

Steele returned their salute. "What are you two doing here?"

"Captain Schmidt told us to pack Corporal Garrison's things. There's a new man coming in later today to replace him."

Steele narrowed his eyes at their words. He'd known it wouldn't be long before Brian was replaced, but damn . . .

This was too soon. He wasn't ready. He needed more time to come to grips with the gaping hole inside him that ached every minute of every day for the friend — no, the brother — he'd lost. There would never be anyone who could replace what Brian had been to him.

Heartsick, he watched as the two privates started going through Brian's things and placing them in one of the lockers. There were stacks of pictures from their home in Fort Benning that Teresa had sent of herself and Cody. Pictures Cody had colored and drawn in his class. A small pillow Teresa had sent, scented with the perfume she always wore.

Images of Brian holding that pillow to his face before he lay down to sleep at night went through him. Brian had loved that woman more than anything. They had met as sophomores in college at a Laundromat and had fallen in love instantly. Teresa had been the first thing Brian had talked about in the morning and the last thing he thought about before he slept.

Brian had died with a picture of her and Cody in his pocket.

Steele frowned as he saw one of the men tearing pages out of Brian's notebook, where he kept a diary of their days in hell. Brian had been extremely proud of it. *"One day, Cody will want to know what his dad did while he was away. This way, he'll know exactly how many times I thought of him and his mother."*

"What are you doing?" Steele asked the private.

"The captain said to confiscate anything that might contain classified material so that the platoon sergeant could go through it later."

Steele glared at him. "Those are diary entries for his wife and kid."

"They could compromise us."

Compromise them?

Now that was funny as hell, coming from their captain.

Steele shot to his feet with his rifle habitually in his hand, but he knew it wouldn't do any good to attack these men; they were just following orders. "Brian didn't put anything in there that would —"

His words broke off as he saw the other private sorting through pictures. He was pulling out anything that showed Brian in uniform, which was almost all of them.

Those pictures and Brian's letters were all Teresa and Cody had left of the man they'd both loved.

This was bullshit! His anger burning through him, he grabbed the notebook out of the private's hand and headed for their illustrious captain.

With every step that Steele took, his temper mounted. What they were doing wasn't right. Brian hadn't been a replaceable cog. He'd been a man with a future. One with a family who loved and needed him.

You're a soldier. You know the life.

Steele was from generations of soldiers. Men died in war. It was to be expected.

And yet he couldn't get over Brian's death that easily. He'd been too close to the man. Brian hadn't been just another soldier to Steele.

He'd been a brother.

Steele paused as he neared the captain's tent. He could hear him speaking on the phone. "No, sir. I'm not sure how the men got lost." The captain actually laughed. "You know how the desert is. It's not exactly teeming with landmarks. Accidents happen, and out here, they happen a lot."

Steele felt a tic starting in his jaw.

"No, sir. They were only to scout out the lay of the land. Sergeant Steele wasn't supposed to engage the enemy. I'm still trying to figure out what happened myself."

Bullshit. That sonofabitch had sent them out with a clear objective. It had blown up in their face — the enemy had known they were coming, and now the bastard was trying to say that he had no knowledge of it. . . .

Steele gripped his rifle even tighter as the captain continued to make light of the whole affair that had cost Brian his life.

After a few seconds, the captain hung up.

14

Before Steele could get a handle on his emotions and enter the tent, the captain came outside.

"We were lost?" The words were out of his mouth before he could stop them.

The captain, who hadn't even realized he was there, stopped dead in his tracks and turned to face him. His brown eyes narrowed dangerously on Steele. "Is there something bothering you, Sergeant?"

"We weren't lost —" He waited deliberately before he added, "Sir. We were right where *you* ordered us to be. And we did *exactly* what we were ordered to do."

He could tell by the captain's body language that he was pushing the man too far. But he didn't care. The man's stupidity had killed Brian, and he wasn't about to let him get away with this.

Not about to allow him to laugh this off.

The captain moved forward in that age-old military method of trying to intimidate. It might have worked better had the man not been five inches shorter than Steele.

Then again, Steele had been immune to that tactic since he'd grown up with his father trying to use it on him constantly.

The captain spoke in a low, deadly tone. "You will *never* speak of this event again with another living soul. Do you understand me, soldier?"

Steele ground his teeth as rage whipped through him, and he kept his mouth closed to prevent himself from saying something that was guaranteed to get him into trouble.

"Do. You. Understand?"

"Yes, sir."

The captain nodded. "Good. You will be assigned a new spotter this afternoon. At sixteen hundred hours, report to my tent for your next assignment."

Steele knew to keep his mouth shut, but he couldn't stop himself. "Is this another mission where we get lost, sir?"

The hatred in the man's eyes was tangible. "Don't mess with me, Sergeant. You know weapons malfunctions happen to even the best of us. Be a damned shame for a man with your talents to have a defective rifle when he needed it, wouldn't it, Sergeant?"

Now the bastard was threatening him? It was all he could do not to punch him straight in that smug face. But he knew better than to try it. All it would get him was arrested.

"Yes, sir," Steele said from between clenched teeth.

The captain spent another three seconds glaring at him before he withdrew. "You will do what you're told, soldier, and you will remember who is in charge here."

Steele watched as the man made his way toward the south end of the tents, but with every step he took, Steele's rage increased.

That cocky fucking bastard had no business being in charge of anything.

He looked down at the notebook in his hand and saw the neatly written words.

Hi Cody,
Another note from Dad. I was thinking of you today and missing you like crazy. I know you're taking good care of your mom for me . . .

Brian's face flashed through his mind . . . followed by the sight of his death.

Even now he could feel Brian's warm, sticky blood as it splattered across his face.

"Malfunctions happen to even the best of us . . ."

That threat was more than he could stand. Dropping the notebook, Steele lifted his rifle and took aim.

Before any rational thought could waylay his emotions, he squeezed off a single round.

The helmet on the captain's head went flying. It landed with a thump against the sand as it sprayed particles around it. Total silence descended as everyone tried to figure out if it'd been a shot or a backfire they'd heard unexpectedly.

The only two who knew what had happened were him and his target.

And as the captain pissed his pants there in front of everyone, Steele's satisfaction was mitigated by one single thought.

That was without a doubt the dumbest move of his life.

One

"Sister, I have found *the* man for you . . ."

Sydney Westbrook laughed at Tee's joyful words as she swiveled her chair away from her desk to see her boss standing behind her at the entrance of her cubicle. They weren't really sisters, as was evidenced by the fact that Tee was Vietnamese-American, while Syd was Portuguese, Italian, and English — an odd genetic combination that gave her a strangely exotic look. One that hadn't been bad until Angelina Jolie had stepped onto the Hollywood scene.

Try being an undercover agent with a very famous lookalike. There were times when she absolutely hated a woman she'd never even met.

But if she had to be the twin of what she often referred to as "that woman," she wished that she'd been given the body to match. Unfortunately, nature hadn't been quite that kind to her, and she was cursed with not only being short, but with big hips to match. Not to mention, she hadn't been the dress size of her famous counterpart since elementary school.

"You've got a man for me, huh?"

Tee nodded. "Yes, ma'am, and he's just what the doctor ordered." Tee handed her a folder. "Joshua Daniel Steele the second. Likes to scuba dive, restore vintage motorcycles, and play with firearms. He's six-two, dark-haired, dark-eyed. Ex-army. He's absolutely perfect for you."

As she scanned the folder's contents, she saw exactly why he was *ex*-Army, and it wasn't comforting in the least. "He's doing time?"

Tee shrugged. "A slight bump in the road, but we can go around it if you're interested."

Hmm . . . She paused to consider that. Convicts tended to come with a lot of emotional baggage, and the last thing she needed was a crybaby or a loon. Syd had never liked playing wet nurse to anyone. What she needed was a man with no issues who could do what she wanted without complaint or question — something that seemed to be impossible to find.

What was it with all these men who wanted to do things *their* way? Ugh!

But as Syd skimmed his dossier, she had to admit this man had some serious potential. "He's impressive."

And as she flipped to the pictures of him that were attached to the back of the folder, she amended that thought to *very* impressive.

The guy was definitely built for sin. His body was lean and hard from hours of Army training. He had dark, seductive eyes and a smile that should grace the cover of *GQ*. It was all she could do not to whistle at the package he presented.

No man should be that ripped and tanned.

At least, not unless he was in her bed a night or two . . .

Squelching that line of thought, she closed the folder, then handed it back to Tee. "I have to be honest, I wasn't really looking for a pretty boy."

Before Tee could respond, a male voice rang out. "Oh, sheez, what's Syd Vicious doing back in town?"

Syd expelled an exasperated breath as the handsome, albeit stupid, Hunter Thornton-Payne paused outside her cube, just behind Tee. It was a pity the man was such a pompous jerk. He had the kind of smooth, sexy looks that were almost impossible to resist — until he opened his mouth. Then he was more repellent than a wildebeest in heat.

She arched a brow at him. "How'd the testicle retrieval go, Payne? You still limping?"

He narrowed his eyes at her before he continued on his way to his desk.

"Thought so," Syd said in a loud voice. "I got the thank-you card from Planned Parenthood last week. Seems they want to honor me for saving the gene pool."

She heard a chorus of laughter from the other federal agents in the office.

"You are so vicious," Tee said with a light laugh.

"Hence the nickname."

Tee shook her head. "You know it's bad when you make me look like Glinda the Good Witch, right?"

"Just call me Elphaba. But don't drop a house on me, 'kay?"

As usual, Tee played right along with her humor. "All right, El. Is this one a go?"

Syd hesitated as she considered it. "I don't know."

Tee pulled out the picture of him, bare-chested and sweaty as he did sit-ups that showed off every bit of his eight-pack of abs. She waved it in front of her, like a piece of delectable chocolate.

"C'mon, Syd. Trust me. You *want* to talk to this one. You *need* to talk to this one."

Then she deepened her voice. "C'mon, baby, I'm too sexy for my shirt . . ."

Laughing, Syd shook her head. Tee was incorrigible. "Only if you promise me he won't be chasing after a quick lay. I don't need or want any more playboys in my life." Syd had had her fill of men like that. She'd made a blood oath that the next time such a man entered her life, she'd shoot him herself.

Or give him a taste of what she'd given Hunter.

Tee returned the picture to her folder. "All right, then. We'll head out to meet him within the hour. Can you be ready?"

Syd glanced at her computer. She had a lot of work to do, but she needed to make sure this one would work out. She couldn't afford to have another man let her down.

It wasn't easy to find a cold-blooded killer who could go in and complete this assignment without any remorse, questions, or hiccups.

From his file, Steele looked to be just what the doctor ordered, and Army men were good at following orders.

But then, convicts weren't . . .

Syd sighed as she ran through the good and bad of dealing with this man. If he didn't pan out for whatever reason, there wouldn't be time to find a replacement sniper. They'd already been through countless files of Marines, SWAT, Army . . . the works. None of them had been right.

Scuba-diving convict loon that Steele was, he was all or nothing.

God help them.

"Yeah. I'll tag along for a look-see."

"Good. Oh, and I almost forgot the best part. . . . you know our friends at Asset Protection?"

Syd ground her teeth at the mention of the "security" company that was a known front for organized crime, mercenaries, and hired assassins. "What about them?"

"They've been in contact with our boy Steele. I have it on good authority that they even made an employment offer not too long back."

A slow smile spread across her face. Oh, yeah, he *was* perfect.

Tee winked at her. "Do whatever you need to to get ready while I go arm-wrestle Joe into this."

Syd watched as Tee made her way back to the private office that she shared with their director, Joe Public. When Syd had signed on with the agency, her agenda had been solely to protect those who couldn't protect themselves.

It was an oath she took most seriously. If she failed in this mission, there was no telling what repercussions could affect not just her life, but millions of others.

Who would have ever thought that the best way to save lives was to take one? But then that was what Joe had preached to her from the first day on her job.

He even had a name for it. Political pruning. In order to make the tree grow, the dead, diseased, and contaminated limbs had to be removed. If they didn't fall off on their own, then you had to get the chain saw out and cut them loose. At first she'd been naive enough to think that she could never be so jaded. But time and missions had finally succeeded in bringing her around to Joe's way of thinking.

It was a dog-eat-dog world, and she had the biggest bite of all.

Two

"The man took a potshot at his commanding officer."

Ignoring his comment, Tee leaned against Joe's desk to read over his shoulder. He was looking at the folder she'd handed him, which contained the dossier for her latest possible recruit: Joshua Steele, former Army sniper, now semi-permanent resident of Fort Leavenworth, Kansas.

She couldn't understand Joe's reticence about that one little fact that had sent Steele to jail. Normally he saw good potential whenever she handed it to him.

"Yeah, so? He's surly, ill-tempered. Marches to his own tune and makes quick decisions. Okay, granted, shooting at the CO, not bright, but we all do stupid things from time to time. Other than that one tiny critical error in judgment, he sounds like a perfect recruit for the Bureau of American Defense."

Joe gave her a droll stare as he closed the

file. "He took a potshot at his commanding officer."

For her life, Tee couldn't understand why he was hung up on that. "So? He's even passed Syd's scrutiny, and I know I don't have to tell you what a death-defying feat that is."

"*I* would be his commanding officer, Tiger. Don't you think you've already gotten me shot enough times in my career?"

She rolled her eyes at him and snatched the folder from his hands. "You're never going to get over Prague, are you?"

He gave her an indignant glare as he slapped at his leg. "You shot me in the thigh."

She snorted. "It was only the fleshy part."

"Fleshy part, my ass. Another millimeter or two more, and the boys would have been history."

She waved a hand dismissively as she returned to her metal desk, which was set just across from his. Unlike his, which always kept scrupulously clean, hers was littered with catalogs, files, papers and several small Amy Brown statues that she collected. "Yeah, yeah, be glad I was tired and my aim was off." She put the folder in her large black briefcase. "Now stop being a baby and make the call."

He continued to glare at her. "Why is it when I'm the one shot, I'm a baby, but when it's you, it's a matter of life and death and national security?"

"Because I'm cuter in a short skirt. Now make the call, Joe."

"Make the call, Joe," he mocked as he reached for his antiquated Rolodex. Personally, she much preferred her small PDA, but Joe was virtually a technophobe — he hated anything that was electronic. Except for the TV remote, and that was one penchant she didn't want to even think about.

He opened the cover and started spinning through the cards. "You do realize that I am the head of this agency, right?"

Tee made a rude noise at him as she opened up her filing drawer and rooted around in it for the rest of Steele's paperwork, which she'd already gathered. "Figurehead, you mean. You couldn't find the key to the door in the morning unless I handed it to you first."

He continued to flip through the cards without looking at her. "Only because I'm not a morning person."

She gave him an arch stare. "And you're not a night person either. Face it, babe.

You've only got two good minutes a day. The minute before noon and the minute right after."

He cast a feral glare at her that might have actually scared her if she wasn't packing an even higher-caliber weapon than he was. "You know, I could fire you. I could even arrange to get you killed. Or kill you myself."

Tee organized some of the more errant papers on her desk while he blustered at her. "Ooo, big scary threat. That might hold water if it wasn't for the fact that I know how much you hate paperwork."

"I do know how to operate a computer."

She had to force herself not to laugh at that one. The first thing she'd learned years ago when they had been partners in the CIA was that Joe Public would rather be hit in the head with a tack hammer than sit at a desk, working on a computer.

"Yeah, right. What was it you said just ten minutes ago? Get this damned thing off my desk before I shoot it? Now make the call, Mr. Hunt-and-Peck."

Joe tossed a piece of rolled-up paper at her before he dialed the phone.

Tee caught it, kissed it, then hurled it back at him.

It rebounded off his head.

He growled at her as he bent over, like any good obsessive-compulsive, picked it up from the floor, and tossed it into the garbage can. "I really should fire you."

Tee would have commented that she wasn't that lucky, but just as she opened her mouth, he started talking to their Army contact. She forced herself not to smile at the fact that she was getting her way . . . again. But then she almost always did with Joe. He was like a big surly bear in a cave. You poked him, he growled threateningly, then moved aside as he rubbed his tush and glared menacingly at you.

Then again, Joe only did that for her.

Deep down, she knew the truth. Joe Public was never a pushover. He was hard-nosed, callous, and stern, one of the best agents the CIA had ever trained. Joe didn't know the meaning of the word *play.*

Which was a shame, given just how good the man looked. He had long, dark brown hair that he usually wore pulled back in a ponytail, eyes that were so blue, they should be illegal, and a butt so fine that Hollywood agents would jump to sign it.

She'd seen him shirtless a time or two on assignments and had never fully recovered from the sight. Lean and taut, his body could rival that of any male gymnast. And

30

every time she saw glimpses of it, she was possessed with a raw need to lick every inch of him . . .

Tee clamped down those thoughts — as she always did. Work and play didn't mix.

Joe was her ex-partner and, at the end of the day, her boss. There could never be anything more than that between them, and she knew it.

But deep down in places she shouldn't acknowledge, she wanted a lot more than just a working relationship with him.

She listened to that take-no-shit tone of his as he talked to their contact. A New York City boy, Joe was able to disguise his accent 99 percent of the time. But when he was trying to intimidate or take control, that accent came out full force.

And something about it was sexy as hell. But then, his voice always was. Deep and resonant, it had a way of sending chills up and down her spine.

Joe hung up the phone.

"Well?" she asked, hiding the fact that she was embarrassed to admit she'd been so focused on him that she hadn't been listening to his conversation.

"Book us a flight to Kansas, Dorothy. Let's see if Toto can bark."

Three

It was just another day in hell as far as Steele was concerned. Why he had ever thought it would be preferable to do time in an orange uniform instead of a green one, he wasn't sure.

But two years ago, when he'd decided to shoot the helmet off his CO in a fit of anger, he'd figured anything, even court-martial and jail, was better than what the Army had in store for him.

Boy, was he ever wrong.

Now he'd spend the next twenty-five years inside these walls, listening to the other inmates spiel bullshit while he had to fight daily to maintain the fact that he was cock of the walk, and if anyone wanted a piece of him, they were going to die for it.

Yee-haw, his life was great.

"Steele?"

He looked up from the carrots he was skinning with a spoon to see one of the guards eyeing him.

"You have visitors."

It took a full twenty seconds for those unexpected words to register.

Visitors? Him?

What were the odds of that? His family had abandoned him the day he'd been arrested.

So had all of his friends. Not that he'd ever had that many to begin with. He'd always been a loner for the most part, some of which came from being an Army brat whose family was transferred from post to post every three to four years. The only real friends he'd ever had had been crazy old Jack and Brian. Jack was now holed up in a bunker away from the world, where he most likely had no idea what had happened to Steele, and Brian . . .

He winced as pain tore through him like glycerin on glass. How could his family have cut him loose so easily? He'd have never done this to anyone, but for all intents and purposes, he'd been completely orphaned and abandoned by everyone he'd mistakenly thought he was close to. None of them wanted the taint of his incarceration to stick to them. Like they were the ones who had to live the horror of his life.

In the last eighteen months the only people who'd come to see him were his lawyer and one stupid asshole who'd wanted to hire him to kill people.

Yeah, right. He was through with killing for a paycheck. If Uncle Sam couldn't get him to do it, no one else could either.

His days of pulling a trigger were over.

Steele turned off the oh-so-manly food processor, then wiped his hands on his equally manly apron. He pulled the apron off over his head and hung it up on the wall hook.

"He can't leave," the head cook shouted at the guard, who was a good three inches taller than Steele. With a stocky build, Hank wasn't the most benevolent of prison guards. He was more like the kind who generally gave them all a bad name. But for fate, no doubt the man would have been in Steele's shoes behind the bars Hank liked to clank with his nightstick as he walked down the hallways at night. Steele really detested the bastard. "We've got to get this meal finished."

"Then you better find yourself someone else to run the food processor," Hank said. "These people aren't the kind to wait."

Steele snorted. "What? We got the fucking president out there or something?"

Hank curled his lip. "Stow it, Steele. These aren't the kind of folks you piss off."

Yeah, right. Everyone was the kind of person you pissed off at some point. No one, not even the president, was that big. "Maybe you don't, Hank, but we'll see about me."

Hank looked less than impressed by his attitude. "Your funeral."

The guard led him out to the hallway, where they were waiting to cuff him. Steele stiffened. Part of him wanted to fight rather than submit, but he'd learned the first few weeks of his unfortunate incarceration that fighting the guards really didn't pay.

Here at Club Leavenworth, daily humiliation was just par for the course. And if he was really lucky, they might even wake him up in the middle of the night and let him scrub toilets with his toothbrush again.

Oh, goody.

Grinding his teeth, he forced himself not to react as Hank grabbed his arm and hauled him toward the visitation room that was reserved for conferring with attorneys. It was one he hadn't seen any more of since his attorney had told him that the last appeal they could make had been turned down flat. Now the attorney, who had cost him every dime he'd had, wouldn't even return his calls. Yeah . . . his life was just a bowl full of laughs.

Needless to say, he wasn't particularly thrilled by being here again as those repressed emotions went through him, stoking his anger.

Once they reached the correct room — which, as fate would have it, happened to be the one where he'd lost his last hope — the guard opened the door, then shoved him into it.

Steele stumbled a step before he caught his balance and went ramrod stiff. His nostrils flared as he kept his anger leashed and his gaze carefully on the floor. He wanted desperately to glare at Hank, but he knew better than to even try it. Instead, he felt a muscle working in his jaw as he righted himself to look at the people who were there to speak with him.

Like the rest of the prison, the room was drab, but even if the walls had been painted hot pink with naked hookers on them, the intense people waiting on him would have stood out.

They were government-trained. He could smell it. It bled from every pore of their bodies, even though they were dressed as civilians, and the man had hair longer than the woman sitting beside him. Steele's gaze went to the man's right arm, where a tattoo was peeking out from underneath his long, dark blue sleeve. He had on black pleated pants and a red-striped tie, but not even that could cover the fact that the man wasn't as refined as he wanted to appear.

There was something about him that was raw and deadly — the kind of guy you'd have to fight in a bar because his woman dared to look at you.

And God help you if you were dumb enough to speak to her.

The woman beside him was a strange dichotomy. She was a tiny, petite Asian woman — Vietnamese-American, if he didn't miss his guess. Dressed in a white blouse and short black skirt, she appeared sedate and calm. Yet his instincts told him it was only a facade. Her movements were too precise. Too studied. He sensed that she was as acutely aware of him as he was of her. Her short black hair was a perfect frame for her attractive face as she watched him from behind a pair of soulless black eyes.

But it was the woman standing in the corner with her arms crossed over her chest who held his attention most. Her expression totally blank, she was dressed in a pair of jeans with a loose red top and a dark brown leather blazer. She wasn't very tall, only about five-four or so. She wasn't petite or heavy, but rather built solidly.

An image of an Amazon warrior popped into his mind. Yeah, he could see her like that. Sword in one hand, whip in the other as she stood toe to toe with an enemy.

Or better yet, naked over the guy she'd tied to her bed.

That thought almost made him smile. Only the pain of his sudden erection kept him from it. It'd been way too long since he'd last spoken to a woman. Never mind being close enough to one that she could actually tie him up to something.

What he wouldn't give to have five minutes alone with her . . .

Steele forced himself not to betray those thoughts, but it was hard.

Her long black hair was pulled back into a braid that fell to the middle of her back. No doubt it would be soft to touch. Like silk against his face as he nuzzled her neck . . .

It was enough to make him want to whimper.

She wore a pair of round tortoiseshell-framed glasses that didn't even come close to hiding her green eyes, which had a feline slant to them. Something hot and wicked went through him as he watched her.

Every part of him seemed strangely attuned to her presence. Yeah, he'd been in prison way too long. She wasn't his type by a long shot. She looked more likely to kick a man's ass than to ride it.

And still he had to force himself not to stare at her, and he wasn't even sure why. Her lips and eyes were a bit too large, her stance a little too masculine.

Even so, there was something about her that was absolutely compelling.

The guard led him toward a chair across the table from them.

"Uncuff his hands," the unknown man said in a bored tone.

"That's against protocol."

"Un. Cuff. His. Hands," he repeated, stressing the syllables of each word without looking at the guard.

Hank glared at the man an instant before he roughly complied. Steele forced himself not to grimace as Hank wrenched his hand so hard, he half expected it to break.

"Fine, if he attacks you —"

"He'll be dead before he hits the floor," the seated woman said in a distracted tone as she rummaged through her large black leather briefcase. "And I'm sure he knows it."

Steele rubbed his wrists as he hooked a heel against the chair leg to pull it out. He sat down and eyed the seated pair sullenly.

The guard took a stance inside the door.

"Wait outside," the man said.

"That's —"

"Wait. Out. Side," he stressed again.

Oh, yeah, there would be hell for him to pay later after these three were gone and Hank could prove himself superior. Steele couldn't wait.

The guard cast a feral sneer at them before he complied.

"Thanks," Steele said sarcastically as his anger swelled again. "Can't wait for the walk back. You guys specialize in something other than acid enemas?"

The Vietnamese woman's eyes gleamed at that as she set her briefcase on the floor. "Ooo, he's snotty. I like him already."

The man, like the woman who still continued to stand off to the side, was completely stone-faced. Steele had to admire that. It took a lot of practice to show absolutely no emotion. He knew that well enough, since he practiced it religiously.

When the man spoke, his tone was as cold as his body language. "We're here with a special offer for you, Mr. Steele. A once-in-a-lifetime type of opportunity."

Steele snorted. "Oh, wait, I've seen this movie. I do a job for you, and you let me go. So who am I? I can't be Eddie Murphy, wrong ethnicity. I'm not bald, so I can't be Vin Diesel. So where does that leave me?"

The woman gave him an evil smile. "Think Snake Plissken. You know . . . *Escape from New York*? You do this job, and if you don't fuck it up, we let you live."

"Yeah, I've seen that movie. At the end they try to kill him anyway."

The man still didn't crack any sort of emotion. "Good, then you're already acquainted with our methods. Saves me a lot of training time and you a lot of surprises."

Steele shook his head. They were full of more shit than a cow pasture. "Look, don't jerk me off. I don't have time for this —"

"Don't you?" the woman asked. "Seems to me time is the only thing you have a lot of."

He glared at her. "Ha. Ha. Why don't you go find some other slob for this suicide adventure? I know the Army isn't going to just let me go."

"And neither are we," the man said. "We never let our people just go."

Why didn't that surprise him? Probably because they all wore the demeanor of . . . well, for lack of a better term, Satan. "What are you? Wolfram and Hart?"

The Vietnamese-American woman laughed as she caught his reference to the

Angel television show. "Oh, no, sweetie, they just take your soul for service. We intend to take even more than that."

Now that was comforting.

The man rubbed his right eye. "Here's the deal we're offering. You work our project to our complete satisfaction, and instead of spending the next twenty-five years peeling potatoes and doing embroidery for the Army, you work for us. In effect, we own you, night and day."

Now that just sounded dandy . . . not. He wasn't about to trade one crap-ass situation for another one.

"Slavery is against the Constitution."

"Tell it to the warden," the Vietnamese-American woman said.

Steele watched as she opened a manila folder and flipped through its contents.

He didn't believe them for a minute about any of this, but his curiosity had got the better of him. He tilted his head back to try and see what she was looking at, but he couldn't tell.

Instinctively though, he already knew this scenario.

"So, who do you want me to kill?"

The man was the one who answered. "No one said —"

"Cut the bullshit," Steele snapped, interrupting him. He wanted the truth, and he wanted it in plain English. "I'm not stupid. I only have one skill in life. I'm a sniper. For you to be here, it means you have someone you want dead, pretty damn badly, and you can't find anyone else dumb enough to do it."

"Not true." The standing woman spoke finally, in a voice that reminded him of Lauren Bacall. It was deep and lightly laced with a New England accent of some sort. "There are plenty of men dumb enough for it. Just none that are as talented as you are, Mr. Steele."

He laughed bitterly at that. "I hate it whenever someone calls me Mr. Steele. It reminds me of my third-grade teacher, who'd gone to parochial schools as a kid. She'd use that right before she whacked my knuckles with a ruler or embarrassed me in front of the other students."

She narrowed those green eyes on him as if she was torn between being ticked and amused. "Be that as it may, we do need you in particular to complete this assignment."

He snorted at that. Assignment. What a great euphemism for what they wanted. "What is it with you government assholes that you just can't say anything in plain English? You always have to beat around the bush and use euphemisms or fucked-up acronyms for everything."

"Fine." The green-eyed woman moved forward to glare at him. She stood just a few inches from the table. Close enough that he could tell she was wearing expensive perfume that seemed at odds with her tough stance. "We need *you* to kill an assassin before he executes his target. Either you eat the bear, or the bear eats you, Mr. Steele. Or, to humor you, in plain English — you find and kill the assassin, or we kill you. End of story."

Steele scoffed. "If you're so gung-ho to kill someone, why don't you kill the assassin yourself?"

She shrugged nonchalantly. "I would if I knew who he was. But unfortunately, I don't. Nor do I have the skills you possess."

The other woman shut the folder and placed it on the table. "We know all about your training in the Shadow Corps, Mr. Steele. We even have one of your old comrades on our payroll, but he unfortunately cracked himself into a tree while extreme skiing and put a severe crimp in our plans. Since he's out of commission for a while, he recommended you as a replacement. It appears he was unaware of your current housing status."

The man slid the folder toward him. "If you agree to work for us, we are in position to fully expunge your record. You will be given an honorable discharge from the Army, and this little jail stint will be erased from all but your nightmares."

Now that was something he'd kill for . . . Maybe.

Steele opened the folder that held the discharge papers, already signed, as well as an order from the Pentagon and the governor releasing him from custody.

He was impressed. And when he looked at the paper underneath that outlined his new pay and benefits, he was even more impressed.

But there were still a lot of unanswered questions. "Who are you people?"

The man sat back. "You don't need to know that right now. After you accept our offer, then we'll talk more about the details."

It sounded good. Too good, in fact, and he wasn't doe-eyed enough to think for one minute that they were being benevolent toward him. Nothing in life came without a price that was usually too steep to comprehend until it was too late. "There's one detail I want answered now."

"And that is?"

"After I do this job, what happens to me?"

The man's blue eyes pierced him. "You will continue working for us. We in effect are your parole officers."

"Only we carry guns," the green-eyed woman said. "*Big* guns. And we have no inhibitions against using them. You screw us, you betray us and we kill you. Clear-cut. Bye-bye, Mr. Steele. Is that plain enough for you?"

He shook his head at her coldness. "I'll bet you sleep well at night."

"You have no idea."

Steele flipped through the pages in the folder as he thought about what they were offering him. How could he say no?

How could he say yes?

Most importantly, what the hell was he getting himself into? He suddenly felt like Joe Hardy standing in front of Mr. Applegate. Vaguely he wondered if the sassy woman who was still standing was named Lola.

But then, the devil was always portrayed as an old man, and the one in front of him . . .

Well, then again, there was something almost evil about him.

"So how long do I have to make my decision?"

The   Vietnamese-American   woman

shrugged. "The judge said twenty-five years without the possibility of parole. That'll make you what, fifty-four years old when you get out? Really sucks, doesn't it? No hot women in short skirts to chase after because you're an old geezer with no prospects. Best years of your life gone while you fight off men who think you have a cute little ass they'd love to jump on —"

Steele screwed his face up in disgust. "Is she like this at home?"

Still the man showed no emotion. "Trust me, she's being nice to you. She's usually much worse." He looked at the woman by his side. "You feeling okay, Tiger?"

"Never better."

Steele drew a deep breath, but at the end of it, he knew what they did. He didn't really have a choice. The last thing he wanted was to waste his life behind bars.

Like the green-eyed woman had said, it sucked being here.

He sat back as he eyed the three of them. "Don't you guys want to know if I'm innocent of trying to kill him?"

"It doesn't matter to us," the man said quietly. "Besides, even if you'd meant to kill him, you'd lie and say you didn't."

Steele rose slowly to his feet and slid the folder across the table toward the man. He

looked at the women, then stared unflinch-
ingly at the guy. His anger poured through
him, and he was sure it was gleaming at
them from his eyes. "If I'd meant to kill that
sonovabitch, he'd have been dead where he
stood. I don't make those kinds of mistakes.
One shot. One kill. I live and die by my
sniper's code."

"And that's why we want you, Mr. Steele,"
the seated woman said calmly.

The man stared at him without blinking.
"So what's your answer?"

"Get me the fuck out of here."

The man and woman stood up in unison.
The Vietnamese-American woman lifted a
small shopping bag from the floor, then
handed it to him while the other woman and
man moved toward the door.

"Welcome back to the world, Mr. Steele,"
she said with a smile that was an odd combination of demure and evil. "Get dressed,
and Joe will be waiting outside to walk you
out of here."

Steele was amazed by her words. It
couldn't be that easy, could it?

He took the plastic bag and opened it to
find a pair of jeans and a button-down
denim shirt, along with a pair of Nike running shoes. All of them were in his size.

Yeah, these people were definitely spooks.

"I'm Joe," the man said at last. "Just knock on the door when you're ready to leave."

Steele stood in silence as they left him alone. This had to be the most surreal moment of his life. It was even stranger than his first day in prison.

"Oh God, don't think about that."

There should be a way to permanently burn certain memories out of the human mind.

But soon, if they were to be believed, this whole thing would be behind him. Part of him still couldn't believe it. To be outside again without some asshole standing over him with a rifle . . .

Happiness rushed through him as he peeled off his prison clothes and swapped them for the jeans and shirt. He almost felt human again.

Almost.

"Yeah, but what are they going to do when they realize I'm not willing to kill anyone anymore?"

They should have delved a little deeper into his file to see exactly why he'd taken that shot at his CO.

Oh, well. How much could a bullet in the head hurt anyway? At least then it would put him out of his misery.

Fuck that. If they tried to shoot him, he'd teach them what had made him the best sniper in his unit.

Four

Steele quickly learned that Joe was far from a chatty Cathy as he led him from the prison to a waiting helicopter. In fact, Joe didn't seem to like to speak at all.

He paused as Joe slid open the door to the helicopter. Trained on military choppers, Steele wasn't expecting what had to be the helicopter equivalent to a corporate jet. The interior could only hold six people, but each of the seats was made out of thickly padded tan leather. There were cup holders, plug-ins for laptops, and such. It was incredibly lush.

The women, whose names they still hadn't bothered to divulge, were already seated inside.

"Damn," Steele muttered, "this is nicer than any place I've ever owned."

Joe didn't comment as he took a seat next to the Vietnamese-American lady.

After Steele was seated, Joe inclined his head toward the pilots up front, who were doing preflight checks. "Joshua Steele, meet Jake Malone and Tony Casella. If in the future, you're dropped into a high-risk area, they and Retter — who you'll meet later — are the ones who will pull your ass out of the fire. So be nice to them. Your life depends on it."

Wearing a pilot's helmet that completely obscured his face, Jake turned around and offered him his hand. "Welcome aboard."

"Thanks," Steele said, shaking his hand.

"You go by Josh?" Jake asked.

"Steele. Just Steele."

"No problem."

Tony offered his hand next. "Don't worry if I lay my head back and start to snore while we're flying. It's normal. I'm just here in case Jake has a stroke and dies."

Steele tensed. "That's not real comforting."

"Yeah, but it's true. But don't worry. Jake only passed out once, and Joe woke me up real fast. He has great reflexes."

"I did not pass out," Jake said between clenched teeth.

"Yes, you did." He turned back to look at Steele. "Of course that was 'cause he'd downed a fifth of tequila, and I told him not to fly. But he didn't listen. 'No one touches my baby but me,' " Tony said in a mocking voice. "He was disgusting. He threw up everywhere — it even short-circuited the landing gear, which seriously pissed off those of us who were sober and aware of what was happening. But that's okay. Once Joe figured out you can't get the scent of vomit out of leather, he bought us a new toy."

Jake shoved good-naturedly at his copilot. "Shut up and go back to sleep, Tone. You're starting to annoy me again."

Steele looked at Joe. "Is there any way to put up some kind of divider between us and them?"

Joe laughed. "Actually, there is, but you don't have to worry. Tony doesn't talk much once the blades start spinning. The sound of the motor lulls him to sleep."

"Great," Steele said, his gut shrinking at the thought. "I always wanted to fly with a narcoleptic pilot."

The woman beside him smiled. "Don't worry, Steele. Jake has a hot date tonight. He won't crash us until she breaks up with him."

"Jeez!" Jake snapped. "That was only once, people. I swear you're all elephants. You can't ever let a guy forget one little mistake."

Tony snorted. "That little mistake had me hospitalized for three weeks, and it almost cost me my leg."

Steele frowned at those words. Oh, what the hell was he doing on this thing with these people?

Jake glanced over at Joe. "Are we ready, boss?"

"Home, Jake."

Jake groaned as if it were an old bad joke between them. He turned around and fired the engines, which whirred at a dull drone through the insulation.

Joe tossed him a pair of noise-canceling headphones as Jake lifted them off the helipad. "In case the drone gets to you."

As they ascended, he noticed Joe rubbing his right eye again and frowning. The Vietnamese-American woman gave him a concerned look before she tapped her right eyebrow twice.

Joe nodded.

She winced in response before she pointed at his pants pocket. Joe held his hands up and made an expression that essentially said, "I know I screwed up."

Rolling her eyes at him, the woman grabbed her briefcase and rummaged through it, pulling out a small gray plastic case. She opened it to remove a small foil pouch that she handed to Joe. The look on his face said he was truly grateful as he took the pouch and opened it.

He popped a small tablet into his mouth while the woman opened her Coke, then handed it to him.

Joe took a drink before he passed it back to her.

Steele frowned at their actions. There was a familiarity with each other that said they were intimately involved.

He looked at the left hands. No wedding bands, no engagement ring.

Hmm . . .

Joe leaned his head back and closed his eyes while the woman picked up a romance novel and started reading it. Jake was busy flying while Tony really did have his head back and his eyes closed.

That just added so much confidence.

He glanced to his side, where the other woman was seated reading the book *Blink: The Power of Thinking Without Thinking*.

Okay . . . this was an interesting group. What the hell was he doing here again?

Leavenworth. Just keep thinking it's better than prison, and you'll be okay.

Maybe. He glanced at the *Blink* title again and grimaced. The whole thinking-without-thinking concept was seriously screwing with his head. If he had to put his life in someone's hands, he would much prefer they think with thinking.

Nothing you can do about it now.

He'd already made the pact with the devil so to speak. Now he had no choice except to see it through.

Steele crossed his arms over his chest and leaned back as he wondered just where they were headed. He probably should have asked before he jumped on board the helicopter. But what the hell. It had to be better than where he'd been.

Then again, being on a helicopter with one narcoleptic pilot, another who had a penchant for crashing, and people who'd already told him that they had no compunction about killing him might be construed as an act of total stupidity.

But he was Army trained to put his trust in strangers and to blindly obey orders . . . r-i-g-h-t. Some training, no matter how zealous, never seemed to sink all the way in.

Not that it mattered. These people had come to him, and they had been able to get him released. Obviously they were legit and had a lot of pull.

He didn't know all the details about the assignment they were about to give him, but whatever it was, it had to beat peeling carrots with a spoon and then feeding them into a food processor for his fellow inmates because no one dared trust him with a knife or a potato peeler.

He closed his eyes and tried to focus, but before he knew it, he was sound asleep.

Syd looked up to see Joe with his head back and eyes closed, while Tee was heavily engrossed in the latest Rachel Fire novel. Glad they weren't paying any attention to her, she slid her gaze sideways to see Steele resting in a stance much like Joe's.

His head was back against the wall of the chopper, his legs open wide, his hands resting on his thighs. She'd known from the pictures in his file that he was good-looking, but what she'd never expected had been his overwhelmingly sexual charisma.

Even while he was resting, she could feel his power. He was all manly sex appeal. His voice had been incredibly deep, with just a hint of a southern drawl to it. His dark hair looked soft. Inviting.

And his dark brown eyes . . .

They weren't just intelligent, they were spooky. Even handcuffed, he'd come into the room like he owned it. Swept that midnight gaze around and sized them up with what she was sure was unerring accuracy.

He was completely confident.

Most of all, he was delectable.

Stop it, Syd. Work and play were a lethal mixture, especially when it involved two agents.

You can look, but don't ever touch.

She sighed irritably at that. Figures the only man she'd been attracted to in more months than she wanted to factor would be one she couldn't even consider.

He shifted slightly, stretching his shirt tight over his chest.

Oh, man . . .

She could use a cold shower right about now. Uncomfortable with the effect he had on her, she quickly glanced back at her book.

But even as she attempted to read, she wondered what had made Steele snap. If what he'd said to Joe about shooting at his CO and not killing him was true, why had he done it? He had to know the repercussions of taking that shot. From what she'd read, he hadn't even tried to argue it was an accident. He'd simply pled nolo to the charges and taken the sentence.

What would make a man throw away his life?

And even more importantly, would he snap under the pressures of this latest mission?

Maybe her desperation for getting to the

hired gun had caused her to make a fatal error in judgment.

She rubbed her chin as that thought chased itself around her mind. Could she trust Steele to remain calm and collected under severe duress? That was *the* question to be answered.

The last thing they could afford would be an agent who couldn't pull the trigger.

Steele was dreaming of Sunday dinner at his parents' house. He could see his mother welcoming him home, see his father reaching out to shake his hand. His sister was there, home from college.

Everything was just as it'd been before his arrest . . .

And then he felt someone touch his arm.

Reacting on instinct born of one too many nights spent in prison, he came awake ready to fight off whoever was disturbing him.

Joe caught his hand before it made contact with his jaw and held it in an iron grip that actually surprised him. The man was a lot stronger and quicker than he appeared.

"We're here," Joe said, releasing his arm.

Frowning, Steele straightened up to find them landed in what appeared to be the parking lot of some stadium. He pulled the headphones off. "Where are we?"

"Nashville," Joe said as he climbed out of the helicopter.

Completely baffled by this location, Steele followed him out of the copter. "Tennessee?"

Joe snorted as he pulled on a pair of sunglasses. "There's only one Nashville."

Steele looked around the attractive and unusual cityscape, but for the life of him he couldn't figure out why they were here. "What the hell am I doing in Nashville? What — you want me to shoot Minnie Pearl?"

Joe gave him a droll look. "No. She's not the target. Not to mention, she's already dead."

Steele returned Joe's bad-ass tit-for-tat. "So what? Garth Brooks is a spy, or did he just piss you off? Do I get to shoot him?"

The Vietnamese-American woman gave him a dry stare. "No, but if you happen to shoot Big & Rich, I wouldn't complain. If I have to hear that stupid 'Save a Horse (Ride a Cowboy)' song one more time, I might shoot someone myself." She shifted her gaze meaningfully to Joe.

"I like that song," Joe said defensively.

"Yeah, I've seen the shirt," she said, her

voice even drier than her expression as she led them across the parking lot. "Trust me, Joe. You're not a cowboy. The only cows you ever saw as a kid came under a plastic wrap in the grocery store or in a paper wrapper from McDonald's."

Joe made a face at her as he walked behind her.

"Do they always do that?" he asked the other woman, who strangely reminded him of Angelina Jolie. He wasn't sure why, but something about her dark looks and confidence was reminiscent of the actress. Though this woman looked like she actually enjoyed food and took in more than a lettuce leaf every three weeks.

She pulled her glasses off and tucked them in her pocket before she shifted her book to rest under her arm. "Always. You'll get used to it."

Yawning, Steele turned to look over his shoulder as Jake and Tony took off with the helicopter. Oblivious to their departure, Joe and the dark-eyed woman led them toward a small black Mercedes sedan.

"Keys," Joe said, holding his hand out to her while he and mini-Angelina waited by the back doors.

The Vietnamese woman stared at him. "You have a migraine."

He gave her a charming, almost boyish grin. "Thanks to you and Maxalt, it's gone, but if I let you drive, I know it'll come right back."

She narrowed her eyes. "I just got it painted from the last time you drove it."

Joe poked his lip out and pouted.

She made a disgusted noise. "You so much as near a curb, and I will cut" — she dropped her gaze to his groin — "*it* off."

He snorted as he took the keys from her. "Never hit a curb in my life."

"Beirut? Paris? Oh, and don't get me started on Madrid."

Joe made a mocking face as he unlocked the doors with the remote. "You nag like your mother."

"Don't you dare start on my mother. I'll invite her down for a visit if you do."

"Sorry," Joe said instantly. "I'll never mention her again . . . or your sister either."

Steele frowned at them. "Are you two married or something?"

"No," the woman said. "I know too much about him to be that stupid."

"Thank you, Tiger." Joe got into the car.

"You're welcome, Joseph," she said as she joined him.

Taking his cue, Steele got into the back at

about the same time as the mini-Angelina. As soon as he had the seat belt on, he understood Tiger's trepidation about her car. Joe drove like a man with a death wish.

"Where'd you learn to drive?" Steele asked as they took a corner so fast, he swore the car was only on two wheels.

"Richard Petty's School of Driving. Had a great instructor there named Steven Norbert who showed me how to dog the shit out of an engine. Why?"

Steele shook his head, wondering if it were sarcasm or truth.

"He's joking," Tiger said. "He learned to drive from a Mafia bagman."

Joe cleared his throat. "I've told you a million times, Tiger, we don't use that term. It's fiction." He paused. "My uncle Fish was simply connected."

Tiger rolled her eyes until Joe cut too close to a slow-moving car. "Watch the bumper!"

Steele cringed, expecting a wreck, but they missed the other car by the skin of their teeth.

Luckily, they were only a few blocks from their destination. Joe slung them into a parking garage, up the ramp, and into a parking space so fast that he swore he heard a sonic boom from the back end.

"Not a mark on it," Joe said triumphantly to Tiger as he put the car into park.

"Yeah. Wanna check the backseat, where Steele is sitting? I'll bet there's a big stain there."

"Hey, I resent that," Steele said. "I assure you, my nerves can take anything you two dish out."

Mini-Angelina laughed. "Don't be so cocky. You've no idea how mean they can be."

"Yeah," Tiger said. "Besides, I'm sure you'll be resenting a lot more comments made by me in the very near future."

"And you can take that to the bank," Joe said as he handed off the keys to Tiger.

Joe and Tiger were an odd couple, but in a weird way, he liked them. They got out of the car and headed toward the elevator to take them out of the garage. "So when do I get to learn more about my new job?"

Joe pressed the button. "In the offices, where we can't be overheard."

The women were making small talk while he and Joe said nothing.

Once they reached the peaceful, shaded street outside the garage, Steele paused as he saw the building across from them. It was . . . different. Made of blue glass and white concrete, it shot up probably a good six hundred plus feet from the ground. The very top of it had two slender towers that looked like something out of a science fiction movie. A bridgelike structure connecting the towers was emblazoned with the word *BellSouth* and a blue circle with white stars just below it.

He'd never seen anything like it . . . and Joe and the women were heading straight for it.

Steele made a mental note of the address: 333 Commerce Street. He hastened to catch up to them. "You work for the phone company?"

"No," Tiger said as they walked around the modern art of the north plaza. "Ma Bell owns the building, which is affectionately called the Bat Tower."

That fit it perfectly. It looked like something out of a *Batman* comic.

Joe glanced at him over his shoulder. "We rent space in it for our offices."

Steele nodded as they entered the posh lobby through a revolving glass door. It was rather dark inside, and overwhelmingly brown, with a lot of green plants that overflowed their containers. There was a security station to the back with a uniformed guard and a woman talking.

Joe headed left toward the elevator banks,

which were almost hidden by the foliage of the lobby.

"We're an insurance agency," Joe said as he entered the elevator.

Steele laughed at the irony. "That's clever."

"Yeah, but it's true," Tiger said.

Steele opened his mouth to respond, but before he could, mini-Angelina elbowed him.

"Save it for the office." She indicated a corner of the ceiling, where there was probably a security camera hidden. "Remember, walls have eyes and ears."

And he'd thought the Army was bad. "You guys aren't paranoid, are you? What? You think there are trained killers in the elevator?"

Joe and the women laughed evilly as the doors opened into a small lobby area.

As soon as the doors closed behind them, Tiger turned to give him smile. "We rode up in them, didn't we?"

She had a point.

If it wasn't for the fact that they carried themselves like professionals, he might think she was kidding — but he knew better.

The small upstairs lobby they entered reminded him a bit of an Army reception area. A petite receptionist was dwarfed by a large brown workstation. Even so, he had a clear shot of her sitting there, doing computer work. She had her blond hair pulled up into a tight bun and was dressed in a thin light-blue sweater set and a pair of khaki pants.

"Hi, guys," she said as she watched them approach her. "He the new guy?"

Joe nodded. "Steele, meet Kristen Delinsky."

Kristen, who appeared unassuming and sweet, held her small hand out to him. "Nice to meet you, Steele."

He shook her hand and noticed that like Joe, she was surprisingly strong. "You, too."

She let go, then reached for a small package on her desk. She handed it to Joe. "Here's his badges, parking sticker, and such. Decker has everything else waiting on your approval."

"Thanks," Joe said as he took it.

As she moved back toward her seat, Steele glimpsed the black leather holster underneath Kristen's sweater.

"So do all your receptionists pack heat?" he asked Joe as he led him toward the large door behind Kristen's desk.

"You'll find they change out frequently," Tiger said. "You get shot, and you'll take a stint at the desk, too. We're an equal-opportunity abuser here." She gave him an appreciative look. "Nice powers of perception."

"That's why you wanted me, isn't it?"

She didn't comment.

Steele paused as he entered the "office." On the surface, it looked typical enough. A cubicle section held desks behind tan fabric walls. On his left, an office area was encased in glass, with tan mini-blinds that were currently open.

That office was empty. No doubt it belonged to Joe and Tiger, who seemed to be the ones in charge.

People started popping out of the cubes to take a look at him. Most of them he could peg as government agents. There was a demeanor that most trained agents had that was unmistakable. But a couple of them he would have placed as criminals — sharks, con men, and other things best left unsaid.

"You sure we left Kansas?" he asked Joe.

"How so?"

He indicated the heads popping up. "Looks like a gopher farm."

The women laughed.

Suddenly, he heard a dog barking. Three seconds later, a small golden Pomeranian with a black face came running out of the glass office to launch itself into the arms of

Tiger. "Petey!" she said happily as she nuzzled him.

Steele started to pet the dog, only to have it snap at him and growl viciously.

"Don't take it personally," Joe said. "Petey hates everyone except Tiger and Retter."

"That's 'cause Petey has taste, yes he does," Tiger said in a high-pitched voice as she played with her pet.

Holding the dog close, she and Joe led him toward the office without introducing him to anyone. Steele wasn't sure if that was a good sign or not.

But he noticed that many of the agents were following them.

One of them, a tall blond man who was so clean-cut he looked more like a fashion model than an agent, cleared his throat before he addressed him. "So what do you think of our assistant director?"

Steele frowned as the guy pointed to the names on the door. In big block letters, it read "Joe Q. Public, Director," and underneath it was "The Thi Ho, Assistant Director."

But what was really strange was the handwritten sign taped below the names: "The truth is in here, so don't bug me with your bullshit."

Still, the unknown man was pointing to the woman's name.

Steele knew instantly the guy was trying to set him up. He glanced at Tiger and paraphrased her earlier words. "I like Tee already. She's snotty."

Tee/Tiger laughed out loud before she kissed Petey's head.

The guy gave her an aggravated stare. "No fair, Tee, you told him."

"No, I didn't," she said as she set her dog down so that he could run into the office, where Steele saw a small dog bed waiting for him. "He's just smarter than you are, Hunter. Then again, most people are."

Hunter screwed his face up in disgust before he looked back at Steele. "Did she tell you her name?"

"No," Steele said honestly. "I have a Vietnamese aunt."

Hunter huffed, then pulled out his wallet and handed two twenties to Joe. "I really hate you two."

Joe gave a laugh that reminded him of Snidely Whiplash. "Yeah, I know. Now get your ass back to work."

Grumbling, Hunter made his way back toward the cube farm along with mini-Angelina.

Steele felt a strange urge to call her back,

though he didn't know why. Even though they'd barely spoken, he somehow felt like she was on his side.

Yeah . . . he was losing his mind.

With his hand splayed over the glass, Joe held the door open with one arm for them to enter. Tee directed Steele to a pair of chairs in front of Joe's desk while Joe shut the door, then closed the blinds.

"We'll handle introductions to the others later. For now, let's take care of business."

Steele nodded. "One question, though."

Joe sat down behind his gray metal desk while Tee took a seat next to Steele. "Sure."

"Are those your real names?"

Joe didn't look amused.

"Yes," Tee answered in a dry tone as her dog jumped up into her lap. "He's really Joseph Quincy Public, and I'm Ho Thi The, or in American The Thi Ho."

Interesting names. He wondered briefly if their parents had held a grudge against them.

But that wasn't the most important matter on his mind. "So do I get any more information about my future now?"

Tee stroked her dog's ears. "Basically we're a shadow agency, much like the group you were a part of in the Army. No one knows who we are, and we like it that way.

You will be listed on payroll as a civilian contractor with government retirement and bennies. We have international jurisdiction, and if you get caught, no one will help you. We will deny all knowledge of you and your missions. Always."

Yep, that sounded like Shadow Corps. "So you're basically telling me that I'm dead to Uncle Sam."

She nodded. "We're based out of Nashville, but we have a few field offices scattered around the world. Your first assignment will be with another agent in the D.C. area."

Steele thought about that for a minute. "Just out of curiosity, why are you based in Nashville, when all other federal groups are based in the D.C. area? You guys do know that the Beltway is the hub of American government activity, right?"

It was Joe who answered. "We're roughly in the center of America. It gives us easy access to the rest of the country should we need to go somewhere in a hurry. Not to mention that when they drop the bomb on D.C., our agency will still be standing intact."

"Yeah," Tee said. "Haven't you ever seen the movies? D.C. and New York always get toasted. Once the bureaucrats go, Joe will be president."

Joe snorted. "I'd rather see Petey as president. Let them shoot the dog."

She dropped her jaw as if the mere thought offended her. "Hey! Insult my dog, and I *will* kill you."

Steele shook his head. "She's a lovely little thing, isn't she?"

"You've no idea." Joe pushed the box that Kristen had given him across the desk.

Steele opened it up. His jaw went slack at the contents. There was literally a badge for every known federal agency in there and they weren't even all American. CIA, ATF, DEA, FBI, NSA, even Interpol and Europol. Freakily enough, they all had his picture on them and looked completely legit. "Humor me for a second. Who exactly do I work for?"

"You work for me," Joe said, his eyes deadly earnest. "We are BAD — the Bureau of American Defense. But no one outside of this organization, other than the president — who will never admit we exist — has ever heard of us, and we intend to keep it that way. We are multijurisdictional, and we work with a variety of international governments who think we belong to other agencies, hence the badges. If you need one to gain admittance into an area, use it. You'll be given a series of phone numbers that will appear legit when called, and will verify you work with whatever agency you claim."

Before he could ask anything more, Tee spoke up. "Your partner is Sydney Westbrook. She'll show you the ropes and fill you in on any details."

Steele curled his lip at the upper-crust name. Sydney. Westbrook. Yeah. That was someone he wanted to train him in this. He could just imagine the tall, blond WASP goddess who would be more concerned with her manicure than their assignment.

"I don't work with rich socialites."

"Sydney knows her job," Tee assured him. "She's fully committed."

Steele tried not to roll his eyes. "Where's she from? Connecticut?"

"Boston. She's a Harvard graduate."

This time he couldn't stop himself. He rolled his eyes. "Let me guess, daddy's a banker?"

"Stockbroker, actually."

Steele turned at the deep, incredibly sexy voice of the woman who'd come in with them. This mission was really beginning to suck.

Tee inclined her head to Sydney. "She's your spotter."

Ah, hell nah.

Every piece of him screamed out at those

words. Steele rose to his feet. "I don't work with a spotter, especially not a woman."

Sydney gave him a droll stare. "All snipers work with a spotter, and the fact that I'm a woman has nothing to do with anything."

"No, we don't, and *I* absolutely will not." He turned to face Joe. "And you can stick my ass back in Leavenworth before I work with her now."

Joe's face hardened. "You will do as you're told."

"Fuck you."

"Do you kiss your mother with that mouth?" Sydney asked, her face aghast.

He turned on her with a snarl. "No. She disowned me."

Syd felt the pain that he was doing his best to hide. She wanted to ask if he was serious, but the look on his face and his irate demeanor told her that he wasn't joking in the least. "Why did you shoot at your CO?"

His dark eyes singed her with fire. "He. Pissed. Me. Off."

"I can relate," Syd said calmly. "Joe pisses me off constantly, but I've never taken a shot at him."

"I have," Tee muttered.

Syd frowned at Tee, who had her attention on Petey. She looked back at Steele, who was still tense and angry. "Look, we are on the brink of a potential international disaster that could hit us any day now. Remember how the first world war started?"

"Archduke Ferdinand and his wife Sophie were shot and killed while visiting in Sarajevo."

Thank God the man had a brain and knew his history. "That's right. And in a few days a foreign dignitary from a former Soviet bloc country will be here for an important meeting in D.C. with the president. Just like Franz and Sophie, he's been marked for assassination by a group of rebels. Our job is to save his life. If we fail, not only America, but his and other countries are completely screwed. We can't let him die on American soil. Understand? We need you to nail his assassin before the assassin nails him."

"Why don't you just tell him to stay home?"

It was Joe who answered. "A, you don't just tell another president he's not welcome here. It looks bad in the press. B, whether he dies here or at home, we're screwed politically. The best place to protect him is here, where we can nail his executioner before the hit takes place."

"You make that sound so easy," Steele said sarcastically. "And just when and where is this going to take place?"

Syd cringed at his question. "We don't know exactly. Basically, we have two ways to go about this. In the first, I'll go over his published itinerary with you, and your job is to pick out the most likely position for the hit. We'll set up an observation point and take out the assassin whenever he moves in on the president."

His eyes narrowed. "President of what?"

"Uhbukistan."

He shook his head. "The Kabukis are coming for us? Yeah, that's a big threat."

Syd ground her teeth at his flippant attitude as anger whipped through her. "Not Kabukis. The Uhbukistanis, and they're not to be taken lightly, Mr. Steele. They were part of the former Soviet Union and are strategically placed just north of Georgia and between the Caspian and Black Seas. Their lands are rich in oil reserves and are highly coveted in the region. As a border country, the USSR stockpiled them with nuclear weapons during the Cold War, and after the collapse, no one has reclaimed those weapons. President Kaskamanov is an ally to us, and he wants to disarm his country and join the European Community. His son, on the other hand, isn't our friend. He's a mercenary bastard who wants to sell the weapons to the highest bidder."

"Let me guess. America ain't it."

She nodded. "So his son thinks that if his father dies here, he can blame us, take control of the country, and then deal with whomever pays him the most. And I don't think I have to tell you what will happen if those weapons fall into the wrong hands. There's no telling how many people could die."

Steele folded his arms over his chest and gave her a bored stare. "Look, I don't care what the Ooga-Boogas do. It sounds like they need a family counselor, not a sniper."

She was going to kill him. Why was he being so stubborn?

Didn't he care?

"They're not Ooga-Boogas, they're Uhbukistanis."

Still he gave her that cold, dispassionate stare. "Whatever. My personal belief is that we should leave Ooga-Booga Land to the Oompa-Loompas. Let them fight it out with the Snozzwangers, Wangdoodles, and the mean Vermicious Knids. I'd rather go peel carrots with a spoon."

He started past her.

Syd grabbed his arm to stop him. "What kind of soldier are you that you're going to just sit in a cell while the world is thrown into chaos? Do you not understand what could happen if those weapons fall into the wrong hands? How could you be so selfish?"

"Selfish?" he asked angrily. His eyes darkened even more. "*I'm* selfish? Look, Agent Westbrook, your daddy's a Boston stockbroker. I'm a death broker. I'm sure you don't lecture Daddy on finance, so don't even try to lecture me on assassination politics. I know all about them. Some bureaucratic ass-wipe sitting in a pristine office that's totally isolated from the rest of the world decides the son of King Oompa-Loompa is a threat. He then hands down orders to people like me to go off King Oompa-Loompa's son. Like an idiot, I do what he says without question. I hunt my target down, using information that is mostly bullshit and unreliable, gathered by someone like you who assured me it was correct at the time. But hey, it changes minute by minute, and God forbid we pass that along to you."

He backed her up against the wall as his eyes continued to singe her. She wasn't afraid of him, but his anger was so fierce it was tangible, and she was all too aware that he could hurt her before she could draw her weapon.

"So me and my spotter lie in the grass, sand, or snow for days on end, cramped and hungry, never able to move more than a millimeter an hour until I have that one perfect shot I've been waiting for for days. I take it, and then we lay there like pieces of dirt until we can inch our way back to safety, where hopefully the helicopter team will remember that they were supposed to retrieve us."

She swallowed at what he described.

"Have you any idea of the nerves it takes to do what I do? To lie there on the ground while other armed men search for you? Have them step on you and not be able to even breathe or wince because if you do, it's not only your life, but the life of your spotter?"

Her heart clenched at that, and when he spoke the next words, she actually gasped.

"Do you know what it's like to have the brains of your best friend sprayed into your face and not be able to render aid to him because you know he's dead and if you do, you'll be killed too?" His low, deep voice was trembling now. "I have been into the bowels of hell and back, *Miz* Westbrook. I have stared down the devil and made him sweat. So don't tell me I don't take this seriously. Believe me, there is nothing in life I know better than what I was trained to do."

Syd nodded at his words as she finally

understood him completely. "Your spotter was killed."

A tic worked in his jaw as ultimate pain flared deep in those chocolate eyes. "He wasn't just my spotter, Agent. He was my best friend. I swore to his wife that I'd bring him home in one piece. And *I* let him die."

"He knew the risks."

He sneered at her. "Save it. I've heard the spiel from the army psychologists and everyone else. Had I listened to myself and not taken up position where they told me to because they knew best, Brian would be alive now. I'm not going into another setup planned by a federally trained spook to get someone else killed. Ever. I'm through with this."

Syd felt for the man. She couldn't imagine the horror of lying next to a friend who'd been killed in front of her. It was a wonder he was still sane.

But it didn't change anything. They needed him.

"How did you escape?" she asked him.

His gaze turned cloudy, as if the scene were replaying through his mind. "I fought my way out in a manner that would have made Rambo proud. And when I got home without his body because I couldn't pull him out without getting myself killed, I got slapped in my face by everyone around me. So don't talk to me about death, little girl. I wrote the book on it."

"And that's why we need you," she said quietly, wanting to reach out and touch him, but knowing he was in no mood to be coddled. There were no words or actions that could erase the hell he'd been through.

He shook his head. "There are other snipers out there. Granted, not as good as I am, but they're good enough to get you killed."

"No," she said earnestly. "Not with your training. You were taught to shoot by the single most successful sniper in military history. I'm assuming your father taught you everything he knows."

That went over him like toxic waste. His entire body tensed, and she swore she could almost taste his anger. "Then hire my father. I'm out of this, and I'm out of here."

As he started for the door, Joe spoke up. "Where are you going, Steele?"

Steele froze as that single, innocuous question went through him like a knife. For the second time since he'd walked into this office, he felt savaged by his emotions.

He had no car. No money. No home. No family. No friends.

Nothing.

He hadn't owned anything in more than two years.

And he'd never in his life felt so helpless. So worthless. He turned around to face Joe, who watched him carefully. Something in the man's eyes said Joe fully understood what he felt right now, though to be honest, he had no idea how he possibly could.

Steele swallowed the pain that had gathered in his throat, choking him. The first thing his father had taught him as a boy was never to betray his emotions. It was that cold, dead person he showed to Joe and the women now. "I refuse to lie down beside another spotter and see her die while there's nothing I can do to stop it. I'm through with this."

Joe nodded. "Understood. But you know, we've been looking for a backup sniper for the last three years, and you're the only one we've ever brought here to Nashville to interview. You're the only one to ever see this office, or Petey."

Joe's humor was lost on him at the moment. "Why me?"

Those blue eyes were as cold as Steele's nerves. "Because you know what tragedy can happen when you don't exercise free thought. We don't want anyone here who's by the book. Anyone who has to be told what to do, when to do it, and how to do it. We need agents who can think on their own and execute their missions without someone micromanaging them."

Steele folded his arms over his chest. "There are plenty of snipers who can do that."

"And we need someone who won't be missed," Tee said coldly. "Someone without any family or friend entanglements. In the four years since this agency was founded, you are only the second sniper we've found who met all of our needs."

That just made him feel all warm and fuzzy inside. They wanted him because, unlike Brian, if someone blew his brains out no one would shed a single tear.

Boy, he had the life, huh?

"Tell you what," Joe said, his features softening a degree. "Why don't you take a few hours and rest. Get used to being free for a while. Get a good night's sleep where you don't have to worry about being vulnerable. If you still feel like this tomorrow, we'll put you right back where you were. No harm, no foul. Deal?"

Steele wasn't sure about that. He had a feeling the harm had already been done. "I have no place to stay."

Joe pushed an intercom button on his desk. "Kristen, have Carlos come in."

A few seconds later, the office door opened to show him a tall Hispanic male. "Yo, bossman? You rang?"

Joe indicated Steele with a tilt of his head. "Carlos, meet Steele."

Carlos held his hand out to him. *"Hola."*

Steele hesitated before he shook it. "Hi."

"Steele is a special recruit who doesn't have any place to stay. He needs some downtime, so I was wondering if he could bunk with you for the night."

"Sure, *jefe.*"

"Gracias."

"De nada." Carlos opened the door again. "You ready to leave now, or do you need a few more minutes?"

Steele looked at Joe.

"We're done . . . for now."

He glanced at Sydney, who was watching him with an angry tic in her jaw. Part of him hated that he'd ruined her plans. But she'd find another fool to do her bidding. All he wanted was to be left alone.

She met his gaze with heat burning deep in those green eyes. There was a time when the accusation there would have spurred him to take this mission just to prove her wrong. But he'd done a lot of growing up over the last two years. Dares didn't motivate him anymore.

Nothing did.

"Hasta la vista," he said to her as he started for the door.

Her response in Spanish caught him completely off guard. "Don't let the door hit you in the ass."

Shaking his head at her, he followed Carlos out of the office.

Syd didn't move until she was alone with Tee and Joe. "So you're just going to let him leave?"

Joe sat back in his chair to watch her with that blank expression he was famous for. "We can't make him shoot someone, Syd. That's against the Constitution."

Frustration consumed her. She'd come so close to having what she needed. "So what am I supposed to do now? We have less than three weeks to put this together."

Joe glanced at Tee, who was feeding Petey a dog biscuit, before he answered. "Have faith."

"No offense, my faith died ten years ago."

Joe looked back at her. "I know, but sometimes you have to believe in other people, Syd. Many times they'll surprise you."

Yeah, right. "I'm all right with that so long

as the surprise is a good one. In my experience, though, it usually isn't."

And something inside told her that Steele wasn't the kind of guy to just blithely change his mind. He was gone, and now she had nowhere else to turn.

She hated feeling like this. She could see the future ahead of them, and it terrified her.

Five

Steele followed Carlos out of the office, past Kristen, who was on the phone, speaking flawless German to someone. She paused to wave at them. There was something strangely surreal about all this. Like he'd walked into a movie or a dream, and that at any moment he'd find himself snatched back to his jail cell. It just didn't seem like it was possible that he was here, away from prison, surrounded by such an odd cast of people.

Without a word, Carlos headed to the elevator and pressed the down button. Immediately after the light came on, Carlos moved to the side of the doors with his back against the wall as if he half expected the doors to open and someone to jump out and shoot him. He even put his hand under his jacket, no doubt over his weapon.

"Been an agent long?" he asked Carlos.

Carlos let out an evil laugh. "You could say that."

Maybe, but there was something about

the man that denied it. He reminded Steele more of the criminals he'd been locked up with. The way he moved, like a hungry predator who knew it had to kill or be killed. It wasn't the arrogance that most Feds had. It was something else. Something almost diabolical. "You don't strike me as a typical Fed."

The doors opened. Carlos lifted his head away from the wall to scan the inside before he moved away from the wall. "I'm not a typical Fed." He literally crept into the elevator and scanned all the way up to the ceiling before he relaxed.

"I really don't want to be this paranoid," Steele muttered as he entered the elevator.

Carlos laughed. "My paranoia has nothing to do with my current job. It's a holdover from my past, and those who would like to ensure I have no future." Carlos pressed the button for the lobby.

"And what was your past employment?"

Carlos smirked at him. "I don't know you well enough to answer that . . . yet."

Steele couldn't fault him there. His past wasn't something he liked to talk about either. And they were strangers, so it made sense that Carlos was defensive.

"So do you speak Spanish?" Carlos asked.

Actually he did, but Steele had learned

the value of discretion early on. "Only what I've learned in *Terminator* movies, *Sesame Street,* and from Speedy Gonzales."

Carlos shook his head. "It's all right. I understand. I personally learned to speak English from Hanna-Barbera cartoons."

Steele gave him a droll stare.

"It's true." He made the sign of the cross over his heart. "For years though, I kept trying to find 'ruh-roh' " — he imitated Scooby-Doo's voice — "in dictionaries. It wasn't until my little brother went to college in Miami that he finally told me it wasn't a real word. Talk about feeling stupid. Thanks, Scooby. But what the hell, my brother got a good laugh out of it."

Steele forced himself not to laugh. He doubted if the man would appreciate it.

The doors opened to the lobby.

"*Hola,* Tracy," Carlos said to a petite blond knockout who was waiting to enter the elevator they were leaving.

She gave them both a spectacular smile. "Hi, Carlos. How's it going?"

"It'll go better the day you leave your boyfriend and give me a date." He winked at her.

She all but beamed at him. "The day I leave him, you're the first one I'll call," she said with a laugh as she entered the car.

Carlos covered his heart with his hand as if he were in pain. "Ah, you break my heart, little dove." He blew her a kiss as the doors closed.

Once they were alone, Carlos growled deep in his throat as he led the way across the lobby, toward the doors that opened onto the street. "You should see her boyfriend. He's a total ass. Completely undeserving of something that fine and tasty."

It'd been over two years since Steele had seen anything in the flesh as good-looking as Tracy was. But what struck him the most was that he wasn't nearly as attracted to her as he'd been to Syd.

I've been in jail way too long.

And if he had to go back tomorrow, he'd like nothing better than finding some action tonight. Twenty-three more years was a long time to go without a woman, and that's what he was looking at if Joe sent him back to Kansas.

The mere thought of it made his cock jerk.

They left the building and headed toward the garage across the street. His gut tightened as he realized how close he was to losing his freedom again. He glanced around at the people on the shaded street. Two women were heading into a restaurant as they chatted about work. A family that was obviously touring the stores and town crossed the street. The dad looked flustered as the two kids fought and the mother snapped at them.

A guy was on the corner, yelling at someone on the cell phone. . . .

None of them had any idea how lucky they were to be living out their lives in such a normal way. There wasn't anyone telling them what time to get up, what time to go to sleep. They didn't have to make roll call. They weren't referred to by their inmate number.

They were just people who had no idea how quickly their entire existence could change.

One stupid move . . .

On the morning he'd been arrested, the day had started out like any other. He'd gotten up without enough sleep, had shaved, dressed, and gone to work, expecting it to be just another day.

And in one split second, because of one stupid decision, he'd thrown it all away.

Don't be stupid again . . .

He could return to this world with nothing more than a few words of commitment. Tomorrow he could stay here, or he could be headed back to hell.

It was all up to him.

"Damn you, Joe," he muttered as they crossed the street. That bastard had known exactly what he was doing when he'd sent him out here to mix with regular people.

"They're coming into D.C. this week, Joe."

Joe looked up from his file on a European case he was working on to see Syd standing in the doorway of his office. "You sure?"

She nodded. "I just got the confirmation from Retter, and they've made six phone calls to APS this week alone to confirm their 'protection.' "

Asset Protection System, or APS, was the front for a known company of freelance mercenaries and contract killers. BAD had been trying to monitor it for a long time, but it was next to impossible. They could trace incoming calls only, and even those were infrequent.

Joe could hear the panic in her voice. But unlike Syd, he knew Steele wasn't about to leave them. Jail wasn't a picnic, and as distasteful as Steele found this work, it beat the hell out of prison detail.

"Don't worry, we haven't lost him yet."

She pulled her glasses off as she fretted. "Yeah, but what if we do?"

"Trust me, Syd. The best people to fight for freedom are the ones who've lost their own. They understand the importance of it a lot more than those who've never been without."

Syd wished she could believe that. But at the moment everything seemed so hopeless. "Maybe I should head out to D.C. and start looking for a way —"

"Give me twenty-four hours, Syd. That's all we need."

She wasn't so sure about that. "But it could be twenty-four hours wasted that I could spend trying to find a way into APS."

Joe got up from his desk. He picked something up and moved to stand in front of her. "You ever been to the Ryman?"

She scowled at his question. "What has that got to do with anything?"

"It's a special show tonight. They're actually broadcasting the Grand Ole Opry live from the stage like they used to in the good old days."

Okay . . . she was worried about national defense, and Joe was off on a nostalgia high. The only problem was, she really needed him to put down the crack pipe and join the rest of them in reality.

He handed her a ticket. "You should go."

She stared at the ticket in her hand as if it

were an alien object. "You've completely lost your mind, haven't you?"

He gave her a good-natured grin. "Be there, Syd. It's an order."

She wrinkled her nose in distaste. "I really hate country music."

His face turned deadly serious. "You know, there's a lot of things in life that I hate that I have to tolerate. Traffic. Lines. Tee's driving. Disco Muzak. But you get used to it." He paused to give her that "don't argue" stare. "Be there, Syd. It'll be good for you."

He walked past her, out of the office.

Syd sighed heavily as she stared at the ticket. "Someone shoot me, please."

"Any particular place you prefer?"

She turned to see Tee entering the office. "The head. Right between my eyes."

Tee frowned. "Okay. What has you so upset?"

She held up the ticket.

Tee laughed before she shook her head. "That man and his Opry. He's downright scary with it."

"Do I really have to go?"

"It's not so bad."

She was surprised by Tee's defense. She knew for a fact Tee's favorite bands were the Black-eyed Peas and Godsmack. "You've been?"

Tee shrugged as she moved to her desk and opened a drawer. "Joe likes it." Petey looked up from his bed, then settled back down to sleep. Ignoring her prized dog, Tee pulled out a small lime green iPod. "And this helps immensely."

Syd looked at it as if it were the Holy Grail. "Can I *please* borrow it?"

Tee tossed it to her.

She grabbed it and held it like a lifeline, which is exactly what it would be. "Thanks, Tee."

"No problem. Just promise me you won't shoot Joe."

"I'll try, but I can't promise the impossible." Syd left the office and headed back to her desk. But as she sat down, it wasn't her case that was on her mind.

It was Steele.

Over and over, she saw the pain in his eyes. Heard the pain in his voice. She was lucky. She still had her family. Granted, they had *no* idea what she did for a living. They only knew she was a federal employee. If she ever told them the truth, they would be worried constantly.

Joe didn't take many agents who had such attachments. Tee had told her that all of Joe's family had died before he turned twenty. Having experienced such loss firsthand, he didn't want to create a bureau of widows and orphans.

He also believed that having a family made an agent weak, vulnerable. It gave your enemies a target.

Syd wasn't so sure about that. Her mother could wield a mean garden hoe when she wanted to. There were enough snakes who'd given up their ghost because they dared venture into her yard to prove it. And her dad . . . get him talking on stocks and bonds, and he could bore anyone to death — even the meanest terrorist out there.

When it came to her sister, Martha, she could shoot even straighter and better than Syd. While growing up, Martha had wanted to join a Wild West show, courtesy of the Clint Eastwood movies. It had broken her heart when she'd found out that such things no longer existed. But it gave her a legacy that Smith and Wesson would envy.

Yeah, her family was about as loony as they came, but at least they were there for her. All she had to do was pick up the phone, and she could talk to any one of them any time she needed to.

Poor Steele. No one should live their life abandoned by their loved ones.

Sighing, she forced herself to focus on her

work. Still, it all came back to one basic thing.

She needed a man who didn't want any part of *her,* or of this assignment. How could she ever convince him to help her protect the Uhbukistani president?

Sighing, she tucked the iPod in her purse, then slid it back into her drawer. "C'mon, Steele. Don't disappoint me. I need one man in my life who's dependable."

"Hey, Syd?"

She looked up to see Andre Moore in the opening of her cube. At an even six feet in height, Andre was a handsome African-American man who served as one of the intelligence experts. More than that, he was an amateur inventor. And as always, he was impeccably dressed in a white button-down shirt, a dark blue tie, and a pair of pleated trousers.

Since she'd been in Nashville, he'd been helping her prep for the Uhbukistani situation. "What'cha need, Andre?"

"I got some real bad news. The agent we had on this over in Europe has just been found in Georgia. His throat was cut."

"Yuri?"

He nodded.

Syd hissed as pain from that hit her. She always hated to hear about the death of an agent, and this one in particular hit her hard.

A draft from the CIA, Yuri Korjev had been a dedicated agent who had never let them down. The grandson of Russian immigrants, he'd been convinced that he could infiltrate the Uhbukistani inner circle and keep tabs on the president's son.

Obviously his failure had proven fatal.

She winced as an image of one of his famous grins went through her mind.

Don't worry, Yuri, she thought with conviction. *We'll get them.* But that was cold comfort for a man who was now dead.

"And it gets even better."

"Of course it does," she said quietly. Didn't it always? "What?"

"I looked into employment opportunities with APS. The only way in is by invitation. You have to be scouted. They're so paranoid, they make Howard Hughes look normal. I can't even get a bug in there."

"Great. So it's Steele or nothing."

He nodded. "If he turns us down, there's nothing else to be done. He's our only way into that door. The game is over before it begins."

And Yuri would have died for nothing . . .

There was no way she was going to see this fail.

"All right, then. Let's turn up the heat on our man."

"How so?"

"Leak the word that he's escaped from jail. If he's listed as a jailbreak, they'll lengthen his sentence, and he won't have any place to go to escape us."

Andre sucked his breath in sharply between his teeth. "That's awfully harsh, Syd."

"So is life, Andre. And until he agrees to help us, it's about to get a lot harsher for Steele."

Six

Steele entered Carlos Delgado's apartment on Church Street with a lot of trepidation as to what might be awaiting him. Especially after he'd had to battle the untold stack of McDonald's wrappers, files, gun/car magazines, and receipts for a seat in Carlos's Corvette.

He'd been in enough homes of his Army buddies to know to be afraid of another man's housekeeping abilities. Very afraid. Granted, he had a high tolerance for messes and dirty underwear, but he drew the line at left-out food, dirty dishes, and filth.

But he had to give the man credit. Carlos's apartment, unlike his car, was immaculate.

"You live alone?" he asked Carlos.

Carlos snorted as if he understood why Steele was asking that particular question. "I have a cleaning lady who comes in once a week, even though Joe keeps warning me that one day she could turn into La Femme Nikita and shoot me. But I think it's worth the risk. I'd much rather take the chance on someone trying to kill me than to scrub out my own toilet . . . or, Dios forbid, do laundry." He shivered.

Steele could respect that.

"Besides, if she looks like Peta Wilson or Bridget Fonda, it might be worth a bullet or two." He winked and made a clicking noise between his teeth.

Steele shook his head. "I take it you have a thing for blondes."

"Definitely. The longer the legs, the better. Know what I mean?"

Yes, he did. But at the moment he seemed to have a preoccupation with a woman who had very average-sized legs, long dark hair, and accusing green eyes.

Carlos led him around the large living room, toward the breakfast counter that separated it from the kitchen. "There's beer, Coke, and food in the fridge, so help yourself."

"Thanks."

There wasn't a lot of furniture in the apartment — a brown leather sofa with end tables, a coffee table, and two media center recliners. The place was built more for comfort than for entertaining others.

Carlos had a top-of-the-line media center and stereo. There were Corvette and vintage-car *Auto-Trader* magazines piled up on the coffee table under four different remotes.

"Bathroom is down the hall. First door you come to. My bedroom is the next one down, so you can understand why I'm not going to show it to you."

"No worries. I have no interest in it."

"Good."

Carlos walked into the kitchen and opened a drawer where he kept a spare set of keys. "The sofa pulls out into a bed that already has linens and a blanket. There's a spare pillow and more blankets in the hall linen closet across from the bathroom, along with towels and washcloths. The only rule here is if you mess it up, you clean it up, or I kick your *culo*."

Those were rules he could live with. "Seems fair enough."

Carlos handed him the spare keys. "I need to get back and work on my case." He pulled out his wallet and handed Steele a business card that actually listed Carlos as an insurance broker. Joe had thought of everything. "You need anything, give me a call, and I can be here in less than fifteen minutes."

"Thanks." Steele tucked the card in his back pocket.

Carlos nodded before he left him alone in his place — something that again showed an unbelievable amount of trust. For agents, they seemed remarkably trusting. Too much so at times. It didn't jive with what he knew about such beasts, but then these guys seemed to like to thwart tradition. Which made him wonder what they would be like out in the field.

Either they were extremely effective, or total fuckups. He hoped, for the president's sake, they were the former and not the latter.

Steele wandered aimlessly through the small apartment. The furniture around him was mostly black and brown, very contemporary in design. There was a collection of black-and-white photographs on the wall behind the plasma TV. By the looks of the people in them, he'd assume they were Carlos's family. Most of them bore a striking resemblance to the man. And in the center of the photographs was one of a much younger Carlos with a boy around the age of thirteen. They had their arms slung around each other and looked as if they were celebrating something.

It must be the brother he'd mentioned earlier, who had gone to school in Miami.

Steele felt a sharp pang in his chest as he

thought about his baby sister, Tina. As a kid, he'd been the overprotective brother to the point of making her insane. There had always been something very fragile about her, and that frailty had made their father push her constantly as he tried to "toughen her up." It was those two things that made him want to be a buffer between her and the world. To keep her safe no matter how mild or severe the danger. Even so, she'd worshipped him in that little sister-big brother way.

She'd been the only one in his family who had bothered to contact him at all after his arrest. He'd gotten a Christmas card from her with three simple sentences inside it.

Hope you're okay. Please don't tell Mom and Dad I sent this to you.

I love you,
Tina

Even now, the pain of her words cut through him. But at least she'd remembered him.

At least she'd made some kind of effort to contact him, even though they both knew their father would have her head if he ever found out. That man was incredibly unforgiving of any slight, whether imagined or real. God, country, and honor were all that mattered to him. Family be damned if they ever interfered with the above.

Steele winced at the reality of that. There would never be a way to reconcile with his father. He'd embarrassed a man who knew nothing of forgiveness.

Seeking some refuge from the grief of all he'd lost, he walked outside onto a small concrete balcony that overlooked the city. There was a small white plastic table and two matching plastic chairs. One was so close to the table that it was obvious that it wasn't used much. The other was angled so that Carlos could sit out here and enjoy the scenery. Oddly enough, there was an empty bottle of Black Label Jack Daniel's under it.

Steele frowned at the sight as he wondered how lonely Carlos must be that he sat out here drinking, alone.

Not willing to think about that, he continued to scope out the view. Carlos had a great view of the skyline and downtown area. Nashville was an interesting place. It was a comforting city — not too large, not too small. There was something familiar and inviting about it. It could be Anyplace, USA.

And before he knew what he was doing, Steele left the apartment to wander around the downtown streets.

God, it'd been way too long since he'd last been able to do this. He had no duties, no obligations.

No one knew his past. He was just another guy on the street. Not a trained sniper. Not a convict.

He was just Joe Average again. And it felt great.

Smiling to himself, he walked for blocks, doing nothing more than just enjoying the sunlight on his skin. There were numerous shops in the downtown area that were alive with activity. Nestled among a wide variety of restaurants and businesses, most of them paid tribute to country music.

He lost track of time as he drifted in and out of the stores, talking to people for the first time in months. No one here knew who he was or what he'd done. They spoke to him like a human being. Like a friend.

He was on top of the world.

Until he happened past a small café. Steele froze as he saw a flash of the Leavenworth prison in an aerial shot, along with the words "breaking news."

His heart pounding in trepidation, he pushed open the door to listen.

"Convicted of attempted murder against a senior ranking officer, Joshua Daniel Steele is believed to be armed and dangerous. He's said to be heading west, but details are sketchy at present. Local law enforcement officers have been given his picture and are preparing a massive multi-state hunt for the fugitive. . . . "

And then they flashed his mug shot. Oh, what a beautiful picture that was. His head was bald, and he had a lovely smirk on his face that made him look like a serial killer. No doubt his mother would be so proud of her son's newfound celebrity status. He could imagine his father spewing his coffee right about now and cursing violently from his home in Manassas, Virginia.

Steele felt as if he'd been sucker-punched. This couldn't be happening . . .

Damn them! Why the hell would they do this to him?

Rage darkening his gaze, he glanced around the slightly crowded room slowly, grateful that no one except for one waitress seemed to be paying attention to the TV — and luckily, that one woman hadn't looked his way yet. Trying not to look nervous or suspicious, he backed out of the café before someone recognized him.

"So much for going back to jail," he snarled under his breath. He was now an escaped felon who would have additional time tacked onto his sentence — just what he needed.

Apparently BAD had just screwed him. But little did they know, he wasn't the kind of guy to just bend over and take it. Oh, no. They'd turned on the wrong person this time, and he fully intended to make them pay.

"Syd, you've got *no* people skills."

Syd let out a disgusted breath as Joe chewed her a new one. Angry over his lecture, she clutched the arms of her chair while he sat on the opposite side of his desk, glaring at her. "We *need* him. Now he'll have no choice except to join BAD."

Joe's eyes turned even icier. "You should have consulted me before you alerted the media. Dammit, woman, this is not the way to start off this assignment. Have you any idea how hard he's going to be to hide? Not to mention how pissed off he is? And now you expect me to hand a loaded rifle to a man who no doubt wants all of our heads on a platter? Yeah . . . brilliant plan, Agent Westbrook. Got any more great ones in there? Tell you what, why don't we just call up the Uhbukistanis and turn over our plans and IDs to them too? Sounds good, huh?"

She really didn't need his sarcasm. "I didn't have time to wait."

Joe came to his feet, an angry tic keeping time with her rapid heartbeat in his left jaw. "Look, I don't issue orders often, but dammit, when I do, I expect them to be obeyed. You don't ever go around me again, do you understand?"

She didn't respond.

"Answer me," he snapped.

She rose slowly to her feet. "I understand. I also understand that time is critical and that my mandate is to use any means necessary to achieve my directive."

The look on Joe's face chilled her. For an instant, she truly feared for her life. Joe was so easygoing and even-keeled most days that it was all too easy to forget just how dangerous the man could be.

"Don't you ever —"

His dire words were cut off by the speaker buzzing. He continued to glare at her as he answered it.

"Hey, Joe, Steele just —" Before Kristen could finish her sentence, the door to Joe's office was slung open with so much force, it actually rattled on its hinges. Steele stood in the doorway with a look of hell's fury on his face. His dark brown hair was brushed back from his face, one lock of it falling into his eyes. Every muscle in his body was tense, as if he were fighting to keep from attacking them.

Syd took a step back at the look of rage on Steele's face. He made Joe's look paltry by comparison.

"What the hell went through your mind?" Steele asked from between clenched teeth.

Syd swallowed, waiting for Joe to turn her in for what she'd done.

He didn't. Instead, Joe's face went so blank that it was hard to believe three minutes ago, he'd looked much like Steele. "We needed to close the escape door for you. Sorry."

Steele's dark brown eyes narrowed. "You're not half as sorry as you're going to be."

Joe tensed as he faced Steele's anger without flinching. "You need to calm down."

"Like hell." Steele took a step toward Joe, who braced himself as if getting ready to defend or attack.

"Joe didn't do it." Syd couldn't believe her stupidity at saying that, but she wasn't a coward. She wasn't about to let Joe bear the brunt of Steele's anger when she'd been the one who caused it. "I did."

That at least succeeded in stunning him enough that he only frowned at her. "Why?"

"Unlike Joe, I don't trust in the nature of people to do the right thing. I needed you, so I took the steps I thought necessary to guarantee your cooperation."

He lifted his hand as if he wanted to reach for her throat. Instead, he raked a tense hand through his dark hair. "Have you any idea how badly you have fucked up my life?"

"No worse than you did on your own."

The look on his face said he hated her at that moment, and in truth, she felt awful for hurting him. She reached out toward him. "Steele —"

"Don't touch me," he snarled. He glanced at Joe, then grimaced at her. "You people don't own me. And no one pushes me around." He met her gaze with a heated intensity that should have scorched her. "If you think I'm afraid of jail, little girl, then you better think again. All you've done is piss me off."

He turned his head toward Joe. "I'm out of this. I'm turning myself in to the first cop I see."

The angry tic returned to Joe's jaw. "I understand. But before you do something rash, head back to Carlos's and relax for a while. I think we all need a break from each other to clear our heads."

Steele's face said that he wanted to argue.

"Don't," Joe said calmly. "One night, Steele. That's all I'm asking. If you still want to turn yourself in tomorrow, I have a friend on the force who can pick you up first thing. I'll personally make sure that you don't get any time added onto your sentence."

Steele nodded. He started for the door, only to stop next to her.

Syd trembled at the ferocity of his presence, even though she refused to show it.

"You need to learn to be a little nicer to people, lady. The next time you take it upon yourself to screw me over, you better kill me. 'Cause if you don't, I *will* kill you."

The sternness of that dark stare said it wasn't an idle threat. He meant it.

"I don't take threats."

"And I don't make them." His gaze hardened even more. "That's a promise between me, you, and God."

Syd stiffened. How she wanted a snappy comeback to that. Something biting and clever. But nothing came to her mind as he walked out the door.

It wasn't fair.

She turned to find Joe watching her. She felt suddenly drained and tired.

"What now? You just took all the bite out of my plan. He still has a choice."

Joe shook his head. "Syd, I appreciate your passion for the job. But you need to find a little compassion for people."

How she wished it were that simple. But it wasn't. "One tree isn't more important than the entire forest, Joe. You taught me that. Remember? Political pruning."

"Yeah, but every forest is always destroyed one tree at a time. You take care of those individual trees because each one that falls brings you closer to deforestation. You only prune what's rotten. You don't cut down a good tree for no reason."

Syd ground her teeth. "Has anyone ever won an argument with you?"

"Just Tee, and I was drunk and wounded at the time."

It was about half past six before Steele returned to the apartment building. After leaving the BAD offices, he'd ventured over on foot to the pedestrian bridge that connected the downtown area to the stadium. The rebellious part of him had wanted a cop to spot him just to have the decision taken out of his hands. It would serve all of them right to lose him to their own stupidity, but then, they had sprung him once. Most likely they could spring him again.

The more intelligent part had wanted to

run as far from here as he could. But how far could he run from someone like Joe or Syd? He had no money. No car. No ID. No family.

The only friend who might help him was eleven hours away, and that was in a car, not on foot or by bus. The law was looking for him and had his face plastered all over the news.

Face it, bud, the odds are not with you on this one.

Steele had no doubt that BAD could track him down faster than a herd of hounds. It was what they did for a living, and after being in the Army, Steele knew firsthand some of the more creative toys the spooks had at their disposal.

As much as he hated it, running wasn't an option. Not to mention, he'd never been the kind of man to run from anything. He believed in taking the devil by the horns and wrestling the SOB to the ground.

In the end, he knew he had no real choice except to see this through. So he returned to the apartment building and headed back to Carlos's crib.

Completely pissed off by this day, he opened the door to find Carlos on the cell phone.

As soon as he saw Steele entering the

apartment, Carlos hung up. "There you are. I was beginning to think you were dumb enough to run from us."

"I honestly thought about it. But the only way to run would be to steal from an innocent bystander. Just because I'm a convict, it doesn't mean I'm a criminal. Besides, I figured you guys would bring me back in chains."

He snorted. "I wouldn't have, but Syd would, and she'd be kicking your ass every step of the way."

"As long as she did it in high heels, it might be worth it."

Carlos shook his head. "You like to live dangerously, don't you?"

"Yes, I do."

"Yeah, you go after her, and I suggest you invest in a steel plated jock-strap. Last guy who said something sexual to her and pissed her off is still limping around the office. So, are you ready?"

Steele frowned. "For what?"

"Joe told me to throw a burger at you and run you to the Ryman."

Was that English? "What's the Ryman?"

Carlos slipped his phone into the plastic holster on his hip. "Oh, man, what? You grow up in a hole? I'm from Bolivia, and even I know what the Ryman is. You know,

Grand Ole Opry? Home of country music? Land of the Rube?"

Steele gave him a droll stare. "Why on earth would I want to go there?"

"Because Joe said so." The answer was automatic.

What? Were they three years old? "You do everything Joe says?"

"Mostly. If it suits me . . . oh, hell, yeah. Trust me, it doesn't pay to jerk him off. The last guy who did still hasn't been found."

Steele scoffed. "Joe doesn't scare me."

"Then you're *loco, amigo.*" Carlos's face was deadly sincere. "He scares the shit out of me, and I used to work for people who made Freddie Krueger look like Mr. Rogers." He indicated the door with a tilt of his head. "C'mon."

What the hell? It wasn't like he had anything more pressing to do with his time. And he did need to eat. Since he had no money on him, getting food without Carlos was impossible unless he wanted to add petty larceny to his rap sheet.

Carlos drove him to a restaurant across the street, and as soon as they ate, he took him over to the Ryman Auditorium on Fifth Avenue. The large red building with its white-paned Gothic windows was hard to miss. It was a splash of yesterday nestled among the much more modern buildings that surrounded it. The Ryman was without a doubt the most famed resident of Nashville.

Steele expected Carlos to get out with him, but he didn't. Instead, Carlos handed him a ticket and pointed to a set of doors at the rear of the building. "Go on in."

"You're not coming?"

He shook his head. "Wasn't invited."

Carlos left so fast, Steele barely had time to shut the car door before he roared away. Perplexed by this latest turn of events and by the bizarre day as a whole, Steele stepped up on the curb and headed toward the building.

For all the international renown of the place, it looked like any other theater in America from the back. He entered the set of doors and saw the box-office windows on his right, with bathrooms on his left. There were a few people milling about and chatting, but nothing like he would have expected.

It wasn't until he went farther into the building and saw the statue of Minnie Pearl seated beside Roy Acuff on a bench that the history of the place fully hit him. There was something eerie and magical about a building that was such a cultural landmark.

It was here between these very walls that an entire style of music and identity had been formed.

He glanced up at the stairs that led to the upper seats of the old revival hall. This had been a church before it became the famed home of country music, and it still bore all traces of its proud heritage.

"Can I help you, honey?"

He turned to see an older woman with a staff badge drawing near. "I just need to find my seat, I guess." He honestly had no idea why he was even here. This whole day had been oddly surreal.

He handed her the ticket that Carlos had given him.

She glanced at it and smiled. "You need to be upstairs, sugar, in the Confederate Gallery. You're in section twelve, row A, seat seven." She lowered her voice as if imparting some great secret to him. "It's a real good one. Just go right on up those stairs, and you can't miss it."

"Thanks."

She patted him kindly on the arm. "Anytime. My name's Carla. You need anything else, you just let me know."

He smiled in spite of himself. One thing he'd noticed all day, the people in Nashville were nothing if not friendly. Heading left, he went up the divided stairs to the upper doors and looked for his seat. The place was only about half full. But the woman was right; he had a great view that was right above center stage.

He took a seat and watched as several people had their pictures taken in a roped-off area of the stage, where a mic bearing the WSM logo and a guitar were staged. The whole group looked thrilled to be standing on the same stage where Elvis Presley, Hank Snow, Patsy Cline, and countless others had once performed.

"Popcorn?"

Steele looked up at the familiar voice and about fell off his chair at the sight of Joe. His hair was still pulled back into a pony-tail, but he now wore a black cowboy hat and a tight black T-shirt that showed off every tattoo the man had on both of his arms.

All semblance of refinement was gone. Joe might not have the shit-kicking accent, but he definitely had the bearing.

Steele took the popcorn from Joe as he sat in the empty seat next to him. When Joe handed him a beer, he realized something. There was a tattoo on Joe's right forearm, a broken heart with the name *Jane* in it. Angel wings were on each side of the name, as if flying it away. But what struck him most was its style, which he'd seen countless times in the last two years. It was unmistakable.

"You've done time too."

Joe took a leisurely swig from his longneck beer as he stared straight in front of him. "We all make mistakes, Steele. It's what we do afterward that defines us more than the actual incident that led to the mistake." He glanced at him. "You done any thinking today?"

"Yeah."

"Good. You calm yet?"

Steele let out a tired breath. "The food helped."

Joe snorted before he inclined his head toward a group of people on the floor seats below them. "You know what I love about this place?"

"I hope it's not the decor."

Without betraying any emotion, Joe took another drink of beer before he spoke. "The people. You see the grandmother down there with her son and grandson? They've probably been coming here for years together. Or maybe it's their first trip. Either way, it's three generations sitting down together, laying aside their differences for one night to be a family."

Joe gave him a hard stare. "This is humanity, Steele. This is what we're fighting for. Family. People. Pride. It's our differences that make up our strength. BAD isn't about patriotism. It's about saving individuals. Not just those in America, but all the ones who are out there going about their lives with little to no care about politics. Men, women, and children who only want to live peacefully while others are looking for ways to use them as pawns in a deadly game they don't even want to play."

To emphasize his words, he pointed the top of his beer to indicate an African-American couple on their right. Three seats over from them was an Asian family.

"When I was a boy living in New York, every summer my mother would send me to North Carolina to stay with my Italian grandmother, who had come over here right after World War II. She'd gone blind from a work accident in the factory where she used to slave fourteen-hour shifts to earn pennies, but every night she'd sit and listen to the radio like she'd done as a girl. There was nothing she loved more than the Grand Ole Opry shows. To her it was wholesome — the epitome of America and why she'd come over here in the first place." Sadness showed in Joe's pale blue eyes. "All she wanted in her life was to come to the Ryman and attend the Opry in person, just once."

"Did she?"

He shook his head. "She died a few hours before I got to her house to surprise her with tickets for a show."

Joe's pain reached out to him.

"My grandmother used to have a saying. 'Joe, don't ever take your life for granted. There's a big world out there, and it's waiting for you. Don't waste your time. It's too finite, and before you know it, it's gone.' " He looked back at him. "I'm giving you a second chance, Steele. I know you're going to do the right thing with it."

In that moment, Steele hated Joe. "What makes you so damned sure?"

"Because you have a little sister, and she sent you a Christmas card."

A chill went down Steele's spine. "How do you know about that?"

Joe gave him a lopsided grin. "I'm a spook. It's what I do. And I know that you won't let Tina live under the threat of a nuclear bomb from a country she probably doesn't even know exists. Am I right?"

Before he could answer, he heard a shocked gasp.

"Joe?"

Steele jerked his head up at the deep femi-

123

nine voice that made every nerve in his body sit up and take notice. But that was quickly followed by a fierce wave of anger.

"Hi, Syd," Joe drawled.

Syd couldn't keep herself from gaping as she caught a look at the Joe she never knew. Good grief, the man even had on cowboy boots! In the office and out in the field, he always wore dress clothes. Dress clothes that had never given her a clue as to how ripped the man really was.

She could do laundry on that stomach. And his arms . . . they were well-muscled and powerful. How on earth did Tee manage to share an office with this man day in and day out and not succumb to uncontrollable lust?

Joe stood up and vacated his seat, which she realized was hers. He handed her the box of popcorn in his hands. "You two need a night of relaxation. Enjoy the show. I'm sure afterward you can give Steele a ride back to Carlos's. Right?"

"Sure."

He looked back at Steele. "Be nice."

The expression on Steele's face said, Not likely.

Joe tipped his hat to her before he walked past her, into the aisle.

Still stunned, she watched as he headed

124

up toward the back row, where, she realized, Tee was waiting for him. Unlike her, Tee didn't seem to think there was anything odd about Joe's clothing. She merely moved her knees aside so that Joe could take his seat on the other side of her. And after he sat down, Tee took his hat off his head and placed it on her own. Joe gave her an irritated smirk before he reached for her popcorn.

"What are you doing here? Trying to find a new way to screw up my life?"

She looked down to where Steele was seated. He was definitely still angry at her. Not that she blamed him.

"I don't think you need any help in that department. It seems to me you did a fine job screwing it up yourself."

As soon as those words were out of her mouth, she regretted them.

Sighing, she took her seat and placed the popcorn between her legs while she balanced her Coke on her knee.

Steele started to get up to leave. Syd reached over and touched his taut arm to keep him still. He glared his hatred at her, and it made her stomach ache.

"I really am sorry," she said, enunciating every word carefully.

"There are some things that sorry don't fix."

"You're right." His face registered surprise at her apology. "If it makes you feel better, Joe already crawled all over me about it."

"It doesn't. I still have to keep looking over my shoulder for cops."

"I know." She raked her hand through the popcorn as she considered some way to make this mission work. "I screwed up today, okay? I don't do it often, and I'm sorry that you got caught in the crossfire."

"You practice that speech long?"

She gave him a sheepish smile. "Does it show?"

Still, his face was absolute stone. "Yes, and for an agent, you suck at lying."

She stiffened at his criticism. "And you can do better?"

"Of course I can."

She scoffed at him. "Sure you can."

"I can."

But she knew better. "That's what they all think."

Before she could move, Steele took her chin in his hand. His look changed from anger to one of heated passion. His dark eyes traced the lines of her face as he moved ever so slightly closer to her.

That look was so hot that she could feel that gaze like a human touch. It made the skin of her face tingle. Made her lips long to taste his.

"Has anyone ever told you that you have the sexiest mouth this side of a movie screen?"

Syd swallowed at his deep voice. Every nerve ending in her body stood at attention as desire coiled through her. "Excuse me?"

"It's true," he said, his tone breathless. "If I had you alone for five minutes . . ."

"What?" she asked, dying to know.

His gaze turned instantly back to anger as he released her chin and returned to his beer. "I'd probably beat the crap out of you for calling the cops on me."

Her own anger flared. "You bastard!"

He glanced sideways at her. "You didn't really think I was serious, did you? And I did that without practicing a single syllable. Like I said, you suck at lying."

Syd seethed. She hadn't been this stung since the guy she had a crush on in high school had ignored her. "You better be glad I need you, or I'd shoot you myself."

He snorted. "I should be so lucky."

Syd turned to look at Joe and Tee, who were laughing together. If not for their presence, she'd be out of here by now. But Joe would probably make her return to her seat.

More people started coming in as an awkward silence fell between them.

Steele had to shift as a man and woman stepped past him. When he did, it brought him close enough to Syd that he could smell the sweetness of her perfume. It went through him like a jolt. He was suddenly so hard that he could barely breathe.

There hadn't been nearly as much acting with her as he'd wanted. The plain truth was that, even though she'd stabbed him in the back, the male part of him was still attracted to her.

Syd frowned. "You okay?"

"Fine," he said, even though the odd thought went through his mind — could a man die of blue balls?

"You sure? You look kind of . . . strained."

That was a good word for it. "Fine. Really. Fine."

Her gaze dropped to his lap an instant before her eyes widened and her cheeks turned bright red.

"Yeah, you're a great actor," she murmured as she quickly turned her attention to the stage below them.

Fighting the urge to say something caustic, Steele rubbed his hand over his eyes as complete embarrassment hit him. He might as well be fourteen again and called to the front of the room for a presentation.

The lights dimmed.

Thanks a lot. Why couldn't they have done that three seconds ago and saved him the humiliation?

Syd cleared her throat as she forced herself not to look at Steele at all, but it was hard.

Not as hard as he is.

She had to press her lips together to keep from laughing at that. *Jeez, Syd, you're awful!* No doubt he was embarrassed by it. He'd been in jail going on two years now. It was bound to happen.

But the worst part about it was the curiosity that was begging for her to look again.

No!

She'd sooner have both her eyes poked out and die. Okay, that wasn't true. But she couldn't look. The man was a total jerk. He irritated her. Mocked her.

She didn't even like him.

From the corner of her eye, she could see him take a swig of his beer.

His jerkiness aside, he was a gorgeous man. There was something about Steele that was absolutely delectable, and she didn't say that about most men. His dark hair was brushed back from a face that was intrinsically masculine. His cheeks were dusted by shadow, adding a rugged quality to him.

In spite of her ire, a wicked part of her wanted to reach out and trace that sculpted jaw.

And then an even more wicked thought went through her . . . he'd been in prison. She wondered how many fights he'd been in with other inmates who thought he was cute too.

Most of all, she wondered if he'd lost any.

Don't go there, Syd. But she couldn't help it. It must have been awful to be that good-looking in jail. She couldn't imagine many things worse.

At least, not until the music started. She tried to listen with an open mind, but this was so not her taste. She grabbed her purse from the floor to pull out Tee's iPod. It wasn't until she had it on and playing Papa Roach's "Getting Away with Murder" that she could breathe again.

Ah, that was so much better.

She glanced up to find Steele glaring at her. "What?" she asked, pulling one of the tiny earphones out.

His gaze narrowed. "You're something else, you know that?"

She honestly couldn't imagine what she'd

done now to irritate him. "I'm not doing anything to you. So sod off."

Unfortunately, he didn't. Instead, he grabbed her iPod and took it from her.

"Hey!"

"Sh!"

Syd cringed as the people next to them gave her a sinister glare. "Give me that back," she said from between clenched teeth as she lowered her tone.

"No."

He was an evil bastard. Crossing her arms over her chest, she stared sullenly at the stage while Pam Tillis told stories about how her father, Mel Tillis, had placed her in his guitar case backstage at the Opry when she'd been nothing more than an infant.

And as she listened, a part of her became charmed by the stories.

At least until the singing began. Syd cringed, wanting to leave. Just when she was sure she couldn't stand it anymore, Steele did the most unexpected thing of all. He offered her one of the earbuds.

Startled by his actions, she looked up at him.

"I'm not as cruel as you are."

She wasn't sure if she should be grateful or ticked off. But as she moved closer to him so that they could share Tee's playlist, her ire at him melted. Their faces were so close that they were practically touching. She could easily feel the heat of his skin. His warm, masculine scent permeated her head as she became acutely aware of his muscled biceps pressed against her upper arm while they listened to Papa Roach sing "Tyranny of Normality."

They stayed that way until the curtain closed and the musicians took a break.

Steele tilted the iPod in his hand. "How long do you think the batteries will last in this thing?"

"I don't know. How long is this show?"

He shrugged. "I have no idea. But I'm thinking jail was better. At least there cruel and unusual punishment can get the warden sued."

She laughed.

Steele tensed at the pleasant sound of her laughter. But more than that, the gesture softened her face and made her seem almost kind. A sudden impulse to kiss her came over him, but he quickly squelched it.

And in the back of his mind was the thought that even though he didn't like the music and wasn't fond of the woman, this moment was the best one he'd had in over two years.

He wanted his life back like it had been before he'd been arrested.

He wanted to live.

Syd's breath caught as she saw the look on Steele's face. Gone was the hatred and suspicion. His expression was completely unguarded and open. And something in it reminded her of a boy.

For the first time, she understood what had made Joe so angry. She had tampered with this man's life. Used him like a pawn.

She really was no better than the people they were after. Dear Lord, she'd pushed Steele's back against the wall, and for what? She had no right to put him in this kind of danger. No right to interfere with his decisions.

Suddenly ashamed of herself, she touched his arm. "Look, Steele, I really am sorry if I offended you earlier. I tend to be a little overzealous sometimes."

Steele frowned as he heard her honesty for the first time. He wanted to maintain his anger, but in spite of himself, it melted.

She was making an effort to lay the matter to rest. And he'd never been the kind of man to carry a grudge . . . much.

"It's okay."

"No," she said, her eyes burning him with their intensity, "not really. If you want to go back . . . well, I can't lie and say I like it. I don't. We really do need you, for a multitude of reasons. But there are a lot of things in this world that are bigger than me and my ego."

He doubted that.

She hesitated, and even though she was trying to hide her vulnerability, he saw it plainly. "I would really like for you to help us. I can prep you if you're willing to do the job, and if you want to go solo . . . I won't get in your way."

Steele could sense how much those words stuck in her craw. Yet craw and all, she'd said them. He had to admire that.

"All right, Sydney. If you agree to listen to me and do things my way, I'll do it."

She actually smiled at him. It was an honest, open smile that struck him like a blow. It was precious and sweet, a total antithesis to the hard-nosed agent she'd been so far.

"Thank you, Steele."

He inclined his head to her.

She turned to look back up at Joe before she pulled the earbud from his ear. "Since we're on the same team now, why don't we blow this gig and do some real work?"

He glanced behind them to the seats where Joe had taken his hat back and looked

134

to be fussing at Tee as he adjusted the brim of it. "Think the boss will shoot us on our way out?"

She laughed again. "Only one way to find out."

They got up and headed up the aisle.

Joe arched a brow at them as they started past him. Syd pulled Steele to a stop.

"You're not leaving so soon, are you?" Joe asked her.

Syd wrinkled her nose. "No offense, it's not really my cup of tea. Besides, we're going to go over some details back at the office."

Joe looked to Steele. "So he's in?"

Steele nodded.

"Good man." He pulled a wallet out from his back pocket, then handed it over to Steele. "By the way, I charged the tickets to you."

Steele scowled. "How? I don't have a credit card."

Joe indicated the wallet with a tilt of his head. "Look inside."

Syd narrowed her eyes at Joe's arrogance. "Come on. Be honest, you had to have some doubt about whether or not he'd join us."

"None whatsoever. I wouldn't have brought him to the offices if I'd thought there was any chance he'd opt out."

Just once, she would love to see Joe be wrong about something. But at least this time, she was grateful he understood people so well.

Syd indicated their vacated seats with her hand. "Since we're leaving, you two want our seats?"

Joe looked delighted, while Tee had a look of ultimate distaste.

"You two have fun," Joe said as he brushed past them to head down the stairs.

"They will," Tee muttered as she moved toward them. "Meanwhile I'll be in hell."

Syd shook her head at Tee's dire tone before she handed Tee the iPod.

"Bless you," Tee said gratefully as she took it.

"Why did you come if you hate it so much?" Syd asked.

Tee looked at Joe, who was walking down the stairs. When she spoke, it was the perfect imitation of a Southern drawl. "I might not like the music, but that there's the best view in town."

Syd laughed at Tee. "One day, my sister, you have got to tell that man how you feel about him."

Tee gave her a meaningful stare. "I can look, but we both know I can't touch. Work is work, and pleasure is pleasure."

It was true. She more than understood Tee's feelings about work and play. Unlike Tee, she'd been burned enough to know exactly why work and play didn't mix. It was a lesson she'd more than taken to heart.

Giving her a quick hug, she left Tee to move closer to the stage with Joe.

Syd followed after Steele, who tossed his drink and popcorn into the garbage can. She followed suit before they left the auditorium and headed for the parking lot outside, where she'd parked her Honda.

While they walked, she noticed that Steele was holding the wallet like a lifeline. His grip was tight and, at the same time, almost loving.

"What did Joe give you?" she asked.

"My life back," he said in a reverent tone. He handed the wallet to her.

Syd opened it to see what had gotten into him. As soon as she saw the contents, she fully understood.

There was a Tennessee driver's license with his name and picture on it, two credit cards, and a little over a hundred dollars in cash. It looked just like any other guy's wallet, and that was probably what had struck him most about it.

How long had it been since he'd been just another normal guy on the street?

She smiled at Joe's thoughtfulness. "We take care of our own."

Steele didn't say anything as she returned the wallet to him and he slid it into his back pocket. Not since his initial arrest, over two years ago, had he felt this human. With what Joe had given him, he could leave and never look back. It was a lot of trust.

He wasn't about to betray it.

And in that moment, he realized something. Joe was right. For the first time ever, he understood what it meant to live. To have a life. He could eat when he wanted, leave when he wanted. Do anything and not have to answer to anyone. There were no armed guards eyeing him nervously right now. No isolation chamber when he stepped out of line. No one to fight for everyday necessities. No gangs to deal with. Nothing.

God, it felt good.

"You okay?"

He glanced down at Syd and offered her a hesitant smile. "Yeah. I think I am." He paused in the parking lot and pulled her to a stop.

And then he did something he hadn't done since the afternoon he'd taken that shot at his CO . . .

He acted on pure impulse.

Pulling her close, he dipped his head

down and kissed that full, lush mouth of hers that had been beckoning him since the moment he first saw her. Steele closed his eyes as he tasted her for the first time. It'd been way too long since he'd last held a woman, and he couldn't remember any tasting better than this one. Her mouth was salty and sweet from her soda and popcorn, but most of all, it tasted like Syd.

Passionate. Fiery.

Most of all, it tasted of lust.

Syd fisted her hand in Steele's dark hair as she inhaled the innately masculine scent of him. Maybe she should be offended by the way he'd kissed, but she wasn't. Part of her had been wondering far too long what he tasted like.

Now she knew.

He was all man and all skill. No one had ever kissed her like this. And it made her wonder what else he was good at . . .

He pulled back with a most unabashed grin. "Sorry. I couldn't help myself."

"I thought snipers never acted on impulse."

"That's only when we're after something we intend to kill." He brushed the hair back from her face, then cupped her cheek in his palm. He traced the contour of her bottom lip with his thumb.

"I thought you did want to kill me."

"You have your moments . . . but this isn't one of them."

Syd wanted to melt at the gentleness of his touch. But even as she softened, a long-buried memory leapt forward, reminding her of why she couldn't allow herself to *ever* consort with her coworkers.

She pulled back immediately. "We need to start prepping you on the details of the case."

Steele wanted to curse as he felt the wall come up between them. It was arctic and irritating.

Damn.

Just go find another woman. All you need is a one-night stand.

Even as that thought went through his mind, he knew better. Sex might take the edge off him, but he didn't want sex with just anyone. His body was aching for Syd-the-viper. How stupid was he? The last thing he needed was to trust a woman who had already shown herself to be less than trustworthy.

What was wrong with him? Had he lost *all* reason?

He sighed irritably as she approached a silver Honda Accord. The car was extremely sedate and practical, which, given what she probably made a year, said a lot about the woman.

"Not a speed junkie, huh?"

She laughed evilly. "As they say, looks are so often deceiving."

He opened his door. "How so?"

She slammed the door shut, then buckled herself in. "This little baby has four-fifty horsepower under the hood and will go from zero to sixty in about two-point-two seconds. She's not even street-legal."

He was impressed by that. "Really?"

"Oh, yeah. She's souped up and ready for just about anything. Drecker and Norbert are our official mechanics. They can make a car do just about anything you can imagine. I'm sure Joe will have them hook you up soon enough."

Steele didn't speak as he fastened his seat belt and Syd started the car.

He studied her in the dim light. She was confident and quick, but even so she seemed an odd choice for a federal agent. Not that he was an expert on them by any means. There was just something about her that seemed like it would be more at home in another line of work.

"So what made you decide to become an agent?"

"March twenty-third, 1992. Eleven a.m."

Steele frowned as those words went through his head and he couldn't peg the time or a place. "Should I know that date?"

"No," she said quietly, "most likely not. It barely made more than the local news." She sighed as if that thought hurt her. "My mother always called such events Darwinian moments. You know, those crystal-clear times in your life that change you forever. When I was a little girl, she used to talk about being in her classroom the day Kennedy was assassinated and how she remembered every detail of it. March twenty-third is that way for me. I remember everything I had on, every detail of that morning . . ." Her grip tightened on the wheel.

It was the only reaction she gave.

"What happened?"

She took a ragged breath as she stopped at a traffic light. "I was in my poli-sci class, bored out of my mind, counting the minutes until it was over. Then a woman from admin came into the room to speak with the professor. He pointed at me, and my heart sank. Two minutes later, I was out in the hallway while she told me that my brother-in-law and nephew had been killed that morning in a boating accident."

Inwardly, he cringed at that. It must have

been hard to hear something like that at such a young age.

She ground her teeth and cursed. "My nephew, Chad, was only five years old. My sister had taken my niece to the doctor that morning, and her husband, Bobby, had volunteered to watch Chad while she was gone. Bobby was a lobster fisherman in Maine and had taken Chad out countless times with him — his dad owned the boat, and it was a family business."

Steele's frown deepend as she spoke. He knew it had to be something more than a simple accident. Her anger was too raw, too bitter all these years later.

She turned them down another street, toward the Bat Tower. "That same morning some environmentalist group had decided to make a point about overfishing lobsters and had picked four boats as targets. Bobby's was one of them. Those bastards had rigged a small explosive to sink it while they were out at sea. Chad had wandered over to the place on deck right over the bomb. Bobby had gone to get him when it went off and caught both of them in the blast. In one instant, they destroyed more than just a stupid boat."

Steele felt for her. He knew firsthand how bad grief like that burned inside. Without thinking, he reached over to take her hand and squeeze it.

He saw the tears in her eyes and was shocked by them. She was such a strong woman that for her to betray those tears told him just how much that day had scarred her.

He could feel her pain as she returned the gesture. She quickly blinked the tears away and cleared her throat. "When the people who were responsible found out what had happened to Chad and Bobby, they shrugged it off by saying that's what they deserved for harvesting lobsters. . . . Yeah, a five-year-old really deserved being blown to pieces over seafood."

She pulled her hand away from his to wipe at her eyes as she cleared her throat again. "I hate extremists with a passion. They get so wrapped up in their cause that they think nothing of killing anyone who doesn't agree with them. It's just so wrong . . . so wrong."

Steele wished he could ease the pain of her loss, but he knew better. Some wounds never healed and those to the heart were particularly nasty. "So you went into this to keep it from happening again."

She nodded. "At least, that was the thought. What I quickly found out is there's so much red tape and bureaucracy involved in trying to get things done that I was ready to quit the FBI and never look back. Like you, I'd fought my superiors so many times that they were just about to can me."

It really spooked him at times how much she and Joe knew about his past.

"That's when Joe came in. BAD was only about a year old then, and he was looking for recruits. I'd been reported so much for insubordination that he'd flagged me as a possibility. As soon as he explained to me that I could actually do my job without having to file reports and requisitions, I threw in with him and haven't regretted it since."

Steele arched a brow at that. "Not even this afternoon, when he crawled all over you?"

She cast an irritated sideways glance at him. "Don't remind me." She downshifted and took a corner so fast it would most likely make Joe proud.

Well, at least he now understood what had prompted her actions against him. She was one of those idealists who wasn't that different from the extremists she fought against. But at least she recognized that in herself.

Not that he was willing to completely forgive her. But understanding went a long way in soothing his anger toward her.

"So how much insubordination mars *your* record?" he asked her.

"More than I care to recount."

"Really?"

"You don't believe me?"

He shrugged. "Given the length you went to to secure me, I'd believe most anything about you. You strike me as one of those overachievers who probably never made a B in her life."

"Not true. I flunked astronomy my freshman year, and passed ethics by the skin of my teeth."

Now that he didn't swallow. "Really?"

She nodded. "See, you're not as perceptive as you think you are."

Maybe, but at least it gave him a degree of hope that she wasn't as transparent to him as he thought. He wondered what else he'd misjudged her on.

Please let this be one of them. . . .

"So have you ever had a one-night stand?"

She actually turned her head to look at him while she was driving. "Excuse me?"

He turned her head back toward the road. "You heard me. I was wondering what other erroneous conclusions I'd drawn about you."

She stopped at a red light and turned to

146

look at him. "That's one you were right about. I don't do men on a one-time basis."

"Figures," he muttered. "I don't suppose you'd want to change your ways tonight?"

She shook her head at him. "Sleeping with a guy you work with only complicates things. No thanks."

He leaned his head back. Damn.

You don't even like her. . . .

His brain might feel that way, but his body was another story. It wanted her with a vengeance.

"I'm sure there are plenty of women out there who don't work with you and who don't share my standards."

The problem was, he didn't seem to want any of them, and he didn't even know why. "Yeah."

She pulled into the garage that was under the Bat Tower.

He frowned as he realized that it was here. "Why do some people park across the street?"

"They prefer it."

"Why?"

"Call Dionne Warwick or ask one of them what park there. I, myself have no answer for it, since I like to park here."

He shook his head at her. "You are sassy."

She got out of the car with a saucy walk

that only increased his discomfort. He growled low in his throat as he eyed those hips he would love to cup in his hands. Being around her was starting to seriously annoy him.

Syd could feel her heart pounding as she came under the full scrutiny of that incredibly male stare.

Don't go there.

But it was hard not to. Trying to force her hormones back into submission, she headed for the elevator that led to the upper floors.

Steele came up behind her and stood so close, she could feel the heat from his body.

"You know, I have to say this has been a hell of a day. When I woke up this morning, the last thing I expected was to be here in Nashville tonight."

She glanced up at the lights to see the elevator still had a ways to go before it arrived.

"Has anyone ever told you how good you kiss?"

She glanced over her shoulder to see him eyeing her like a predator. "Steele —"

He placed his finger over her lips to silence her. "It's okay, Sydney. I know how to take no for an answer. We'll forget about the kiss."

He dropped his hand away from her face, and she felt the absence of it immediately.

It's for the best.

Then why did she feel so vacant? For that matter, why did she crave another kiss from him, even though she knew better? Kisses only led to relationships, which eventually led to a broken heart, and she'd had her fill of the latter. Her days of being lovesick were over.

She didn't want to be hurt anymore. She had her career and her causes. They were enough to keep her happy.

At least, most of the time — and on the nights when they weren't, it was why the good Lord had created chocolate, and Ben and Jerry's.

Once the elevator arrived, they headed to the offices, while remaining completely silent.

The lobby area was dark, but as she entered the cube area, she realized that several agents were still working.

"Hey, Mark," she said as she paused outside his cube. "This is our newest member, Steele. Steele, meet Mark Thunderheart."

Steele extended his hand out to a man who was obviously Native American. Tall and thin, he had long black hair that hung around an angular face. His jet-black eyes were uncanny with their intelligence.

"Hi."

Mark shook his hand and inclined his head to him. "Nice meeting you."

"You too."

He then bypassed Steele and pulled out a set of papers from his desk, which he handed to Syd. "I got that info for you. It appears your Kabukis have made their financial commitment to our friends at APS. There was a large wire transfer to their Cayman account late this afternoon."

Syd made a sound of disgust in her throat as he used Steele's term for the Uhbukistanis. "Don't even tell me you were listening in this afternoon."

Mark laughed. "I couldn't help myself." He grinned at Steele. "I have to say, I thoroughly enjoyed your take on the conflict."

"Yeah, well, when King Oompa-Loompa is threatened, we all have to get involved."

Syd groaned. "Oh, please spare me before I get an ulcer."

Mark gave her an unrepentant grin. "They requested confirmation of their contact. So I figure if APS hasn't assigned a hit man to the president yet, they will in the next day or two."

"APS?" Steele asked.

"Asset Protection Systems. They're a front for a group of D.C. assassins and mercenaries we've been tracking for some time now."

Steele gave them a dry stare as he finally understood the real reason why he'd been contacted. "You want me to work for them."

Both of them nodded.

Damn. The last thing he wanted was to be involved . . . oh, wait, he'd already been involved with people like this for the last two years. "Who are these people, anyway?"

It was Mark who answered. "They are an independent firm that uses recruiters to find new talent. One of their recruiters goes by the name Dillon Williamon."

Suddenly everything became crystal clear in his mind. "You guys know he contacted me."

Again both Syd and Mark nodded.

That made sense. Dillon had offered him a job about nine months back after Steele had kept his younger brother from becoming another inmate's bitch. Of course, he and Williamon had assumed it would be about twenty years or more before Steele would need employment. . . .

But now they wanted him to take the job from the mobster. Great. Just great.

"So how did you peg them?"

Mark pulled a roster out of a file and handed it to Steele. "There's a lot of ex-military working for APS, some of whom were referred there by Williamon."

Steele scanned the names. "That's normal though. A lot of military people go into security and law enforcement after they get out."

Syd put her hands in her pockets as she watched him. "Yeah, but when you do a background on these guys, you find an interesting array of talents that aren't really suited to a security company."

"Such as?"

"Demolition experts," Mark said. "Dishonorably discharged snipers and my personal fave, bio-weaponry experts."

Steele gave him a pointed look. "You have to love shadow agencies that pretend to be legit." He slid his gaze meaningfully to the American Fidelity Life Insurance logo that was painted on the wall behind Mark.

"Ha, ha," Syd said sarcastically. "But now you know why I had to leak your supposed escape. This way, when you show up on APS's doorstep, you look legit."

"I would still appreciate it if you would call the authorities off."

The look on her face was divinely evil. "You complete this mission, and I will."

He growled at her as she picked up a phone and handed it to him.

Steele took it with a frown. "What's this?"

"We need you to make contact with APS."

He gave her a droll stare. "You don't just call these people up out of the blue, Syd, and ask for a job."

Mark nodded in agreement. "He has a point."

"So then how do we get in?"

Steele winked at her. "We do this my way, remember?" He expected Syd to argue, but for once she remained silent.

Amazed by that, Steele called Information for Metuchen, New Jersey. Once he had the correct number for Williamon, he entered it in while Mark and Syd watched him closely.

"Hi," he said, stepping away from them. "Is Dillon Williamon there?"

"This is Dillon, who are you?"

He bristled at the commanding tone, but forced himself not to respond in kind. "It's Steele from Kansas. You told me to call you whenever I was looking for work."

There was several seconds of silence. "Are you shitting me?"

"No. I could really use a job right now."

"I thought you weren't interested."

"Yeah, well, I saw the light and was liberated."

Evil laughter sounded over the phone. "Your uncle looking for you?"

"Let's just say that I'd like to stay away from the old man for a while. Can you help me?"

"I don't know, man. You ready for this?"

Steele glanced over to Syd and the expectation on her face. He still couldn't believe he was doing this. He must have lost a few brain cells over the last two years. "Don't worry. I can handle myself."

"Yeah, I know. Where you looking to move to?"

"You know me, I don't much cotton to you Yankees. I'm thinking of someplace where I feel comfortable. You got anything around Dallas or D.C.?"

Dillon hissed. "Dallas is dry lately. You sure you don't want to head up this way? I got a lot of people who could use your talents and skills."

"Nah, man. I don't like cities that big. Besides, it'd take me too long to learn my way around. I'd rather stay on familiar turf."

"You got a point. Let me do some checking and call you back."

"That's easier said than done. I'm not exactly steady at the moment. How about I call you back?"

"Okay. Call me in the morning."

"You got it. Thanks." Steele hung up the phone.

"What was all that verbal code talk?" Syd asked.

"That was me interviewing to become a hired killer."

Syd crossed her arms over her chest. "Are you telling me it's that easy to become a contract killer?"

"No, I'm sure there will be more to it than that. But if he can put me in touch with whoever is running APS in D.C., we might be able to find your killer before he makes a move on King Oompa-Loompa."

"That's President Oompa-Loompa," Syd corrected.

Steele smiled as she finally accepted his nickname for the Uhbukistanis. "Sorry."

"Well, he's gotten us closer to them than we've ever been before," Mark said. "I'm impressed. With any luck, he'll let us in the back door yet."

"Yeah, but he knows nothing about undercover work, and we don't have much time to teach him."

"Bullshit," Steele said. "I'm a sniper. I know more about undercover work than all of you combined. First thing I learned was how to make myself invisible to my enemies.

Believe me, I can handle anything they throw at me."

Still Syd looked skeptical. "I hope you're right, 'cause when all things are said and done, they just might be hurling a lot of live artillery your way."

That didn't scare him in the least. "Bring it on and damned be he who first cries, Enough. And I can guarantee you this. It won't be me."

Seven

Syd spent the next four hours briefing Steele on everything she knew about Uhbukistan and the Kaskamanovs. Everything from how the country had broken down after the Soviets pulled back to the coup that had allowed the president to rise to power. It was a position that the man held tenuously at best. With discordant factions who wanted him deposed, and a ne'er-do-well son who couldn't wait to claim his father's power, he had his hands full.

But Viktor Kaskamanov was nothing if not a determined man. Instead of wanting to defect to the Middle Eastern countries that bordered his own, he wanted to keep his country allied to the West. A disciple of Marx and Stalin, Viktor believed that his country must adhere to its Soviet heritage and not be absorbed by the neighboring countries, who wanted its oil and the political advantage that came with its land.

It was a belief that would cost the man his life if they failed.

All in all, Syd was surprised at how quickly Steele absorbed the history and current events of Uhbukistan, even though he persisted in calling them anything but Uhbukistanis.

It was a little after midnight, and everyone except for Mark and Andre had long headed home.

"You look like you've about had it," Steele said softly as he closed the file in front of her.

Syd covered her mouth as she yawned. "I probably should head home. You're probably exhausted too."

He leaned his head to the left to stretch his neck muscles — a gesture that was remarkably seductive and inviting. No man should ever expose such a tantalizing piece of flesh unless he wanted a woman to sink her teeth into it.

"Yeah, I've been up since four a.m."

She gaped at his confession. "Why?"

"I was on kitchen detail. They tend to make us rise early to get breakfast ready for the rest."

She was aghast that he was still going strong, considering that he'd been up for almost twenty-four hours straight with nothing more than that tiny nap on the helicopter. "Why didn't you say something?"

He shrugged. "A good night's sleep isn't something you generally get in prison. After a while, you get used to going without."

Even so, she was amazed he'd stayed sharp for so long. Until he'd mentioned it, she'd had no idea that he was even tired at all. "C'mon, let me take you home with me."

He gave her a painful expression. "Don't tease me, Sydney, when you know I'm dying to get laid."

So much for her tender feelings for him — which was probably good. Every time she started to soften where he was concerned, he invariably said or did something that repelled her. "Is that all you can think about?"

"You know, I entered prison on a long dry spell. Believe me, had I had any inkling I'd have to go two and a half years without touching a woman, I'd have given Wilt Chamberlain a run for his money."

She snorted as she gathered her files and then locked them in her desk drawer. "That has to be the worst come-on line I think I've ever heard. Sleep with me, baby, 'cause I'm fresh out of jail and desperate for a quick lay and I need a warm body. Oooh, baby, lay it on me."

He shook his head at her. "Do you really think that? If all I wanted was a quick lay from any warm body around, I'm relatively sure I could find it."

She rolled her eyes. "I guess you're just incredibly attracted to my razor-sharp wit."

"No," he said in a deep, provocative tone, "I'm incredibly attracted to your sexy lips. Damn, woman, you really should keep those covered. Angelina Jolie has nothing on you."

In spite of herself, she was succumbing to his less than charming words. It would be so easy to give in to him, but she knew better. Men and their hormones with her heart were a lethal combination, and the last thing she wanted was to be fodder for the other agents to mock.

She'd learned a long time ago that she was the type of woman who wore her heart on her sleeve. And that was the one thing she truly hated most about herself. Whenever she was in love, she was *in love.* Instead of being the hard-nosed agent she prided herself on, she became a total doormat for whatever guy held her heart in his careless hands.

Her last relationship had tutored her well on how much crap she could put up with from a man just to keep him around because the thought of living without him was too much to bear. All she'd done was cry and hold on to a relationship that had been cruel to her at best. David had used her as a backup girlfriend while he'd been engaged to his college sweetheart, who lived across the country.

She'd been devastated when he'd told her that instead of going to Cancun like they'd planned for a June vacation, he was getting married that very weekend.

Good Lord, she'd actually shown up at David's house and begged him to take her back. She'd stood on his doorstep and cried like a brokenhearted teenager. The next day, she'd overheard him laughing about it in the office with another coworker, who had quickly bandied that around the water cooler. That was yet another reason she was more than happy to be away from the FBI. At least while working for BAD, she wouldn't have to worry about running into David and that pompous smirk of his.

She would never again trust herself into the hands of a careless man so that he could toy with her. She intended to be her own person from now on, not some man's backup girlfriend.

"Don't play with me, Steele. The last time I slept with a guy I worked with, he wasn't serious about it. I found out the hard way that he had a fiancée back home that he'd forgotten to mention."

"You know in my case that that's not true. I assure you, I didn't leave a fiancée in prison. And I don't have anyone else in the world."

"Yeah, but I'm not doe-eyed enough to think for a minute that in less than twenty-four hours you have developed some lasting bond with me either."

Still, those dark brown eyes tempted her. "My grandfather proposed to my grandmother two hours after he met her on a bus. They married three weeks after that and were in love until the day he died, fifty-three years later."

She arched a brow. "Are you proposing to me?"

He gave her a hopeful look. "Will it get me laid?"

She screwed her face up at him. "You almost had me going there — almost."

She started past him. Steele took her arm gently and pulled her to a stop. "I'm only teasing, Syd."

"About what part?" She dipped her gaze down to where she could see how swollen he was.

"Obviously not about that. But you're the only woman I'm dying for a taste of."

She wasn't buying that either. "With the exception of Tee, who would shoot you if you even tried it, I'm the only woman you've seen in the last two years."

"Not true. I was out and about today, and all I could think of was you . . . you, and not Tee or that bombshell who got into the elevator when Carlos and I were leaving or the cute brunette who passed her number to me when I stopped in her shop to ask what time it was."

Surely he didn't think telling her about those other women was the way into her bed?

The man really had no finesse. "You are so not helping your cause."

He leaned his head back as if he were totally frustrated. "Fine. Get me back to Carlos's so that I can have a nice, long, cold shower."

Syd snatched up her purse and keys, but as she left her cube, she realized that Mark and Andre had heard every word of their exchange.

Her face flamed at the sight of them.

Mark stepped forward and handed Steele his card. "Give me a call tomorrow, and I can hook you up with some very talented women."

Syd glared at him. "What are you? A pimp?"

"No. I'm just trying to help the man out."

Andre laughed. "I don't know, brother, you keep that up and Syd looks like she's going to give you some of what she gave to Hunter last time she was in town."

Mark cringed as if in extreme pain just from the thought of it.

"What did she do?" Steele asked.

"Racked him so hard, she drove his balls up through his nostrils," Mark said. "Hunter still flinches and cups himself anytime she gets near him."

Steele scowled at her. "Why did you do that?"

"He pissed me off, and if we don't change this topic, I know a couple of other men who will learn to fear me and my killer knee." She passed a meaningful glare at both Mark and Andre.

Steele gave her a devilish grin. "I'll take the pain if you promise to kiss the boo-boo afterward."

She made a face at him. "You're disgusting!"

"No, he's desperate," Andre said in sympathy. "You women just don't understand. *Dayam.* Even I feel sorry for him, and I generally don't pity any man."

"I'm out of here." Syd headed for the door.

Andre laughed as Steele followed after

her. "She's hasn't racked you yet," he called. "I'd take that as an encouraging sign from Syd Vicious."

"Thanks."

Ignoring them, Syd left the office and went to the elevators to press the button.

Steele came up behind her.

She turned to glare at him. "I could have done without that embarrassment. You know I really don't like being the office laughingstock."

"No one's laughing at you, Syd."

"Yes, they are." And she hated it. She hated him! She entered the elevator, then turned around to glare at him.

"So why did you rack the guy? Really?"

"He offended me."

"How?"

Before she could stop herself, the truth came pouring out. God, she really was tired and overworked. "He called me frigid and uptight, okay? Are you happy now? He was friends with the guy I used to date. The one who spent two years jerking me around. So the last thing I wanted to hear after all this time was that I was the one with a problem."

"What an asshole."

His indignation on her behalf startled her. "Excuse me?"

"I hope you knocked some sense into

him. Any man who thinks you're frigid is an idiot."

She felt a little better at his words, even though if anyone should think her frigid, he was probably the one. "Thank you."

"You're welcome."

Feeling awkward again — which seemed to be her natural state around Steele — Syd didn't speak until they reached the parking garage.

She led the way to her car.

But as she unlocked the door, his words kept haunting her. And like a needy little puppy, she couldn't stop herself from asking, "Do you really think I'm not frigid?"

He paused to stare sincerely at her. "No woman who's frigid kisses the way you do. Trust me."

In spite of her common sense, she was thrilled with his response. She wasn't sure why, but she needed that reassurance. "Really?"

"Really."

She smiled. "Thanks, Steele."

He inclined his head to her before he got into the car. Syd joined him, and instantly felt a wave of desire coil through her. No man had ever stood up for her like this, and it felt good. Real good.

Don't, Syd.

She couldn't let herself get all fawning and stupid where he was concerned. This was a professional relationship. That was all it would ever be.

As she drove out of the lot, she couldn't stop herself from glancing over at him. The streetlights cut angles across the planes of his handsome face. Even so, she could see how tired he was.

But not even that detracted from the perfect masculine picture he made. If anyone was kissable, it was Steele. And deep inside she was a lot more attracted to him than she wanted to admit to anyone, even herself.

Like him, it had been way too long since she last had sex. But then, she'd never had much luck in that area. She didn't know why. Maybe she was too intense for most men.

Or maybe Hunter had been right, and she was frigid. Fear of it being true was what had caused her to attack him so ferociously.

Yet for a frigid woman, she found herself aching to reach across the seat and cup the part of Steele that was still swollen. She was actually amazed at how long he'd been that way and stunned by the fact that he was able to control himself so completely. It had to be excruciating for him, and yet he said nothing the few minutes it took her to drive over to Church Street.

She pulled up to the front of Carlos's building and stopped. She glanced back at the bulge that seemed to draw her gaze like a magnet.

Maybe it wouldn't be so bad to have a one-night stand — maybe that would end the whole "frigid" debate and doubts.

"You know, Steele, I . . . um . . . I —"

"It's okay, Syd," he said quietly, as if he understood what she was attempting to spit out. "I don't really want a pity fuck. I'm willing to wait."

Before she could respond, he leaned over, kissed her cheek, and was out of the car so fast that she barely had time to draw a breath.

Stunned by his actions, she watched as he made his way toward the dark building.

Her heart hammering, she strained for a glimpse of him, but he'd completely vanished into the darkness.

She still couldn't believe he'd left her when she'd been about to offer to take him home.

"You are a strange bird, Steele," she whispered before she locked her doors and took off.

★ ★ ★

Steele stood in the shadows he knew concealed him and watched as Syd left. *You are such an idiot. She was right there, and you let her go. Have you lost your friggin' mind?*

No, he'd meant what he said. He didn't want her in his bed because she felt sorry for him.

There was nothing worse than lackluster sex.

Well, okay, that was a lie. There were a lot of things worse. But he'd gone this long with nothing, what was a few more days . . .

Weeks . . .

Months . . .

Damn, he was a first-rate idiot. He should have taken her invitation. But then she'd probably hate him in the morning. Women could be so unpredictable that way. She already hated him enough. The last thing he needed was to give her even more reasons.

And even as that thought ended, he could envision what Syd would look like without those glasses. What she would look like with her hair free of that braid, draped over her shoulders as she straddled him . . .

Whimpering, he headed for the elevator. He froze as he reached for the button and caught the lingering scent of Sydney on his clothes. He closed his eyes and savored the sweet, feminine scent.

What he really wanted was that scent on his bare skin.

Grinding his teeth at the image of her naked and under him, he pressed the button and waited. He'd been dealing with this in prison. He could certainly deal with it out of prison.

But as he rode up the elevator, he was tormented by thoughts of Sydney. Thoughts of her breasts in his hands . . . of her legs wrapped around his waist.

Or better yet, his neck.

He hissed as his cock jerked. Yeah, this was what he needed — walking into another man's apartment with the hard-on from hell. There was truly no justice in the world.

He'd barely opened the door before he was grabbed and flung into the wall. Acting on impulse, he turned and attacked. Unable to see his opponent, he grabbed the gun that was aimed at him and twisted it out of the man's hand.

The man backhanded him and said something in Spanish. The metallic taste of blood filled his mouth as he registered the voice.

"Carlos?"

The man went still. "Steele?"

"Yeah," he said sarcastically. "Who else would it be?"

Carlos turned on the lights.

Steele glared at him as he wiped the blood from his lips with the back of his hand. Carlos's hair was tousled from sleep. He had on a pair of flannel pajama bottoms and a black T-shirt.

"Have you lost your friggin' mind?" Steele snarled.

"No, man, I'm sorry. I was sound asleep, and all I heard was someone coming in."

"With a key?"

"I know. I was on autopilot and asleep. I'm really sorry." He pointed to the gun in Steele's hand. "Can I have my weapon back?"

"Hell, no. You might shoot me."

Carlos gave an evil laugh. "I intended to. But you're quick, *culebro.* I'm impressed. I've never had a man disarm me before."

"There's always a first time, and you're lucky I didn't pistol-whip you with it," Steele said as Carlos wiped at the blood on his brow, where he'd caught him in the fight.

"True enough." He reached for the gun.

Steele hesitated. He unloaded the clip before he returned it to Carlos.

Carlos grimaced. "Now what good is this?"

"It's the best you're going to get for the time being. Jeez. What if I have to get up in the middle of the night and piss? I don't want you to shoot me while I'm doing my business, *comprende?*"

Carlos held his hands up in surrender before he returned the gun to Steele. "In case someone else comes in here other than you and I, I'd rather at least one of us be armed."

"That's not comforting."

"I know. But as I said, I have those who would love to find me asleep."

Okay . . . it was nice to know that someone wanting Carlos dead could break in here while he slept. What had Joe been thinking when he offered him this place to rest?

Without another word, Carlos headed to the bedroom in back.

Sighing, Steele returned the clip to the gun and set it on the coffee table. Well, one good thing had come out of it. He was no longer hard. The attack had effectively curbed his desire.

Grateful for that one small comfort, he went to the couch, where Carlos had left a blanket and pillow. He moved the coffee table aside, pulled out the bed, then turned out the lights and undressed. After he lay down and covered himself up with the blanket, he reached for the weapon.

It was a Glock 18, a full automatic pistol. Yep, Carlos had meant business with this. Grateful that his reaction time hadn't slowed during his prison stint, he slid it under his pillow and settled down to sleep. But no sooner had he closed his eyes than images of Sydney tormented him again.

And as he drifted off to sleep, he wondered what she'd look like in a black lace teddy. . . .

"I hear you, Andre," Syd said into the mic of her cell phone as she navigated the light morning traffic from the Bat Tower to Church Street. Carlos had shown up an hour ago at the office without Steele in tow.

"I didn't know you wanted me to bring him in. No one told me that."

She adored Carlos, but there were times when the man didn't think things through. He'd warned her that he'd left Steele asleep on the pull-out couch. Since Carlos didn't have a land line, she had no way to even call Steele to see if he was ready to get started.

Andre was on the other end of the phone, headed for the stadium where the chopper would land so that they could all head out to D.C.

"I'm thinking he should be up and ready to go when I get there." At least, she hoped so.

"I don't know, Syd. I think the man likes to harass you. He might still be sleeping just to piss you off. Or maybe he is *up and ready,* and he ventured out to relieve his pain. For all you know, he's off in flagrante delicto with some hot babe he found on the street when he went for coffee."

For some unknown reason, that thought really pissed her off. "You're not funny, Andre."

"Oooh, someone's cranky this morning."

"Just have that damn helicopter ready to go when we get there."

"Yes, ma'am, Miz Scarlett. You got any more orders for me?"

She let out an exasperated breath at his words. "I didn't mean it that way, and you know it."

"I know. Gather our boy up, and I'll see you shortly."

"All right. I'll see you in a few." Syd hung up the phone as she stopped in front of the building and parked. She pulled her headset off and left it in the passenger seat before she got out and headed for the door. She clipped the cell phone to her purse as she made her way up the sidewalk.

The building was completely silent as she made her way to Carlos's apartment. As soon as she reached it, she knocked on the door.

No one answered.

Andre's words about Steele having found a willing woman haunted her. Angry that he might be right, Syd leaned closer to the door and listened carefully. She held her breath as she waited for the telltale sounds of sex. But there was no sound inside. Everything seemed completely quiet. More relieved than she wanted to admit, Syd knocked again.

Again there was no response.

Now her anger gave way to fear that something might be wrong. She pulled her weapon out and reached for the spare key Carlos had given her. She opened the door slowly and did a quick sweep of the perimeter, only to find Steele still sleeping on the couch.

Steele was curled on his side, facing the wall. His blanket was twisted around long, tanned limbs that were lightly dusted with dark hairs. But what held her attention was the sight of his bared back and chest.

Holy cripes, the man had a body that was made for sinning. Her mouth was literally watering for a taste of that.

Get a grip.

The problem was, the only thing she wanted to grip was some of that luscious bare skin.

Her heart hammering, she shook her head in disgust at her wayward thoughts. It figured he would still be asleep. Irritated at him for not being up, she put her weapon back in the holster and shut the door.

She crossed the room. "Steele?" she said, reaching out to shake him.

The instant her hand made contact with his skin, he opened his eyes and grabbed her, pulling her completely over him.

"Steele!" she shouted.

"Relax, Sydney," he purred in her ear. "I knew it was you the minute you opened the door and I smelled your Ralph Lauren perfume. I just wanted to have you close to me."

Steele leaned his head back. She felt him relax until she started to pull away. His arms tightened around her as he buried his face in her hair and inhaled.

"You smell like heaven," he said gruffly in her ear.

Syd swallowed as she felt his hard body underneath her hip. There was something strangely erotic about his embrace. She lay completely on top of him with her back to his front.

He lifted one hand up to brush the hair back from her cheek. She knew she should get up, but some part of her was enjoying this way too much.

It'd been too long since a man had held her.

He fingered her cheek a moment before he brushed his lips against her ear. Syd squirmed as unexpected pleasure rushed through her. She'd always been a sucker for anyone who played with her ears. She didn't know why, but that one thing made her instantly hot and needy.

Steele laughed playfully. "Like that, do you?"

She couldn't answer as her body turned molten.

He slid his arms around her to hold her in a gentle hug as he began to tease her ear with his tongue. Syd arched her back as chills swept over her. She could feel his erection pulsing against her as he slowly pressed himself closer to her.

His whiskers scraped against her neck as he moved his hands lower to gently rub against her thighs while he lifted up the hem of her skirt. She licked her lips as desire pounded painfully at the center of her body, begging for a much more intimate touch.

Her body was on fire as he moved with a slowness that was as aggravating as it was thorough and pleasing. He began to gently rub himself against her while his hand stroked her inner thigh. Syd held her breath as he slid his hand up to cup her breasts while he plunged his tongue into her ear.

She moaned in pleasure as his hands worked magic on her body. He left one hand to play on her left breast while he slid the other one slowly back down her body.

Steele was past thinking as he touched her silken inner thigh. He was truly grateful that she didn't have on panty hose under her short skirt. Her skin was completely bare for him, and all he wanted was to feel closer to her. He let his hand slide over her flesh from her knee up high on her thigh, working his way in ever closer to what he really wanted.

He paused at the band of her panties, waiting for her to tell him no.

She didn't.

Smiling in satisfaction, he slowly slid two fingers underneath the satin so that he could feel her crisp hairs tease his hungry fingers.

But that wasn't what he wanted.

As he moved his hand over her, she parted her thighs so that he could have access to the part of her he was dying for. She turned her head and captured his lips with hers as he slid his fingers down her soft, wet cleft.

He growled at the feel of her as he pumped his swollen cock against her buttocks. He wanted inside her so badly that it was all he could do to keep from it. But the last thing he needed was to take a chance on making her pregnant.

Relegating himself to this small pleasure, he toyed with her before he plunged his fingers deep inside her wet heat. She shivered in his arms.

No, there was nothing frigid about this woman.

He lifted his legs between hers so that he held her open for even more exploration.

Syd couldn't breathe as Steele teased her mercilessly. She rubbed herself shamelessly against his hand as he pleasured her. It'd been so long since a man had touched her like this. She hated how much she enjoyed the feel of his hands on her, the feeling of her body burning and aching for more of his touch.

"That's it, baby," he breathed in her ear while she rode his fingers.

Her throat suddenly dry, she reached around her hip to find his erection so that she could cup him tight. He growled in her ear, letting her know just how much he enjoyed having her hold him too. He was incredibly large and thick.

"See what you do to me, Sydney. I haven't been this hard for a woman in a long time."

She wanted to believe that.

"Think of me deep inside you." He plunged his fingers in even deeper, wringing a cry of pleasure from her. His thumb pressed and teased her even while his fingers tormented her. "Now come for me, baby. Let me feel you."

Suddenly her body exploded in pleasure. Throwing her head back, she cried out as wave after wave of ecstasy tore through her.

Steele smiled in satisfaction as she shuddered above him. And still he toyed with her. He wanted to wring every last bit of pleasure out of her body.

And then he felt his own orgasm coming. Holding her close, he moved even faster against her hand until he exploded. He growled as he finally found what he'd been needing in the worst sort of way.

Sydney lay against Steele as her body slowly came back under her control. Heat exploded across her face as she looked to see his legs holding hers open. His hand was still buried underneath her dark green panties, while her hand was under the blanket between their bodies, covered with his warm release.

Steele slid his legs down and pulled his hand up so that he could hold her. "Thanks, Syd. I really needed that."

In a weird way, she felt the same way. "You

ever tell anyone about this, and I'll cut your balls off."

He laughed warmly in her ear. "I don't do that, baby. What's between us stays between us. It's nobody else's business." He moved his hands underneath her blouse to the catch of her bra.

"What are you doing?"

He opened her bra to spill her breasts into his hands. "I just want to feel you for a little bit longer."

She knew she should get up, yet she couldn't seem to make her body cooperate. All it wanted was to feel more of him.

He moved his callused hands over her breasts in a rhythm that actually started another fire inside her. He had an incredibly hot touch that was strangely gentle and firm as he kneaded her breasts. He teased her nipples with his fingertips, making her stomach contract with wave after wave of pleasure.

"You feel so good, Syd."

Syd bit her lip as he toyed with her. No man had ever derived this much pleasure from her body before. He rolled over with her until he had her pinned to the couch's mattress. His eyes flashed hunger at her before he lifted her blouse up so that he could capture her right breast in his mouth.

His rough tongue lapped and teased, making her stomach contract even more with each erotic lick he delivered.

Syd squirmed as her body started throbbing and humming again. Steele grinned at her as he pulled back to stare into her eyes. There was something so charming and sweet about him. It was at total odds with what she knew about him, and yet there was no denying that this tender side of him was there.

She brushed the hair back from his eyes.

"You are beautiful with your hair loose like that."

His compliment warmed her.

His eyes continued to burn her while he tugged at her panties until he had them off. He pushed her skirt higher over her hips as he slowly kissed his way down her body. A part of her was completely embarrassed by his actions, but another, foreign part of her was thrilled as she watched him make his way down her stomach and over her thighs.

Slower and slower he moved while he nudged her thighs farther apart. His warm breath tickled her thigh as he nipped her flesh with his teeth.

He moved his hand to gently separate the tender folds of her body so that he could look at her. Syd shivered at the sight of him studying the most intimate part of her body. He ran one long finger down her before he shifted his weight and took her into his mouth.

Moaning aloud, Syd sank her hand into his hair as he pleased her. He was absolutely incredible, and she wanted to feel more of him.

Steele moaned deep in his throat as he finally tasted her. This was what he'd dreamt of all night long, and now that he had it . . .

He wanted to keep her like this. Warm and supple. No harsh words or feelings. Just the two of them lost in a moment of profound pleasure.

Closing his eyes, he savored her.

In the back of her mind, Syd knew she should be getting him dressed and out of here. But she couldn't think straight with his mouth teasing her so. All she really wanted was to feel him deep inside her.

As if he could hear her silent plea, he sank his fingers deep into her body while his tongue probed and teased. She bit her lip as more and more pleasure built until she couldn't take it anymore.

She screamed out his name as she came again, even more fiercely than the first time.

Hissing, she arched her back, unable to stand the pleasure he was giving to her.

Still he continued to lick and tease until she begged him for mercy.

He pulled back with a triumphant grin. "Now that was worth getting up for." He kissed her soundly before he pulled away. "So what's on the agenda for the day?"

Syd pulled her shirt down as her body continued to pulse. Unlike him, she wasn't comfortable with her nudity. And she was having a hard time remembering what they were supposed to do today.

D.C. . . .

Jake. Andre. Helicopter. Yeah, that was it. They had to go to APS.

"We have a flight to catch."

He stretched like a languid cat. "What about calling Dillon?"

"You can do it from the chopper."

He placed a quick kiss on her cheek before he rose from the couch. Sunlight cut across his naked body, highlighting the ripped perfection of it.

"Have you no modesty?"

His grin was absolutely wicked. "Not a bit." He dipped his head down to capture her lips.

Syd didn't want to be as affected by that kiss as she was. Something about him was completely addictive, even though she wanted to hate him. "You are the devil, aren't you?"

His laugh was warm and deep. "Horny to the end."

She rolled her eyes at him. "Get dressed, hotshot. We have a lot to do, and Andre and Jake are already waiting for us."

Syd put herself back in order while he sauntered to the bathroom to shower. She heard the water come on as she gathered the blanket up. Her actions dislodged his pillow, showing her a Glock that was under it.

She frowned as she recognized Carlos's weapon. Why did Steele have it? How did he have it? Carlos was about as paranoid as anyone could get. It wasn't like him to leave a weapon lying about. Syd unloaded it, then left it in the kitchen drawer before she went back to the sofa bed to make it up.

Deciding the blanket should be washed lest Carlos figure out what they'd done in his place, she went back into the kitchen to search out Carlos's washer and dryer.

As the water came on, she heard Steele curse in the bathroom. "Sorry!" she called, but even so she didn't turn the washer off. She was too afraid she'd forget and leave evidence behind.

She still couldn't believe that she'd allowed Steele to do that to her. "I have to be the dumbest human to ever live and breathe," she whispered to herself. "When am I going to learn?"

But maybe it had been a good thing. Steele no doubt needed the release. Now he should be able to focus.

And maybe she could too.

Maybe.

She jumped as her cell phone rang. Answering it, she found Andre on the other end.

"Where *are* you?"

"We're still in Carlos's apartment. Steele was asleep when I got here, and now he's getting dressed."

"Well, shake a leg. We can't stay here all day."

"I know. We'll be there shortly." As she hung up the phone, Steele left the bathroom . . . still completely naked. Now he was dripping wet and looking way too choice.

She ground her teeth at the damp perfection of that body. "That was Andre, telling us to hurry."

"I'm hurrying," he said with a wink. "Can't you tell?"

"No. You look like you're crawling from here."

Tsking playfully at her, he walked past to grab his clothes from the floor by the couch.

Syd frowned as she realized he didn't have anything else to wear. "Remind me, we need to get you some clothes later."

He snorted. "I'd much rather you get me naked again later."

Her stomach shrank at his teasing tone. "Look, Steele, this didn't happen, okay? We didn't do anything here as far as I'm concerned."

A hurt look flashed across his face before he concealed it. "Don't worry, Syd. I've had enough one-night stands in my life to know how to behave afterward."

Now it was her turn to be stung. "I'll bet you have. You're probably one of those guys who promises to call and then never does."

He tugged his shirt over his head. "I've never in my life made a promise I didn't keep. Never."

"Then promise me that you'll forget all about this and never mention it to anyone."

"Done. Didn't happen. It's forgotten already." He turned his back on her and folded up the bed back into the couch.

Even though those words should thrill her, they didn't. Instead, it left a hole in her stomach that ached.

It's for the best.

Still, that hole was there. Burning. Empty. Consuming. Swallowing against the pain of it, she nodded as she led him toward the door.

As she opened the door, Steele caught her and pulled her to a stop. "But answer me one thing, Syd."

"What?"

"Can *you* forget about it?"

Syd didn't answer him. As he'd pointed out, she wasn't that good a liar. "We have people waiting on us."

The look on his face was harsh and condemning. "One day, Sydney, you're going to have to face me."

She lifted her chin until their gazes were locked. "I have no trouble facing you. But tell *me* something, *Steele.* Why is it you never use your given name? Could it be you're even more afraid of intimacy than I am?"

By the expression on his face, she knew she'd struck the truth.

"Yeah," she said in a meaningful tone. "We can talk about what happened here today when you let me call you something other than Steele."

But even as she walked out the door, she didn't feel any satisfaction at being right. She was sad that their encounter hadn't been a tender interlude between lovers. It'd been a hurried encounter between two lonely people who only wanted to keep the world at a distance.

And that made her want to cry, but she was long past tears. This was the way her life had to be. She knew it. She understood it. There was no place in her world for a boyfriend or lover.

Like Steele, she was alone in the world, and that was all there was to it. Yet even as the thought went through her, a tiny, buried part screamed out in denial. It wanted more than this.

It wanted . . .

The impossible. There was no use in pining for something she couldn't allow herself to have. Her heart had been trampled one time too many.

They had a job to do, and that's all she was concerned with. He was out of her system. Her curiosity was appeased, and he'd scratched his itch.

End of story.

It wasn't until they were in the elevator that Steele approached her again. He moved to stand so close to her that she could feel the heat of him. The intensity.

"There's just one thing about this morning that you probably don't want to forget."

"And what is that?" she asked irritably.

His look turned scorching as a wry grin twisted his lips. He leaned down so that he could whisper in her ear. "You forgot to get your panties back, and I have to say that the thought of you standing there with nothing underneath that short skirt is seriously turning me on again."

Eight

Steele wasn't amused, as he had to move covertly from the apartment to the street where a group of three cops were chatting together. They stood only a few feet from Syd's Honda.

She cursed at the sight of them.

"Good call," Steele said sarcastically.

She glared at him as she pulled a pair of sunglasses out of her handbag, then handed them to him. "Put these on and keep your head down. Hopefully they won't even glance at us."

He was disgusted by it, but even so, he put the sunglasses on. "If you hadn't told people I was an escaped murderer, it would help. I ought to let them capture me just to get me out of this."

"Fine," she said, stepping away from him. "There's the door." She indicated the glass double doors that separated him from the police.

He growled. "I really hate you people."

"Yeah well, you should have paid attention to the small print on your contract. Use any means necessary."

"The means suck, Syd."

She paused to look up at him. "How were you ever in the military? You have been resistant to my plans from the beginning."

"The Army taught me well what happens when you blindly follow someone else's orders. All it gets you is a bullet in the head and a lame letter sent to your family saying you died during a training exercise."

"Fine," she said, opening the door. "Get yourself caught then. I'm tired of fighting you."

She paused just outside the doors to look up at him with those gut-wrenchingly green eyes. "Besides, we can't call them off you until after you complete this mission. We need you to be a fugitive to give legitimacy as to how it is you've turned up to work for APS when you're supposed to be serving a twenty-five-year sentence."

He narrowed his eyes on her, something that was less than effective since she couldn't see his eyes for the sunglasses.

What he hated most was the fact that she knew as well as he did that he wasn't about to go back to jail if he could help it. "So how do you propose getting me through airport security later?" he asked before they started toward her car.

"We're not going through the airport. The chopper's waiting a few blocks over at the stadium, but we need to get a move on it. Jake can't stay there long before he gets a crowd gathering."

Steele followed her to the car. The cops stopped talking as they approached.

"Hi, officers," Syd said cheerfully.

Two of them greeted her in kind, but the one who was equal in height to Steele frowned. "Do I know you?" he asked.

Steele shook his head. "I don't think so. Ever been to North Carolina?"

The cop didn't look convinced. "Nah. But I swear I know you from somewhere."

"I just have one of those faces. Good day, gentlemen." Steele moved with a nonchalance he didn't feel as he got into the car and tried not to tell Syd to floor it out of there. They couldn't afford to raise the cop's suspicions any more.

But he could feel Syd's tenseness. He had to give her credit though. She didn't show it. She was remarkably cool and calm as she pulled away from the curb and headed down the street.

Meanwhile, he expected the cops to recognize him at any moment and give chase.

It wasn't until they were out of sight that he began to breathe a little easier. "That was too close."

"Yeah," Syd agreed. "You work well under pressure."

He snorted at that. "You haven't seen pressure, little girl. Trust me. That was easy."

She cast a sideways glance at him. "Kill the arrogance, Steele. I wasn't *that* impressed."

"Trust me. You will be."

She shook her head as she turned a corner toward the stadium. "We'll see."

It only took them a few short minutes to reach the stadium where the helicopter that had brought Steele in was waiting. Syd parked in an empty space nearby, then turned the car off.

They got out and headed for the chopper. Jake and Tony were arguing as they climbed on board.

"Oh, wait," Tony said as he saw them. "They're here. Guess we can't leave them after all."

"Go to sleep, Tone," Jake said.

Syd ignored them as she moved to sit beside Andre, who was already strapped in and waiting for them as well. "Nice of you two to finally join us."

Steele didn't respond as he strapped himself in, but he noticed the sudden flush that came to Syd's skin. She gave him a furtive look, which he ignored, as she pulled the hem of her skirt lower. He had yet to return her panties to her — something he refused to do until she got that stick out of her butt and learned to treat him like a human being.

Not to mention he liked teasing her. But not nearly as much as he liked knowing that there was nothing on underneath that dark blue skirt.

Andre handed him a phone, making him want to curse as it diverted his attention away from the thought of what Syd tasted like.

Andre leaned his head back and shouted at the pilot. "Jake, keep the engines off until I give you the heads-up." He looked back at Steele. "You need to give our friend another buzz. Let him think that you're already in Virginia."

Steele nodded as he pressed the send button. Dillon answered on the second ring.

"Hi, it's Steele."

"I was wondering if you'd changed your mind about that job. I saw on the news last night that there was an escaped convict headed out west. Scary stuff, isn't it?"

He glanced at Syd and for the first time agreed that she'd been right to turn his name over to the media. It did add legitimacy to his story. "The world is a bitch. Hope the poor guy makes it to Pasadena."

"I heard that. It's a long way from Kansas. But, man, with that kind of heat . . . a guy has to be careful, you know?"

"Yes. Yes, I do. So can you help hook me up with some immediate work?"

"Yeah, but I want you to know that I had to call in all kinds of favors on this. It's not the same as if you were working for me, you know? I'm having to send you over to one of my partners and he doesn't like dealing with new talent. He prefers I train the new recruits and then send them over to him after they have a few years on them. But for you . . . I'm willing to bend the rules a little. You're not going to be one of those take-and-forget kind of guys, are you?"

"Never."

"Good. My partner, Randy Wallace, owns a security company down in Georgetown called Asset Protection Systems. You ever heard of it?"

"Not really." Steele gave a thumbs up to Andre and Syd to let them know that it was working.

"Well, it's a good company. I told Randy

you'd be in about three o'clock this after-noon. Can you make it?"

"Sure."

"Good. He'll be able to interview you in person and see if you're suited to the com-pany. You got something to write the ad-dress down with?"

He motioned to Andre's pen that he was holding in his lap. Andre handed it over with a piece of paper.

"I'm ready." Steele wrote the address down as it was given to him. "Thanks, Dillon. I really appreciate this."

"No problem, you just keep your nose clean, kid."

"Don't worry. I fully intend to." Steele hung up the phone and tossed it to Andre. "We've got an appointment with them this afternoon."

"And that is why we needed you," Andre said. He leaned back and smiled in triumph. "Yo, Jake, get us out of here. We got an ap-pointment to keep."

Jake nodded as he started the blades.

Steele watched as Andre and Syd estab-lished what looked like a fully operational command center between their seats. It was impressive. They had all kinds of data, such as the schedule for the Uhbukistani presi-dent's arrival in America and a record of the son's latest phone calls to America. Hell, they even had a list of the call girls the boy had contacted for his first night in town.

Steele frowned as they reviewed the limo route from the airstrip to the hotel. "Won't they change their plans just in case someone like, say, *us,* happens to be planning a coup or murder?"

Andre shook his head. "These were encrypted. They'll think they're absolutely safe."

Yeah, and he was three feet tall and green. One thing Steele had learned as a sniper, the brass could and would change plans at a moment's notice for absolutely no reason at all.

Never rely on intelligence unless you wanted to die.

He watched as Andre pulled up a list of stores the Uhbukistani president wanted to visit while he was in town. "Just out of curiosity. Is there any information you guys can't access?"

Syd shook her head. "Not really. But you'll get used to no privacy."

Maybe. "I still say they'll probably change their plans once they arrive."

She looked a bit . . . well, for lack of a better word, miffed at his insistence. "If there weren't Secret Service men assigned to him, I might agree. But as you well know the Secret Service doesn't like change. Once a plan is set, they usually go through with it even when they have reports that tell them it might not be a prudent thing to do."

Steele didn't comment.

"Now our biggest concern is what to do with you," Syd said as she read over the reports. "We're going to need you to get us info on how the APS personnel files are set up. We can't find them on anything which says that they are hidden under something we're not thinking of. We need to know who their power assassins are. Anything like that that you can give us."

"And if I can't get it?"

"We'll have a dead president on our hands and a major auction for nuclear weapons."

Andre handed him another pair of sunglasses. "This is your mic and your camera. You can wear them outside and I'll be able see and hear everything you do. I'll be in a van a few blocks over, recording and monitoring everything, while you and Syd drive in. When you go inside the offices, hang the sunglasses on your shirt. I need you to keep your arm away from this." He pointed to the right hinge. "This is the camera, and if it's covered, I'm blind."

Steele examined the sunglasses carefully. He had to give Andre credit, there was no way to detect the camera or mic. They were truly a work of art. "Where's the mic located?"

He showed him the earpiece, but for his life Steele couldn't see anything. "You can't tell anything's there."

Andre gave him a gloating stare. "I know. I designed it myself. No one will ever know you're bugged."

"Ego's not Andre's problem," Syd said with a laugh. "But he saves our butts, so we tolerate him."

Steele nodded. "So when they ask me how I escaped, what do I tell them?"

She handed him a piece of paper with bullet points on it. "The story we fed to the media is that you escaped from a work detail."

"And I made it to D.C. on foot? Man, I'm one hell of an athlete."

Syd rolled her eyes. "You climbed out of the window of a public restroom, and your girlfriend was waiting to pick you up in her car."

He arched a brow at that. "My girlfriend?"

"Sara Whitfield."

He frowned at the unknown name. "Who is that?"

She wagged her eyebrows at him.

"Oh, hell, no."

"Oh, yeah," she said in an offended tone. "For all intents and purposes, I'm your gal. Why do you think I'm wearing a skirt and blouse?"

He cleared his throat on that, which caused her to blush again. He could tell by the look on her face that he hadn't won himself any points with that. In fact, he probably just lost quite a few.

Good going, asshole.

Andre opened a case with a hypodermic needle in it.

Steele went cold. "What's that?"

"A homing device. Once we land, I'm going to inject an RFID chip into you."

He shook his head. "You ain't doing shit unless you can show me a medical degree first."

"It's for your own protection."

"No."

"Steele . . . ," Syd said in a warning tone. "It's an RFID transmitter that will allow us to find you should anything happen. I swear it's safe. Jason had one in him and didn't even know it."

"And I don't know Jason. Where is he now? The morgue?"

She gave him a droll look. "No, he's off on vacation with another agent."

"Um-hmm . . ."

Andre snapped the case closed. "Fine. When they find the bug in the sunglasses and decide to take you off in the trunk of a car to kill you, don't expect one of us to find you and save you at the last minute."

"You told me it was undetectable."

"Well, as good as I am, I do, on very rare occasions, make mistakes. I would hate for you to be one of them."

So would he.

Andre looked at Syd. "You know, the Army might already have him tagged. Did you check his records?"

"No one has me tagged."

Syd scoffed. "That's what Jason said too, and they had to dig the tag out of his butt."

"And I can assure you, that area of my body is most sacred, and nothing is *ever* going to be buried there."

She rolled her eyes. "Stop being a baby."

"Then you let him inject you."

"He already has." She lifted her arm up to show him a spot next to her elbow.

"I don't see anything there."

"That's the idea. Andre found a new frequency. It can't even be picked up by tracers. The only way for anyone to find it is to have one of ours."

"And if one of your people turns on you, you're all screwed."

She put her arm down. "That'll never happen."

"How do you know?"

"Because we're family. Andre over there is the crazy uncle no one ever listens to."

"Hey!"

She smiled at him. "But we love him anyway."

That sounded like a nice fable that ranked right up there with unicorns and fairies, and Steele knew better than to ever trust in those. "Everyone has a price."

"No," Andre said earnestly. "They don't. You turn on us, and we'll hunt you down and kill you. We're kind of like the Mafia. No one leaves the family. No one. And once you see exactly how easily we trail people, you'll understand why no one in their right mind would ever betray us."

Steele shook his head at them, hoping he could trust in that, but his trust had worn thin a long time ago. He didn't care what they said. People could turn on you in a heartbeat, and he didn't want to be dead because of it.

They could keep their tracers. There was just too much room for error.

And even more for betrayal.

But even so, the two of them continued to prep him on the mission's parameters and on how to penetrate the organization. Little did they know, he was about to enter his own arena. In his world, they were the novices.

Syd was nervous as she drove Steele toward his rendezvous. As an agent, she knew all the things that could go wrong. For all his military training, Steele wasn't a paid liar.

That was her job. And in spite of what Steele thought, she was very good at it.

"You have your story straight, right?" she asked him.

"Yes."

"Okay. How long have we been dating?"

"Fifteen minutes," he said drily.

"Steele!" she snapped, aggravated that he'd play around with something this serious.

He let out an exasperated breath. "I'm not going to forget, *Sarah.* If there's one thing I know how to do, it's keep my butt low to the ground when it's under fire. I won't forget anything we went over."

"Good." Syd let out her own irritated breath as she edged her way down M Street, only to see that there was nowhere to park near the security company. Damn, she really, truly hated D.C. traffic.

"Just let me out there on the corner."

"No. We'll circle the block and see if someone pulls out." But after the fourth time around, she was beginning to feel like a land shark circling for nonexistent food.

"I'm going to be late," Steele said from between clenched teeth. "And these aren't the kind of people you keep waiting." He pointed to where a green parking sign was. "Park there and wait for me."

She didn't want to, but she realized that she wasn't going to have a choice in this. Even more aggravated, she headed for the public lot and parked.

She turned to face Steele, who was going into a bad situation completely unarmed — and worse, she, unlike Andre, wouldn't even be able to monitor him. "Be careful. Don't do anything stupid."

He grinned at her. "You keep talking like that, and I might actually think you like me."

Before she realized what he was doing, he leaned over and gave her a wickedly hot kiss. "For luck," he said as he pulled away. "Keep my seat warm. *I'll be back.*"

His impression of Arnold didn't do much for her. Unlike the actor in the movie, he wasn't made of invincible steel. He was just a man who hadn't been properly prepared for what he was about to face.

Syd gripped the wheel and forced herself not to follow him. He had to do this alone. If she went anywhere near him, she could very well jeopardize not only the mission, but both of their lives.

"Relax, Syd."

She jumped at Andre's voice in her ear. "Jeez, I forgot you were there. Did you see —"

"Yeah, you kiss pretty good for an agent."

"Shut up, Andre."

His laughter filled her ear from the tiny earbud. But after this, she knew she wouldn't hear anything else from Andre as he taped Steele's conversation. Unlike Andre, she didn't have two-way communication with Steele. Too many receivers might jeopardize his cover. So here she would sit in total silence until he returned . . . hopefully in one piece.

Steele lowered his head as he passed a couple of uniformed cops. Luckily, they were checking out a Georgetown co-ed across the street. Quickening his steps, he headed straight for the security company.

He pushed open the door to find a long gray counter with three women sitting behind it. Two of the women appeared to be college age while the other was closer to fifty. Dressed neatly and tidily, none of them looked like a front for a company of assassins and mercenaries.

In fact the entire place, much like the BAD offices, looked like a legit company, complete with multiline phones and security brochures. The only thing weird was the number of cameras that were trained on the door and counter.

"Can I help you, shug?" the older lady asked.

"I have an appointment with Randy Wallace for three o'clock."

She pulled a large brown book toward her. "Your name?"

Before he could answer, an intercom buzzed. "It's fine, Agnes. I'm expecting him."

She laughed. "Well, the powers that be have spoken. You are able to get in. Just open the door when you hear the buzzer and walk to the end of the hallway. Mr. Wallace will have an escort waiting to show you to his office."

Even if he hadn't known what Wallace did for a living, he'd be suspicious by now. The man had more security than . . .

Leavenworth.

Steele opened the door as the secretary buzzed him in and did just as she said. The hallway was narrow and dark, without a single door or window.

When he reached the end of the hallway, the door opened automatically to show him a large, burly man who was frowning at him.

"You packing?" the man asked gruffly.

"Do you see a suitcase?"

That succeeded in making the man reach out to grab him. Steele caught his arm and twisted it behind his back. He forced the man against the door. "I'm not your bitch, boy," he said from between clenched teeth. "You don't grope me without an invitation."

Steele heard the sound of applause. He looked up to see what appeared to be a balcony, where a dark-haired man stood watching them.

"Nice moves," he said in a voice identical to the one that had buzzed Agnes. "Can you sing too?"

"Not on key, but I can fake it."

"Too bad I'm not hiring a comedian, huh?" His face hardened. "Let go of Bruce."

Steele wrenched his arm a bit more, just to make a point, before he released him.

The man on the balcony, whom he assumed was Randy, folded his arms over his chest as he gave him a withering stare. "You know I'm not going to let you up here until I'm sure you don't have on a wire or a weapon, don't you?"

Steele took the sunglasses off his shirt, then pulled it over his head. He turned around for Wallace's inspection. "Obviously, I ain't tapped or tagged."

Randy shook his head. "You're an arrogant sonofabitch, aren't you?"

"Better than a dumb one or a dead one."

If he didn't know better, he'd swear a look of admiration darkened Randy's face. "Put your shirt on and get up here. Bruce will show you the way."

Steele shrugged his shirt back on, then turned toward Bruce. The man looked like the only thing he wanted to show him was the bottom of the Potomac. "Sorry, man. I just don't like to be manhandled."

Bruce growled at him before he led him toward a door on the right.

Steele put the sunglasses back in place before he followed him.

Wallace's offices were plush and well decorated — except for the line of stag heads on the wall. It looked like something out of a bad movie.

The man sat behind an antique mahogany desk with such a high gloss that it was almost blinding. He rubbed it with a chamois cloth. "Nice, isn't it?"

Steele shrugged. Who was he to judge furniture? He'd never paid much attention to it.

"Have you ever heard of feng shui?" Randy asked as he put the cloth away in a top drawer.

"Yeah. It's the 'put the mirror on your door and sleep in the right direction' bullshit."

Randy's face was stone cold and blank. "The Chinese say that you should never, ever buy a used desk unless you know the history of it. They claim that if it belonged to a bad businessman, his karma will befall you." He indicated his desk with a tilt of his head. "This one here belonged to President Kennedy. So what do you think that means?"

Steele shrugged. "I don't know, but if I were you, I wouldn't ride through Dallas in a convertible in November. Bad feng shui."

Wallace laughed at that. He reached to a wooden box on his desk and opened it. "You smoke?"

"Only when I'm on fire."

His face returned to stone. "I don't appreciate your humor, Mr. Steele."

"It's an acquired taste."

Wallace pulled out a Cuban cigar, then reached for a clipper. He didn't speak as he prepped, then lit, the cigar. He blew out the match, then tossed it in the ashtray. "Dillon tells me that he owes you."

Steele nodded grimly.

Wallace tapped the cigar on the ashtray while he narrowed his eyes on him. "I'm going to be honest with you, Steele. I don't like working with people I don't know. And I don't know anything about you. For all I know, you're some limp-wristed pansy with a few swift moves."

Steele was completely unamused by the man's words. "Hmmm, let's see . . . I cried when Ole Yeller died, but I was young back then. I have a scar on my knee from when Willie Durante knocked me off my bike when I was seven. I beat the shit out of him later, then took his bike and sold it at a pawnshop. Oh, and my favorite color is pink . . . it's really soothing."

Wallace scowled. "What kind of bullshit is that?"

Steele gave him a bored stare. "Look, there's nothing I'm ever going to tell you about me that's the truth. The more you know about me, the shorter your life span is going to be. All you need to know is that I don't miss. In fact, you don't even need to know exactly how good I really am, because if you ever find out, you're going to be dead."

One corner of his mouth turned up. "There you're wrong."

"How you figure?"

Wallace reached into his desk drawer and pulled out a small digital camera. Steele frowned as he took a picture of him, then set the camera aside and checked his watch.

"Haven't you ever wondered how someone such as myself 'interviews' an independent contractor?"

Steele toyed with the arm of his chair. "The thought did cross my mind."

"Well, it's simple, really. That photograph I just took of you will be e-mailed to one of my contractors in twenty minutes and counting. My contractor will then have twenty-four hours to complete training."

"What training is this?"

He smiled snidely. "It's the game of life, Mr. Steele. Survival of the fittest and all that. Whoever makes it back to this office tomorrow at three-thirty will get a bonus and will have a job. Whoever doesn't . . . well, that contractor won't need a job, since he'll be permanently dead. May the best contractor win."

Steele sat there in complete shock. "You've got to be shitting me."

"Do I look like I'm 'shitting' you, Mr. Steele?"

No, he looked serious as all get-out. "I don't even have a weapon."

Wallace shrugged. "Resourcefulness is ninety percent of the trade." He checked his watch. "Fifteen minutes and counting."

Steele glanced over his shoulder at Bruce. He could easily take both men out and stop this here and now. But then the Uhbukistanis would only hire someone else, and Syd would kill him for screwing this up.

Damn. Here was one scenario BAD hadn't seen coming.

He stood up slowly and eyed Wallace with malice. "Your bonus better be worth it. If it's not, I'm going to add your head to the collection on *my* wall."

The bastard actually laughed at him. "Run, Bambi, run."

"Fuck you." His blood boiling, Steele made his way out of the room with Bruce trailing three steps behind him.

So much for all the stories Syd and Andre had prepped him on. Wallace didn't care if he'd really escaped from jail or not. Most likely, that was because he thought Steele would be dead in the next few hours.

Part of him wanted to drive straight back to Nashville and choke Joe for this. The other part just hoped he lived long enough to make it off M Street.

"Y'all have a good day now," the receptionist called after him.

What? Was the woman high? He raised his hand up in mock friendliness.

"You, too," he said in a high-pitched voice. No doubt she had no idea what had just happened. Or maybe she did. For all he knew, she was the one assigned to check him out.

You're paranoid.

Duh to that. He didn't like the thought of a hired killer knowing what he looked like while he was completely in the dark. What's more, he wouldn't be able to go near Andre or anyone else, since he'd be under surveillance.

"This is getting better and better."

Just think, two days ago his worst fear was Frank in the next cell getting frisky. Now it was getting a bullet in his skull.

With a nonchalance he didn't feel, he headed to the lot where he'd left Syd and got into the car.

She looked up at him expectantly. "Well?"

He curled his lip at her. "You people suck."

"Excuse me?"

214

"You heard me."

She looked appalled by his rancor. "Why would you say that?"

"Because by this time tomorrow I will most likely be dead . . . and all thanks to you."

She pressed her earpiece into her ear. "Andre? What is he talking about?"

Before Steele could answer, the hair on the back of his neck rose. It was something that seldom happened, and he wasn't sure what was setting off his instincts.

Before he could look around, he heard an odd snap. It was followed by an unmistakable sting.

"Get us out of here!" he snarled.

"What? What's —"

"I'm shot, Syd! And if you don't get us out of here, we're both going to be dead."

Nine

Syd punched the gas as more glass shattered around them, spraying her and cutting her cheek and arm. "What did you do, Steele?"

He hissed in pain. "Nothing."

She found that hard to believe. "Nothing? Then why are we being shot at?"

" 'Cause the sonofabitch can't tell time."

Andre gave her very sketchy details of why they were under fire. Syd went careening through traffic and traffic lights at a breakneck speed as Andre directed her through the D.C. streets to where there were fewer civilians.

At first she thought it would be easy to escape their pursuer, but a glance in the rearview mirror showed her a large black Escalade swerving and accelerating.

She could see the gun an instant before they opened fire again.

She cursed under her breath.

This was a lot harder in real life than it appeared in movies, especially in such heavy traffic. One wrong move, and not only they but some innocent bystander could die.

From the corner of her eye, she saw Steele brace himself as she took a corner so fast, the car slid sideways. She cringed as they sideswiped a brown sedan an instant later. Still, she kept going. She had no choice.

Syd cursed as they fired again. She leaned forward to expose her back to Steele. "Take my weapon."

His hand was warm as he grabbed it and pulled it free, then he turned and hesitated.

"What's wrong?" she asked.

"Too many civilians. I can't shoot and chance a stray bullet hitting some mom in her minivan full of kids. Unlike Dickhead, I can't live with the knowledge that I killed someone's kid."

Respect for him welled up inside her.

"All right, Andre," she said loudly over the sound of her car braking to miss a slow-moving work van. She swerved around it, narrowly missing two men who had stepped onto the street. They hopped back to the curb just before she ran them over. "We need some assistance. There's a 2005 black Escalade bearing down on us. It's armed and loaded for agents. Steele has already been wounded."

Steele cursed at her words. "What's Andre going to do? Clap?"

She glared at Steele as the Escalade came closer.

"I hate rental cars," she said between clenched teeth. "This is why I love my little four-hundred-horsepower engine." If she were in her Honda, her pursuers would already be lost.

As it was, she could barely stay ahead of them.

"Well, you've got about one-forty in this go-cart, so I hope you can outmaneuver them."

Another bullet went through the back window.

Syd swerved into oncoming traffic as Steele started a string of colorful expletives that said, yes, he'd been in the Army a long time.

"Calm down," she snapped as she deftly dodged cars.

Horns blared as oncoming cars swerved out of her way.

"I'll calm down when I have a clear shot and this bastard in front of me so that I can kill him."

"Well, why didn't you say that?" Syd swerved back into her lane and slammed on the brakes. The Escalade went speeding past.

Steele fired two shots that shattered the back window of the Escalade.

She whipped the car left onto another street as the Escalade did a J-turn to head back for them.

"Andre! Mayday. Mayday. We need help!"

No sooner had she spoken than a string of police cars went streaming past her, toward the Escalade.

"Relax, Syd," Andre said in her ear. "I've got our police contact on a secure line. He's dispatching the police to chase the assassin. They'll pretend to follow you, then drop off so you two can flee."

As she made another turn, two police cars fell in behind them.

Steele's curses picked up in volume. "Ah, hell, this is beautiful."

"Relax."

"How? I'm shot, and once they stop us, my ass is headed back to Kansas. Thanks, Syd."

"They're not going to arrest you."

"Yeah, right. Then how do you propose that we explain my absence from jail, huh?"

"We don't. The police are going to pretend to chase us, and we're going to outrun them."

She gunned the engine and headed out of Georgetown with the police in hot pursuit.

As soon as she was clear and the other police cars had the Escalade headed in the opposite direction, the police cars tailing them fell back — just as Andre had predicted.

Satisfied that the Escalade was off them, at least for the time being, she took the first exit and headed for their rendezvous.

"Don't do it."

She frowned at Steele. "Don't do what?"

"Head for Andre. They'll be watching us."

"There's no way they can be watching us." She glanced at him and felt her heart sink as she saw how badly he was bleeding. He had one hand pressing against his shoulder, but it was doing very little to staunch the blood.

They had to get him help quickly, or he was going to die.

"They'll be watching us," he said through clenched teeth. "How many satellites do you think bear down on D.C. every minute of every day? I assure you, they have us on their radar and are tracking our every movement. If they weren't, the Escalade would still be behind us, police be damned. In fact, Andre needs to cut the communication before they pick up on the wire and use it against us too."

"You're so —"

"I was in the Army, Syd. I know what we can do to track a target and that was two years ago. God only knows what they got now."

"He's right," Andre said in her ear. "Swap out transport and meet up at the hole in two hours. All communication is cut in . . . three . . . two . . . one."

Her earpiece went dead.

Damn.

"Okay," she said, looking over at Steele as they headed west. "We need to get you a doctor."

"Since someone told the authorities that I'm an escaped felon, that's not a wise move, now, is it?"

She ignored his sarcasm. "We can get you —"

"No," he snapped. "Find us a hotel, and I can field-dress it."

She rolled her eyes at his stupidity. "What are you going to do? Dig the bullet out your-self?" she asked, echoing his own sarcasm.

"It won't be the first time."

Syd did a double take sideways at his words. But more than that was the sincerity she heard in his tone. He wasn't kidding. The thought of him lying out in the field someplace with a gaping wound he was dressing by himself brought a peculiar pain to her chest. For some reason she didn't understand, it actually made her hurt for him.

He sat beside her, still holding his shoulder as even more blood covered his hand. A light sheen of perspiration covered his handsome face, which now had a grayish cast.

Unwilling to argue more, since time was critical, she decided to heed his advice. "You still need a doctor."

"Then you and your friends had better sneak one in, otherwise this mission is totally fubarred."

"Fubarred?"

"Fucked up beyond all recognition."

She headed toward what she hoped would be a safe hotel. "We're not fubarred."

"Yeah, we are. Our friend back there in the Escalade has twenty-four hours to kill me, so I have a strong feeling we haven't seen the last of him." He placed her gun on the seat next to him. It was completely covered by blood. "We also need to get me my own weapon of some sort so that I can give him a dose of his own medicine. Let him bring it on when we're on equal footing."

"Wait, wait, wait. Go back to the first thing. What's this twenty-four-hour thing? Andre didn't tell me anything about that."

Steele gave her a mean glare. "You wanted

me to get a job. Well, lady, that's their job-screening. I kill him, or he kills me. Winner gets the job."

"You're kidding."

"Absolutely. I'm not the least bit serious. All of this is one big hallucination. And I'm not sitting over here bleeding to death. But hey, since it's a hallucination, could you please make my arm stop throbbing because right now it hurts like hell." He practically snarled the last bit at her.

"You don't have to be so nasty."

He growled at her like a wounded bear — which she supposed he was. That growling only increased as she pulled up to the Henley Park Hotel and parked off to the side so that their beat-up car wouldn't be quite so obvious.

"What the hell are we doing here?"

She gave him a menacing glare as she put the car in park. "Getting a room."

"In a swanky hotel? Sure. Why not?"

"The assassin won't be looking for us here."

He rolled his eyes at her. "You can't outrun the satellites, Syd. Not to mention the fact that I'm just a little hard to hide right now. How do you propose we get me in there? I think they might get upset if I bleed all over their polished floors."

"Don't worry, Steele. This is one hotel where they have plenty of security. If someone comes into this place who isn't a registered guest, they *will* be stopped. A French politician and his family are here on vacation, and they have elevated their procedures to accommodate him. It's the safest place I know of."

She balanced her weapon on his thigh. "Here. Protect yourself while I sign us in." She hesitated as she saw the agony of his expression. "Hang in there for me, okay?"

He took her weapon grudgingly. "What? You going soft, Syd Vicious?"

She gave him her own growl before she got out and rushed across the sidewalk, toward the entrance.

Steele forced himself not to say anything while she left him out in the open like a neon sign begging the independent contractor to come finish him off.

As he looked around the car, with its obvious bullet holes and shattered glass, he started laughing at the thought of what it must look like outside with the fender damage too. Yeah. They looked like they belonged at a fine hotel, huh? It was a wonder management wasn't calling the police to escort the riffraff off the premises.

He didn't know what would be worse.

Steele's eyes narrowed as an unmarked black sedan entered the lot, then slowed down as it came into view of his car. It crept along, slowing even more as it came alongside him.

He gripped the weapon, ready to fire.

It parked two spaces down. Grinding his teeth against the pain, he pulled the slide back to lock a bullet in the chamber as he held his breath and prepared to shoot.

Until he saw two young women get out of the car. They were chatting together as they put their designer purses on their shoulders and grabbed several shopping bags from the backseat. Completely oblivious to him, they chatted away as they headed for the hotel.

Steele drew a long breath as he switched the safety on and relaxed even though the pain of his shoulder was a throbbing nightmare. He'd learned a long time ago to deal with physical discomfort. The wound would either stop throbbing eventually or kill him.

At the moment, he had no preference. *Just make the damn pain stop.*

Grinding his teeth, he tilted his head back and took long, deep breaths. He wasn't sure how much time had passed before he saw Sydney headed back toward the car.

She ran to his side.

"Stay there a second," she mouthed through the only piece of glass that wasn't shattered.

"You know, I can hear you just fine, since most of the windows are gone," Steele said sarcastically, frowning as he watched her go to the trunk. A few seconds later, she returned with a long coat. She opened the door and made a face of sympathetic pain as she saw the blood that had soaked the faux leather interior of the car.

"Sorry, hon," he said, wiping the sweat from his brow. "I made a mess."

She didn't look amused. "Are you okay?"

"For a guy who's bleeding to death, I'm doing pretty good. You?"

She shook her head at him as she wiped her hand over his face. He closed his eyes at the tenderness of her unexpected actions. He didn't know how her touch could make him feel anything other than the pain of his injury, but it did. Hell, it even made him hard again.

She brushed his hair back from his brow. "We need to get you inside."

"What about the car?"

"It'll be taken care of."

Deciding not to argue, Steele got out slowly and pulled the coat on. He let out a groan as his shoulder flamed even more. He heard Syd hiss in sympathy. She helped him put it on gently, then buttoned it.

It was a bit warm for a coat, and no doubt it would gain them too much attention, but Steele went with it anyway. The coat would be less conspicuous than the blood.

"We need to get to the room before I bleed through this," he mumbled.

She nodded as she tried to help him away from the car.

"I got it, Syd. It'll be too obvious if you help me."

"Okay," she said as she led him toward the hotel.

"I still think it's a mistake to stay here."

"Don't worry. This place is crawling with security."

Was that supposed to make him feel better? The last thing he needed was for any of them to be TV watchers who'd seen his supposed jailbreak.

"We're on the third floor," she said as they entered the lobby and she led him toward the elevators.

He would have put the sunglasses back on, but seeing how dark the lobby was, that would make him look even more suspicious than he already did. So Steele kept his head down, but he was well aware of everyone in the place. Luckily the two desk clerks were busy chatting, and the only man who was obvious in the lobby was sitting with his laptop, working.

Syd pulled out her cell phone and pressed a button. She started speaking in spook talk, which meant she was saying nothing while updating someone on their situation. Steele had no idea who she was talking to, and frankly he didn't care. His head was starting to buzz, and the last thing he could afford was to pass out.

He leaned against the back wall of the elevator car while she pressed the button for their floor. It seemed to take forever before the doors opened onto an elegant hallway. Syd led him out to a room that was halfway down, between the elevator and the stairwell.

"Let me guess," he said as she fumbled with the lock. "Not a coincidence?"

She shook her head as she hung up the phone. "We need an escape route."

"Good woman."

As soon as she had the door open, Steele headed for the bed so that he could finally lie down. But what he really wanted to do was pass out.

If only . . .

Syd bit her lip as she headed for Steele and helped him remove the coat, which was now completely soaked with blood. She sucked her breath in sharply at the sight of his wound. "I'm sorry. I didn't realize how bad it was."

"It's just a flesh wound," he said in a bad rendition from *Monty Python and the Holy Grail.*

"What are you, a loon?" she asked, using another quote from that scene.

He laughed, then groaned. "You like Python?"

She nodded as she dropped the coat to the floor. "See the violence inherent in the system. Help, help, I'm being oppressed."

His eyes were light, even though his brow was creased with pain. "I need some towels, a knife, and a sewing kit with some kind of alcohol to soak it in."

Syd scowled at him. "Oh, you are not seriously going to tend this on your own, are you?"

"The only other way is to cauterize it. In which case I need towels, a knife, and a lighter."

She stared aghast at his calmness. "You're just going to dig it right out of your shoulder all by your lonesome, huh?"

"It would be nice for you to do it, but since I don't trust you not to nick an artery and kill me, I think I should handle it."

"Do this a lot, do you?" she asked as she went for the towels.

"Only when I have to."

And that made her stomach clench. She grabbed two towels and headed back for him. In all honesty, she was worried about him. He didn't look good, but then given his current state there was little wonder about that.

"Lie back," she said as she pressed the towels to the wound. "Andre will be here momentarily with help."

"No!"

She glared at him. "Yes, Steele. We can't afford to have you die on us. We're compromised enough."

She could tell he wanted to argue, but he merely laid his head back and kept his jaw clenched.

Someone knocked on the door. "Housekeeping."

Steele had the gun up and angled at the door before she could even reach for it. She motioned to him to stay down while she approached the door, half expecting it to be the hired killer.

She lifted herself up so that she could see out of the peephole. "Yes?"

"You need extra towels and alcohol?"

She relaxed only a hair at the code words.

Still, she wasn't foolish enough to trust them completely. She glanced back at Steele, who still had the gun up, before she unbolted the door and slowly opened it.

The maid came in slowly, with Andre one step behind.

Steele frowned at the small Hispanic woman in a cleaning lady's uniform as he let his arm with the gun fall to the side. Andre closed and locked the door.

The "maid" had an armload of towels, but instead of heading to the bathroom, she moved toward the bed. He watched as she set them down at his feet and unwrapped a doctor's bag.

"It's all right," she said to him as she moved to cut his shirt from him. "I'm Dr. Vasquez."

"I hope so," he said quietly. "I'd hate to have Alice dig a bullet out of my body. Call me crazy, but I don't think they teach that in cooking school. Not to mention I don't ever recall the episode with Marcia, Greg, or Cindy getting a bullet wound."

She patted his arm before she unwrapped alcohol swabs, then set about cleaning his injury. "I know the pain makes everyone snappish."

"He's always like this," Syd said drily.

He snorted at her. "Oh, I'm barely getting started. Just wait until the pain really gets bad."

Syd didn't say anything as she moved out of the way while the doctor prepared to give him a local.

"Any word on our friend?" she asked Andre.

Andre shook his head. "He lost the cops and vanished on the interstate. He was last seen headed north of here."

Syd sighed as if that information irritated her. "That tells us nothing."

"I know."

Syd looked back to where Steele was watching the doctor dig the bullet out of his shoulder. Her stomach shrank again. The man definitely had guts. She'd give him credit there. There was no way she could watch a doctor work on her without losing her lunch.

She turned back to Andre. "We're going to need a few supplies . . ."

"An M21 rifle," Steele said from the bed. "I also want a handgun, a butterfly knife, and a few smoke bombs. A coded, secure cell phone and a gym bag. I need a Swiss Army knife, clay, wire, and electronic lock picks."

Syd frowned at him. He was really starting to sweat. "How on earth can you concentrate while she's digging a bullet out of your shoulder?"

He gave her a droll stare. "Mind over matter. Not to mention the fact that I don't want to die right now. I've still got a few things I want to do, like shove my foot so far up the assassin's ass that he tastes leather for eternity . . . ow!" he snapped as the doctor twisted the unnumbed part of his arm.

Andre shook his head. "Okay, I have his list. I'll procure a new car, dump the old one, and get started on everything —"

"Let us procure the car," Steele said. "It'll look more authentic that way."

Andre nodded. "All right, refresh. I'll get a car and park it on the street. I'll put everything in the trunk and lock it tight so that it'll look like you stole it. I'm going to assume you know how to hot-wire?"

Steele nodded.

Andre looked at Syd. "You two be careful."

"We will."

At least, she hoped. But it was hard to be certain, since neither of them knew who they were up against.

Syd let Andre out of the room, then didn't speak while the doctor stitched Steele's wound. His strength was absolutely amazing, and she had to admit that she was learning to respect this man. How had someone like him lost his temper to the point he took a shot at his CO?

It didn't make sense.

Which made her wonder what else had happened between them. What had the CO failed to mention, and what secrets was Steele keeping? She had to admit, she was a lot more attracted to him than she wanted to be. But how could a woman not be intrigued by someone who was so calm and capable in such an extreme situation?

She cocked her head as the doctor finished.

"He'll need someone to help him keep the wound clean," Dr. Vasquez said as she wiped the blood from his stitches. "I'm leaving an antibiotic, swabs, and dressing for the wound. Just make sure it doesn't get angry looking. We need to keep as much infection out of it as we can."

"Got it."

Dr. Vasquez handed her a small bottle. "I also have some oxycodone for the pain, but I somehow think he might not want to use it, since it'll make him drowsy. But just in case . . ."

"Thanks."

"You know, I'm right here, Doc," Steele

said. "And I'm not stupid or deaf. I can hear you."

The doctor didn't say anything as she finished packing up. By the time she left the room, the good doctor again looked just like any other hotel maid.

Neither of them spoke as the doctor left with what appeared to be dirty towels.

Syd bolted the door before she returned to Steele, who looked like he was only one step away from passing out. "How you doing?"

"I've been better."

She could imagine. Syd went into the bathroom to get a cool compress.

After wringing it out in the sink, she returned to place it on his damp brow. "I'm sorry, Steele. I didn't know they'd do this to you."

His features relaxed as he closed his eyes. "It's okay, Syd. Who could have imagined that a man who heads up a company of paid assassins and mercenaries would be psychotic?"

She let out a disgusted breath. "Could you please lay off the sarcasm?"

"I can try, but I make no promises. I tend to excel at it."

Yes, he did. "Well, I guess if anyone is entitled to it, you are."

He opened one devilish eye to look up at her. "What a day, huh?" To her complete shock, he pushed himself up.

"What are you doing?"

"We can't afford to stay down."

Syd pushed him back. "I have your back, Steele. You need to rest."

Steele started to fight, but the sensation of her hands on his bare chest did something odd to him. It wasn't in him to trust anyone. It really wasn't, and yet some part of him was betraying that code even as he tensed.

He lay back down.

Syd smiled at him, and his groin jerked in reaction to the way her face softened. She put the cool compress back on his brow before she lightly stroked his hair. It was all he could do not to moan at how good she felt.

He hadn't had a woman take care of him like this since . . .

Ever.

It was true, he realized. Not even his mother had been allowed to coddle him. His father had been adamant that a boy didn't need any kind of sympathy. He'd been afraid of making his son weak. And most of the women he'd dated had been more into their own comforts than his.

"Other than your sister, you got any other siblings, Syd?"

"A younger brother."

He wondered if she'd ever done this for him. "Does your family know what you do for a living?"

"Not a clue. They think I'm a government insurance agent."

"Are they proud of you?" He wasn't even sure why he asked that, but some part of him was curious. His father had never been proud of him. There were times when he suspected that the man couldn't even stand being in the same room with him, and that was even before his arrest. Not that he cared. He'd come to terms with his father's emotionless state years ago.

"They are, but I wonder what they'd think if they ever knew what I really did for a living."

"I'm sure they'd be concerned for your safety."

She nodded. "What about you? Weren't your parents afraid of having a son in the military?"

"Hardly. My dad couldn't wait for the day I turned old enough to join so that he could kick me out of the house. My mom's the kind who would gladly hand me a rifle and tell me not to embarrass her as I head off to war. I think she must have been a Spartan mother in a former life."

She pulled the cloth from his brow.

Steele opened his eyes to find her staring at him with a strange, almost weepy look. "Is that why you don't go by your name?"

"Not really. No one ever really used it. My dad always called me boy, or son. My mom and sister used J.D., and all my friends used my last name just to jerk on me, so Steele stuck long ago."

She cocked her head as she wrinkled her nose at him. "You don't look like a J.D."

"No?"

She shook her head. "Besides, that has too many derogatory meanings."

"Such as?"

"Jury Duty. Justice Department. Juris Doctorate. Juvenile Delinquent."

He gave her a lopsided grin. "Rather appropriate. I am a felon."

She lightly stroked his cheek. "Maybe, but you look more like a Josh to me."

Steele reached up to cup the softness of her cheek. He focused on those lips of hers that always seemed to beg him for a hot kiss. "If I let you call me Josh, will you kiss me?"

"Steele . . . I already told you —"

He pulled her to him and cut her words off with a kiss. Steele sighed as he tasted the sweet warmth of her mouth. For a woman who wanted to put this morning behind them, she had a funny way of responding to his touch. She buried her hand in his hair as she tugged lightly on his bottom lip with her teeth.

And even though his arm hurt like hell, he knew that underneath that little skirt, she was still naked, and he couldn't help wondering if this kiss was making her wet for him.

Syd found it hard to think with him kissing her like this. What was it about him that was so addictive?

He deepened his kiss as he took her hand into his and led it to his cock so that she could feel just how swollen he was. She cupped him through the denim, taking care not to hurt him. She moaned at the size of him as an image of him in her arms tore through her. More than that, she remembered exactly how good he'd felt earlier.

He was right, she couldn't really put it out of her mind.

But she had no choice. Pulling her hand away, she withdrew from his lips.

She saw the look of disappointment in his eyes.

"I know," he said gruffly. "Not the time or place."

"Not to mention you're wounded."

"Yeah, but you know what they say."

She frowned. "About what?"

"You can't feel both pain and pleasure at the same time. Since I can't take the meds, you wouldn't want to ease my ache, would you?"

She made a disgusted face at him. "You have to be the king of bad come-on lines. Have you *ever* had a woman take you up on one of them?"

His look turned devilish. "All the time. Women love my debonair wit. Besides, it was worth a shot."

"You keep talking like that, and you'll have another 'shot' to deal with."

"Yeah, yeah." He reached into his pocket.

Syd frowned as she saw him pull out a wad of dark green fabric. Her face flamed as she realized it was her underwear. "Give me that!"

He held it away from her. "Let me put them on you, and I will."

"You've got to be kidding me."

He shook his head.

Syd glared at him. Honestly, it would be easy to take them back, but to do that would hurt his injury even more. It could even re-open it.

Just do it. Get it over with and get your underwear back.

It wasn't like he hadn't already touched

her. That thought seriously backfired as she remembered exactly how good he'd felt this morning.

"Fine," she said angrily.

His dark eyes were taunting as he unwadded the panties and got up slowly. In all honesty, she couldn't breathe as she watched him kneel on the floor in front of her. With one hand on the wall to steady herself, she lifted one leg and inserted it into the panties.

She knew from his position that he had a perfect view of her underneath her skirt. It was strangely erotic, especially given the heated look on his face. She knew he was thinking of how she'd tasted earlier, and the truth was, she wanted to feel his mouth on her again. Her body was already on fire as she felt the moisture pooling for him. Licking her lips, she lifted the other leg.

Steele pulled the panties up slowly, rising with them until he stood before her. He pulled the hem of her skirt up all the way to her waist before he slid his hand down between their bodies.

"Look me in the eye, Syd, and tell me you're not wet for me. Tell me right now that you're not aching to feel me touch you."

She couldn't speak. He was right. Her

body was absolutely throbbing with bittersweet pain.

As he tugged at her panties, his knuckles grazed against her sensitive cleft. She moaned in spite of herself.

One corner of his mouth quirked up as he released her underwear and ran one long, hard finger against her. She shivered as he wiggled it against the part of her that was swollen for him.

Steele wanted to shout in triumph at how wet she really was and at the fact that she wasn't pulling away from him. Dipping his head down, he kissed those plump, taunting lips. She clutched him to her as he slid his finger deep inside her.

So much for forgetting about this morning, huh? But he would never tease her with that. The truth was, he didn't want her to forget, any more than he wanted her to pull away from him. Pain or no pain, he wanted another taste of her.

More than that, he wanted her to ride his cock the way she rode his fingers.

His body burning, he'd started to reach for his fly when he happened to see a strange shadow flash on the wall beside her.

Syd whimpered slightly as Steele pulled back from her white-hot body. He was now looking at the window and not her.

Scowling, she turned to see what had him distracted.

But before she could do anything more than twist at the waist, Steele sank to his knees and pulled her to the floor with him.

Three seconds later, she heard a pop in the wall. She looked up and went pale.

There was a bullet hole in the vicinity of where her head had been just a second before.

Ten

More shots splattered the beige wall as glass shattered from their windows and bullets tore through the cloth of the muted colored curtains.

"Fucking amateurs," Steele snarled in her ear as he pushed himself away from her so that he could put himself closer to his weapon. "Then again, thank God or you'd be dead."

Somehow that wasn't comforting to her. Syd quickly pulled her underwear up and her skirt down, and tried hard not to think about the fact that their assailant had most likely seen their little interlude through the scope on his rifle.

"Where's he shooting from?" Syd asked.

He gave her a patronizing look. "I don't know. You want to go look out the window and then tell me the answer?"

She gave him her own peeved stare. "I thought you experts could tell these things from the angle of impact and such."

He crawled on the floor until he reached

his weapon. "I could if I stood up to examine the busted drywall. But personally, I'd like to live long enough to shove the barrel of my SR up this guy's —"

His words were broken off by more shots.

But those shots were enough to give her a clue as to where they were originating — from across the parking lot. Rolling to her knees, Syd rose and fired out the shattered window.

Steele cocked his head. "What are you shooting at?"

"Hopefully our attacker."

"Do you have any extra ammo after you exhaust that clip?"

She bridled at his criticism and the fact that he was right. Once the ammo was gone, it was gone.

Steele let out a disgusted breath as more shots were fired haphazardly into their room. "Why is he shooting like this? It doesn't make sense. There are too many witnesses to take such a chance."

She heard the sound of police sirens approaching from outside. "Maybe he's doing it to get you arrested."

He shook his head, and she agreed — that didn't make sense either. Since Steele knew about their undercover club, the last thing they would want was to take a chance on him telling the police about their organization.

So why the dramatic attack? It was as if the assassin wanted to get caught.

More bullets arched through the room.

She glanced to Steele as he cursed again. "You want to run for it?"

His face hardened as if he were ready to stare down the devil and win. "Not really. He's out there waiting for us. We hit the street, and we're ducks in a barrel."

"Isn't that fish in a barrel?"

"Don't fuck with my metaphors right now, Syd. Can't you see that I'm under stress?"

He had a point. But where did that leave them? They couldn't stay here with the police bearing down on them while they were under fire.

"Hotel security!"

Syd added her own curse to his as someone pounded on their door. What kind of idiot would do such a thing?

Couldn't he hear the . . .

The assassin paused his assault — most likely to reload, but he could riddle the door with bullets again at any moment. God help the idiot in the hall if he did.

What was she going to do? There was blood all over the bed. Steele's shirt was cut to pieces beside them on the floor, and the bandage on his shoulder was starting to bleed again. She didn't have any kind of agency ID on her, and neither did Steele.

The last thing they needed right now was hotel security hassling them.

Or worse, the cops outside storming into the building, wanting an ID.

"I think you're going to have to go to jail for a little while," she said to Steele.

He glared at her. "No. I'm not about to be unarmed in a jail cell and at this prick's mercy. Rule two of a sniper — No one takes my weapon from me."

The door lock clicked an instant before it opened slowly.

Before she could move, Steele rushed the man in the red security coat. More bullets sprayed through the room as Steele and the man went crashing to the hallway floor.

"Steele?" she called.

He crawled over the security guard to the other side of the hallway, where he checked his clip as he leaned against the wall. "Stay down!" he ordered the guard, who was still on the floor. "I don't know's shooting at us or why, but he's not stopping his attack."

The guard stopped moving entirely. "What should I do?"

Syd gave him a dry stare. "Breathe shallowly, and whatever you do, don't raise your head. At least, not if you want to keep it."

More bullets sprayed the wall and door-frame.

The security guard covered his head and started praying out loud.

As soon as Syd made her way into the hallway too, Steele grabbed her and ran in a crouching stance with her toward the stairs.

"What are we doing?" she asked. "The police will be —"

"We're heading up," he said, climbing the stairs.

"Why?"

"Because the cops will be coming up to our floor," he said between clenched teeth. "And we can't head down without meeting up with them. I don't know about you, but it's not something I want to do half-naked and bleeding."

They were a bit conspicuous. Personally, she'd rather meet the cops than their attacker, but since she'd been running the show so far, she deferred to Steele to see what he had planned. He led her up two flights of stairs before he left the stairwell.

He went down the hallway until he came to a door on the opposite side of the hotel from theirs.

He knocked roughly on the door. "Hotel security. Is anyone in there?"

Syd remained quiet as her heart beat frantically against her chest. She hated being in a situation where she wasn't in complete control. It didn't happen very often, and she really resented it happening now.

She also hated not knowing who or what was out there, waiting to take their lives.

After a few seconds with no answer, Steele put a card key into the lock and opened the door.

Her jaw went slack. "How did you —"

"I lifted it from the security guard when I threw him to the floor," he said, opening the door. He entered first and scanned the room.

He pulled her in before he shut the door and locked it.

She watched as he went to the drawers and rifled through them until he found a D.C. sweatshirt. He checked the size before he pulled it on over his bare chest.

"Thank God for tourists," he said as he went back to the door and checked the peephole.

Syd repeated his actions as she searched the drawer for a pair of pants. She kicked her heels off and replaced her skirt with a pair of baggy blue jeans, then fluffed her blouse out over them. It wasn't the most attractive outfit, but it would do.

Now if she just had running shoes . . .

"All right," Steele said. "You and I are just a married couple here to sightsee, who know nothing about any of this. Got it?"

"Sure."

"Good."

Syd tossed her pumps in the trash. "If we don't get out of here soon, we're screwed."

He snorted. "I don't know about you, but I've had that feeling since the moment I first met you people. The least you could do, baby, is give me a little more foreplay to ease me into it."

She shook her head at him as she heard a click from outside, probably the police cutting the power lines to the hotel.

Syd tucked her weapon into her waistband. "Speaking of ease, let's ease our way out of here under a police escort."

"Are you insane?"

"No. Think about it. My money says our little sniper out there will be wearing a cop's uniform and will come in here with them to search the hotel. Why else would he shoot at us the way he has unless he wants the cops to come and cover him? He'll shoot you on sight and claim that he recognized you as an escaped felon. In the ensuing chaos, he'll vanish."

She saw the grudging respect in his eyes. "It makes sense, doesn't it? The news would report the incident, and he'd have total verification of the kill. All things considered, it's a good plan."

"Too good. So we need to get out of here before he comes in and shoots you somewhere we can't bandage."

Steele had never been the kind of guy to follow anyone blindly — a fact that had gotten him into serious trouble while in the Army. Yet he was beginning to trust Syd and her instincts almost as much as he trusted his own. He hated to admit it, but she made a good ally.

"What's your plan?"

"To live through this," she said with a wink. "C'mon and follow my lead."

She took him by the hand and led him out into the empty hallway. It was completely dark as they made their way back toward the stairwell, which was now flooded with cops.

They walked down a flight to reach the officers, who were looking up at them in alarm.

Syd immediately launched herself at the nearest one. "Officer, officer, please help us! I'm so scared of all that racket. What's going on?"

Steele had to give her credit. The woman could act when the time called for it.

The cop looked up at him before he extricated himself from Syd's crushing hold. "It's okay, ma'am. There's just a little disturbance."

"My husband said it was gunfire," she said in a light, almost hysterical tone that seemed completely incongruous with the capable woman he knew. "Is it gunfire?"

Steele feigned putting a comforting hand on her shoulder. "Let's not disturb the good officer, hon. He looks busy."

"But I can't help it," Syd wailed. "I don't want anything to happen to my unborn baby." She placed her hands over her stomach as if to protect it. "Please. Where can I go to be safe?"

Steele was even more impressed as tears gathered in her eyes and actually started falling down her cheeks. He took back what he'd said earlier. She should get an Academy Award.

"Where can we hide?" she asked with a sniff.

The officer took her arm comfortingly. "Is this your first baby?"

She sniffed again and nodded.

He turned to a policewoman coming up the stairs. "Mary? We got us a pregnant woman here who's scared. Can you help get them to a safe zone?"

"Absolutely." The female officer smiled up at Syd. "Follow me, ma'am, and I'll get you downstairs to the offices. You'll be safe there."

Steele doubted that any place in the hotel would be safe for them. But at least at the moment the police were so concerned about the sniper outside that they weren't looking at him. God help him if they did.

The female officer led them down the stairwell. There were probably two dozen cops and at least one SWAT unit searching the building. As they neared the bottom, the hair on the back of Steele's neck rose.

His subconscious had picked up on something. He scanned the cops around him. None of them were paying any attention as they nervously went about their jobs.

He skimmed the blue uniforms until he realized something . . .

He spotted the assassin two seconds before Syd did. It was the only cop who wasn't nervous. The only one who was staring straight at them as if he knew exactly who and what they were and what they were up to.

The cop was of average height with non-descript brown hair. To the average observer, there was nothing to make him stick out. Nothing to mark him as a killer.

Except for one thing. The look in the man's brown eyes was chilling — it was a look Steele knew well. That of a trained killer who had no compassion as he sized up his target and waited for the perfect moment to pounce.

Ah shit, they were dead. There was nowhere to run, and the hired killer was already reaching for his gun. If he returned fire on a uniformed officer, every cop there would turn on him and kill him instantly.

It was over.

At least, he thought so until Syd started screaming. "It's him, it's him!" She grabbed the female officer and put her between them.

"Who?"

"My ex-husband, the cop! He's going to kill me and Terry. He said he would if he ever saw us together again. Oh, my God, save us!" Syd continued screaming as she pointed dead at the assassin, who was now starting to look nervous.

"He's not even supposed to be here!" she screamed. "He was suspended from the force for stalking me and threatening to kill me for remarrying. He's a sick, sick man! Help! Help! Someone help us!"

Steele had to force himself not to smile as the assassin quickly made his way out of the hotel before the police could question him.

Syd continued to point at him. "Fake policeman! Stop him before it's too late. He's going to kill me!"

"Stop that man," the female officer shouted to the others. "We need to question him."

The assassin took off running as the police gave chase. Steele shook his head at the sight. If they weren't still in jeopardy, he'd kiss her for her quick thinking.

There was nothing sexier than a woman who could think so fast.

While the police, who had no idea what was going on, started for the assassin, Syd grabbed Steele's hand and pulled him toward the door on the opposite side of the lobby. They could hear more shots being fired from the front of the hotel.

"That should keep him occupied long enough for us to get out of here," Syd said as they surveyed the parking lot.

The scent of burning tires was strong as the black Escalade headed toward the street with several police cars behind it. It was the best thing he'd seen since Syd had been naked in his arms.

Syd wagged her brows at him as she lifted a cell phone and started dialing it.

"Where did you get that?" Steele asked as she led him away from the car chase.

"I took it off the cop when I threw my arms around him."

He looked aghast. "Why, you little thief . . ."

She arched a brow as she looked at his stolen sweatshirt. "Pot," she said saucily. Then she ignored him. "Hi, Andre. Where's the new car?"

Well, he had to give her credit, the contract killer and crew couldn't be listening in on the cop's line, since not even he knew who the cop was. It was a relatively safe line.

She stopped and scanned the street. "Yeah, I see it, . . . By the way, I got a good look at our *friend.* He's not military trained. I agree with Steele about that. He was about five-eight, brown hair, brown eyes. He's left-handed and has a little nervous twitch to his nose."

Damn, she was even better at observation than he was, and that said something.

"I'm banking he's a former cop," she continued. "He wore the uniform too well and mingled with them too easily. I'll uplink and search files once we find a new safe hole."

Steele followed her as she led him toward a parked blue BMW. He cocked his head as he watched the way she moved, confidently, and yet she was all woman. There was a sway to her hips that a man could watch all day long . . .

Even while under fire.

"No," she said, unaware of what she was innocently doing to him, and given the fact that his shoulder was throbbing . . . "I need you to stay put. I think Steele and I can handle it for now. I'll be in touch."

She hung up the phone and tossed it to him.

He caught it with one hand and grinned at her. "You do nice work, Syd Vicious."

She gave him an arrogant smile. "I told you I know what I'm doing."

Yes, she had. It felt good to know she wasn't lying. It'd been way too long since he'd been able to trust in anyone or anything.

Syd opened the door to the BMW, which apparently had been left unlocked. "Okay, my idea about a safe hotel was crap. What'cha got?"

"A splitting headache and a throbbing arm." He opened the door and got in.

Leaning over, he reached to hot-wire the car, only to have Syd stop him.

As he frowned at her, she reached up and flipped down the visor. A set of keys fell into her hand. "Andre set us up."

"How'd he know someone wasn't going to steal this before we got to it?"

She pointed across the street to where an exterminator van was parked. "Smile for his camera. If anyone had come near the car, he'd have shot them." She started the engine. "So what's the plan now, hotshot?"

"I don't know. Our friend out there has got a distinct advantage over us. He knows my name and location, which means he's probably spying on us right now. Damn the satellites and Carnivore system." The latter was a telecommunications nightmare that allowed the government to capture any e-mail or phone conversation bouncing around on wires and satellites, and to file them away for later examination. It was a system that many agencies such as BAD and less-than-legal companies could use to monitor and find people.

The age of privacy was gone, and it was a whole new world of Big Brother that most people didn't even know was out there. It bothered the hell out of him that right now the bad guys could be watching him from more than three miles above the atmosphere and see him as clearly as if they were in the car beside him.

It just wasn't right.

Steele let out an aggravated breath. "If we knew who he was, we could turn it around on him. So . . ." He broke off into laughter.

Syd frowned. "What?"

He laughed even more as he thought about the one ace in the hole that no one would know about. Forget Carnivore and the satellite system. This was the one person who could find anyone. Anywhere. Any place. Any time. The one person who could keep them safe from any threat.

"How far are we from Calverton, Virginia?"

She shrugged. "I'm not sure. I think about forty-five minutes to an hour, depending on traffic, why?"

He didn't answer that question. "You know the way?"

"And again I ask, why?"

"Because I know someone there who can help us."

Syd cast a sideways glance in his direction. He didn't know what it was about that look that was sexy, but something about the expression on her face made him hard. "Is this a prison friend?"

He laughed evilly at that. "He probably should have been in at least a time or two, but no. He's much stranger than any of them could ever hope to be."

"Oh, goody," she said, screwing her face up.

Steele shook his head at her suspicion — not that he blamed her. She had no idea just what she was in for. "He'll keep us covered. I promise. No one messes with Gator Jack and lives. Trust me, you'll be safer than in your mama's arms. Our independent contractor won't stand a chance."

She glanced at him. "Well, we've got a lot of open road between there and here. Our 'other' friend could easily come back and finish what he started."

"In that case, find a place to pull over and let's see if Andre left us anything in the trunk that's worth having."

Syd obeyed, and within a few minutes, they found a rifle case and two suitcases in the trunk. Steele could feel his eyes shining in glee as he caressed the rifle. It was well oiled, without a scratch on it. Even though he'd forsaken his sniper's post, it felt good to touch another sniper rifle after all this time.

Too good.

Maybe Jack had been right when he said that snipers weren't chosen, they were born already made. And once made, the only way to unmake them was to kill them. 'Cause God knew, he hadn't felt like this since the day he'd been arrested. There was a special bond a sniper felt with his weapon. It was like marriage. You took care of it, and it took care of you.

Closing the case and putting those thoughts away, he turned toward Syd. "Get us to Virginia. We have a score to settle."

Syd shook her head at the enthusiasm on Steele's handsome face and the gleam in those deadly brown eyes. He was ready to make the assassin pay, and she couldn't blame him. Personally, she'd like to give the man a piece of her training too.

She headed back to the driver's seat while he took the rifle and a new handgun, along with their ammunition, to his side of the car. She watched as he inspected them.

"You can't have weapons out in the car like that. You know that's illegal in Virginia, right?"

"Only if we get caught."

She rolled her eyes as she drifted back into traffic. Steele reminded her of a kid in his favorite toy store as he went over the weapons.

"Does it all meet your approval?" she asked.

"Andre has good taste." He slammed a loaded clip into the handgun before he locked a bullet into the chamber.

"Yes, he does," she agreed as she kept her senses alert to all the cars around them. She kept expecting the Escalade to turn up again.

"Don't be so paranoid."

She glanced back at Steele, who had his head tilted back and his eyes closed. "Why not?"

"He won't be back right away. He'll give us time to relax our guard. Not to mention he still has to evade the cops and reload and replan."

He was probably right. "How you feeling?"

"Like I got shot and then dragged out of bed."

She frowned at the sight of blood just seeping through the sweatshirt. "You've been holding up like a pro."

He opened his eyes to give her a hard stare. "I am a pro, Syd. Isn't that why you sprung me?"

She nodded. "But you've exceeded all my hopes."

"Don't get soft on me, Vicious. I won't know how to deal with you if you do."

She wondered about his words. He didn't

really seem like he enjoyed interacting with people in general and her in particular. It made her curious as to what he would have been like had they met as two strangers on the street. "Do you know how to deal with anyone?"

"Not really," he whispered. "People skills have never been my forte. It's why it was so easy to be a sniper. I only have to interact with my spotter. Everyone else can go to hell."

"So I take it long-term relationships were never a part of your future plans."

He snorted at that. "Not really. Women either confuse me or they irritate me. Never have I met one I could stand to be around for more than a few months before I'd had enough of her."

She made a disgusted noise at him. "On behalf of my entire gender, I am seriously offended by that."

"Yeah, well, I don't see a ring on your finger either, babe. Why is that?"

Syd gripped the wheel. "None of your business."

"Touché."

Syd had a feeling there was more to his curt dismissal, though. She remembered the file on him that she'd been reading that morning before she'd picked him up. He'd been engaged at the time they'd arrested him. "Does your opinion of women include Melissa?"

He frowned. "Who?"

"Your fiancée?"

"Margaret," he said quietly. "Her name was Margaret."

"Sorry. Didn't she aggravate you too?"

"Yes, which is why we'd broken up a year before my episode with my CO."

"Your file said you were still engaged at the time of your arrest."

"My file," he said in a totally dispassionate voice, "was wrong. I dumped her the day I opened the door to her apartment and found her on her knees with another guy in front of her. Kind of killed any thoughts I had of having a future with her."

Her stomach shrank in sympathy for him. Man, that was a harsh way to learn someone was cheating on you. Poor guy.

"I'm sorry."

"Don't be. It was probably the best thing that could have happened to the two of us. Believe me, there wasn't any love lost. And at least I found out the truth before it cost me half of everything I own. . . . Then again, all I own right now is a headache. Maybe I should have married her after all. I'd love to split this with her."

Syd gave a half laugh at his humor. He was definitely one of a kind. "What was so special about her that ye who profane marriage so emphatically actually asked her to marry you?"

"She could suck the chrome off a trailer hitch. . . . Too bad she didn't limit herself to one make or model."

Syd cringed at his crude words. "You pig! You are so offensive."

He let out a long breath. "Yeah. I try hard at it too."

And in that moment, she understood what he was doing. He was trying to keep the wall up between them . . . and he was doing a good job of it.

"Really, Steele, why did you ask her to marry you?"

He paused as if he were trying to recall the reason himself. "I don't know. It seemed like the thing to do at the time. We'd been going out for a year, and she kept hinting at it. Teresa, my spotter's wife, said that it was time I either made an honest woman of her or let her go."

"So you proposed."

"Yeah. I still don't know why. Not really. She was all right, but the worst part was that after we broke up, I actually felt relieved."

She glanced over at him. "Do you think you asked because you wanted a family?"

Steele didn't speak as her words went through him. Damn, she was astute. Frighteningly so. It wasn't something he liked to talk about, but yes. He'd spent way too many hours watching those corny TV shows as a kid where Dad was there with Mom. His own family had been far too dysfunctional for him.

He'd always wanted that special loving relationship, like some pathetic sitcom. How could a grown man be so stupid as to hold on to such a dream? And yet there was no denying what he felt.

"What about you, Syd? Is there some agent or other hanging around who curls your toes?"

She cast him a feral glare. "No, and there never will be."

"Why not?"

"I don't trust you guys. You're always bragging and strutting around like you own the world. The last thing I want to be is some guy's doormat."

He nodded. "I can respect that." He fell silent as he watched the traffic out the window. "Why does Hollywood fill us so full of shit anyway?"

"What do you mean?"

"You know. The whole one man, one woman for eternity baloney. Here they are, Mr. and Mrs. Brady and their perfect six kids, running around a house with only one bathroom for nine people. No one ever really fighting, and every dilemma in life has a perfect solution that only takes half an hour to reach." He sighed.

"I don't know," she said in a distracted voice, as if she were really thinking about it. "I guess 'cause deep down we all want the fantasy of it. It would be a nice life, wouldn't it?"

One corner of his lips quirked up. "I don't know. You don't strike me as the stay-at-home mom."

She smiled. "Not unless she's undercover and armed to the teeth." She gave him a strange look that made something inside him ache. "Tell me something, Steele."

"What?"

"What is it with you guys that you —" She paused, as if she had caught herself in the middle of a thought. "Never mind."

Even more curious, he sat up in the seat. "Never mind, what?"

"Nothing. It's stupid."

He could tell that she wanted to change the subject, even though he was dying for an answer. Deciding that it wasn't wise to question her further while she was packing heat, he found himself wondering what it would be like to date Syd. She didn't strike him as the kind of woman to dote on a man. No doubt she'd be the kind to kick his ass and make him go get it himself.

"How long has it been since you had a steady boyfriend?"

She shrugged. "I don't know. Define steady."

"Someone who has a key to your place."

She answered without any hesitation. "Never. I don't trust any man with a key to my place. What's mine is mine, and I like to keep it that way."

Hmm . . . he'd misjudged her there. "Why? You cheat too?"

"No!" she said in an extremely offended tone. "I would *never* do that to someone. I think Margaret should have had her butt kicked for doing it to you. You don't hurt people that way."

By her indignation, he could tell that she'd experienced that betrayal firsthand herself. "I agree. A pox on all their houses."

Her face softened into that gentleness that had a way of setting him on fire. "I like your take on Shakespeare."

Steele sat quietly as he watched her navigate traffic. She was still looking around, aware of every car in front and behind them. She was so incredibly capable. But more than that, she was beguiling.

Before long, he found himself staring at those lips again. Lips he could still feel against his. And as he watched her, he realized something. "Where are your glasses, Syd?"

"I'm wearing contacts. I was afraid that we might have to do some running around, and it's hard to shoot straight with them slipping down my nose."

He laughed at the thought of that. God, she was beautiful with her black hair down and her sharp green eyes flashing. After their escapade that morning, he should be sated.

He wasn't. If they weren't being chased, he'd ask her to pull over right now and see about the new ache he had.

But he couldn't afford to do that.

And for that he owed the assassin an ass-whipping before he killed him. Not that it really mattered. Knowing Syd, she'd rack him if he even suggested another romp.

Still, he wanted to reach over and touch her. To bury his face against the softness of her neck and just inhale that sweet perfume of hers. There was something about her that just calmed him down. Made him ache and

269

yet at the same time excited him. If he could have one wish, it would be to have one single day with her in his bed.

Yeah, that would be heaven. . . .

They rode for miles in silence as Syd continued her surveillance and Steele tried his best to ignore her presence.

Steele's body continued to ache as he fought against sleep. The last thing he needed was to be sluggish if Syd needed him. But even so, he found himself drifting in and out of consciousness.

"We're getting near Calverton," Syd said, jerking him out of his catnap. "Where are we headed?"

Clearing his throat, he opened his eyes and looked around. There wasn't much but open farmland surrounding them. "I don't know. Pull over at the first Pop-owned hardware store you see, and I'll make an inquiry."

"What?"

"Have faith in me, Syd. Jack isn't the kind of person to trust others. I'm sure he's holed up somewhere out in the middle of nowhere and has barricaded himself in for the duration. He can go without food, but he'll never go without tools. Since he doesn't like big stores, he'll have bonded with whoever owns the smallest hardware in town."

He half expected her to argue more, but for once she didn't. Instead, she followed his orders as she left the highway and then pulled in at a small, independent hardware store.

Steele took a minute to survey the area in case they'd been followed before he got out and headed into the store, with Syd one step behind him.

A tiny bell sounded as they entered the dusty place.

There were two men inside around the age of fifty, standing at the counter and chatting about the weather and what they thought it would do to the crops.

The one behind the counter, who was dressed in overalls and a dark blue shirt, looked up at him. "Can I help you, son?"

"Yeah. I'm looking for Jack Taylor. I know he comes in here from time to time, and I was wondering if you could direct me to his house."

The customer frowned but didn't speak.

The man behind the counter leaned over to grab a plastic Coke bottle that was under the cash register. He spit his tobacco juice into it, then set it back.

He chewed on the tobacco so slowly that Steele could almost swear he saw the man's mind working on whether or not he should say anything. "I don't know you from Adam, son. Why would I tell you something like that, even if I knew it?"

Steele exchanged a look with Syd over his shoulder. "I'm a friend of his from the Army. If you have his number, you can call him up and verify it."

"I don't know no Jack Taylor. Sorry."

Steele knew the man was lying. He could tell it by his expression. "C'mon. I really need to talk to him. My name is J. D. Steele, and —"

"Steele?" The man burst out laughing as he slapped one hand down on the counter. "You're not the same Steele who lost his rifle during training, are you?" The older man looked over to the other guy with him and patted him on the chest. "Get this, Gil, the rifle was tied to him on a string, and still the poor sumbitch lost it."

They both laughed.

Steele felt the heat crawl over his face at the reminder of one of his less than stellar moments in the military. "Yeah, that was me, and I didn't lose it. An asshole cut the string and stole it, then hid it."

"Sure he did."

Steele growled low in his throat as he turned to see Syd with an expression that said she was trying hard not to laugh too.

Personally, he didn't find it funny, since that little prank had gotten him into all kinds of trouble. A sniper who couldn't keep up with his rifle wasn't exactly a bragging right in the Army.

The man sobered. "How do I know it was you?"

"Because only a complete idiot would admit it was him. Not to mention once I found out who did it, I locked his ass in the portable latrine and turned it over with him inside it. Jack took the blame for it, since he figured I was in enough trouble over the rifle incident."

The man narrowed his gaze as if he were trying to decide if he was lying or not. After a brief debate, he reached for the phone and dialed a number.

"Hey, Jack," he said after a brief pause. "I got a man here what claims he knows you. Says he's your Army buddy Steele who had his rifle taken from him."

The man spit out more tobacco juice as he listened. "Ah-huh. Ah-huh. Nah, I don't think so. Hang on." He held the phone out to Steele. "He wants to talk to you."

Steele gratefully took the phone. "Hey, Jack, long time no hear, huh?"

"Boy, can't you ever stay out of trouble?"

He smiled at the sound of the rough, deep

voice of the man who'd been the closest thing to a father Steele had ever known. "Apparently not. You always said that if there was an easy way to do something, I'd go out of my way to complicate it."

"True enough. Tell Bob to give you a piece of paper and write down where I am."

Steele asked Bob for a pen and paper, then wrote down the directions to Jack's place. As soon as he was finished, he handed the phone back to Bob and turned toward Syd. "I got it. Let's ride."

Bob hung up the phone.

"Thanks, Bob," he said as he folded the paper in half. "I appreciate your help."

Bob inclined his head as they left the store and headed back toward the BMW.

Syd gave him a snide look as they reached the car. "Did you really lose your gun with a string on it?"

He growled at the reminder of something he'd really rather forget had ever happened. "Not exactly. I was exhausted from training, so I closed my eyes for a combat nap. In retrospect, I knew I should have kept my hands on my weapon, but I was only going to close them for a sec, and the rifle was right beside me. Smithy snuck up on me and cut the cord as a joke, then hid it."

"Smithy?"

"One of the assholes in my unit. He couldn't stand the fact that I outshot him, so he was always looking for ways to screw with me. He once stole the firing pin from me when I had my rifle disassembled too."

"And yet you let him live?"

"Believe me, it wasn't by choice."

Syd got into the car and started it while Steele joined her. "How far away is Jack's?"

"Not too far."

As she dropped the car into gear, a weird shiver went down her spine. She looked around the lot and didn't see anything that should have alerted her.

"Blue Nissan, eleven o'clock."

She glanced over to the car Steele had identified. "What about it?"

"Look at the driver."

She did. The driver was an older blond man who bore no resemblance to the man she'd seen earlier. "It's not our guy."

"No, but my money says it's a spotter for him. Notice how intent he is on us."

Steele did have a point. "Maybe he's just a local wondering what we're doing here."

"Do you really believe that?"

"No." And she didn't. Steele was right, he was too focused on them. Damn the government satellite system. It was too easy for those with the know-how to tap into the system and use it to find anyone whenever they wanted to. It was a good thing for them to use to find the bad guys, but a bad thing when it was used against them.

Her first inclination was to go confront the driver, but that would be pointless.

Instead, she pulled out her weapon and checked the clip in case the man decided to get frisky.

"Drive, Syd," Steele said as he took her gun from her hand and placed it on the seat. "I doubt he'll follow us. If he is who we think, then he probably put a tracer on the car while we were inside."

Now that thought gave her an ulcer. "You know, I miss the Hollywood legend that assassins work alone. Wouldn't it be nice if that were reality?"

"Yeah. But they seldom do, and the ones today are high-tech and online."

Sighing in irritation, Syd pulled back onto the highway and headed off into what had to be the most remote area of Calverton. As Steele had pointed out, the other car didn't follow them, which meant they were tagged now.

What a fabulous day.

But at least the assassin was giving them a little breather.

Or so she thought until they pulled up

onto an unmarked dirt road. She'd just started down it when a large bomb went off to her left.

Eleven

Syd jerked the wheel to the right with a curse to avoid the spraying clods of dirt.

"Easy," Steele said in an oddly calm voice, given what had just happened.

"We're under fire!"

"No. Not really. That's just Jack's welcome mat."

She pulled to a stop to gawk at him. Was he serious? "I beg your pardon?"

He nodded. "It's true. It's just his way of letting people know that they're on his land now, and old rules don't apply. Jack is a bit —"

"Psychotic?"

He laughed. "Eccentric. He has a few issues with authority and government, and, well, people in general."

"Uh-huh. And that causes him to arbitrarily bomb cars for no reason?"

"No. That wasn't a bomb. Believe me, if he'd wanted us harmed, we'd be dead by now. That was a motion-triggered explosive to let him know someone's on his property.

I'm sure he has us under surveillance even as we argue. So drive slowly for a few miles until you reach his 1957 red Chevy, which should be parked in the middle of the road."

Was that supposed to make sense to her? "We're not looking for his house?"

"Nope. You're looking for his Chevy."

Sure. Why not? That made about as much sense as everything else that had happened to them thus far. She headed down the unpaved road that was lined with tall wheat growing up on each side of it. A light breeze blew through it, making it wave at them as she tried to see something through it.

She couldn't. The only thing that was clear was the road ahead.

"How well do you know this guy?"

He gave her a wry grin. "About as well as anyone does, which isn't saying much. Jack is unique."

Just what she wanted to hear. That ranked right up there with "he's got a great personality, so go out on the date and have fun." Only difference, this one was trained to kill and seemed to like to play with explosives instead of just being plain ugly.

Oh, joy . . .

Syd edged the car farther down the dusty unpaved drive. The wheat finally gave way to shrubs in bad need of water. The whole area was desolate and unkempt. Jack definitely wasn't into landscaping or rural development. But then why bother, when he had it rigged to explode? Why waste such valuable time?

It was probably a good four and a half miles before she saw the abandoned Chevy. Faded and rusted, it was a vintage icon that had been left untended far too long. Oddly enough, it sat out in the middle of the road with nothing around it.

"Stop here," Steele said.

"You sure?"

"Yeah. That's what Jack said to do."

Still unsure of what would happen next, she parked the car and turned it off. Steele got out first and moved slowly to stand at the front of the Chevy. He motioned for her to join him.

Half-expecting Rod Serling to greet her, she got out and walked over to Steele. As she scanned the area, she realized that there was an ancient, faded wooden cabin that was overgrown with vines.

Surely not even eccentric Jack would live in such a place. Would he?

"Hey, Gator Jack?" Steele called. "We're here."

She noticed that Steele was standing with his hands out, as if to convince this mysterious Jack that he was unarmed. Syd's eyes widened as she heard an odd rumbling sound coming from the ground underneath her feet.

"What the — ?" She jumped to the right as the ground started moving.

Three seconds later, the rumble stopped and a section of the grassy ground beside the Chevy went flying. Syd shielded her face as a large trapdoor was flung open and something that looked like a refugee from an old Mad Max movie came out. Dressed in a khaki jumpsuit, the man had on a pair of goggles that caused part of his thin gray hair to stand on end. A white scarf was wrapped around his face, and he was covered in dirt.

He glanced at her, then paused to stare at Steele. He pulled the goggles off to show a pair of bright blue eyes ringed by dirt before he tugged the scarf off his lower face to pool around his neck.

"Hey, slick!" he said with a laugh. "Long time no see."

"Hi, Gator," Steele said, extending his hand out to him. "I heard through the grapevine that you were living out here in the middle of backwoods Virginia. So when exactly did you turn into a mole?"

Laughing, Jack scratched his neck before he pulled a baseball cap out of his back pocket. It made a strange crinkling sound as he pulled it on over his head. "Oh, I don't know, about five or six years ago when I was thinking that what with all the new gadgets them bastards had, they could probably see straight through my walls to see where I was. I just couldn't stand the thoughts of it, know what I mean? It's spooky to think that some pervert in Russia could pull up a satellite link to see me doing business on the toilet. I just couldn't take it, so I figured I'd move underground to have my privacy and dignity."

Syd couldn't resist teasing him. "You know they have sonar now that can allow them to see what's under the soil too."

Jack snorted in disagreement. "Not my soil, they can't. I made sure of it. I got me a number of them gadgets on eBay and dug myself down so far under the soil and reinforced the walls to the point they can't see shit unless I let them, and I ain't gonna let them."

Steele grinned. "And that's why we're here. I've got a hired gun dead on my heels, and I need a place to confront him so that no one else has to pay for my sins. I'm tired of him shooting up hotels and giving chase on a city street. It's just a matter of time before some innocent person is in the wrong place at the wrong time."

Jack gave him an arch stare. "A hired gun? Boy, what'cha into now?"

"I wish I knew," Steele said, glancing over at her. "I should have listened to you, Jack. The government got me by the short ones, and they won't let me go."

"See," he said triumphantly. "And you thought I was crazy. Who's the crazy one now, huh?"

"I know."

Lifting his hand to the brim of his hat, Jack scoped out the landscape around them. "Well, if that's the case, you two better come on down before they sneak up on us. Last thing we need is to be caught out in the open like geese with our peckers hanging out" — he paused as he noted her — "not that you have a pecker, ma'am. Just a figure of speech," Jack said as he grinned at her. He paused to frown at her bare feet. "You're not pregnant, are you?"

Syd scowled at his odd question. Was he insinuating she was fat? "What would make you think that?"

He looked down at her bare feet. "Barefoot. Pregnant. Them things go hand in hand, 'cause them pregnant women have feet that can swell up to ten times their normal size. You're not expecting, are you?"

"No!"

He appeared relieved. "Good, 'cause there's enough radon down there to give a fetus three heads. I don't want to be responsible for none of that. I only believe in corrupting the ones what come out of the womb and grow to at least five feet in height."

Syd made a noise of disbelief. "You can keep out the NSA, but not radon? Just how sophisticated is your operation?"

Jack blew his cheeks out. "Radon don't bother me none, and I don't bother it. Me and Cletus done grown immune, but this way I figure if anyone else tries to come after us, they can get infected and have their lungs removed."

She frowned at the name. "Cletus?"

"My best friend."

Good grief, there was another one of him? She wondered if Cletus was watching them from the shrubs.

Steele passed an amused look her way. "Pop the trunk and let me pull out our supplies."

"What supplies?" Jack asked.

"Clothes, weapons."

"You can always go naked, but weapons . . . those are important, aren't they Mr. I-Can't-Hang-Onto-My-Rifle?" Jack turned toward her with an evil grin. "Did he ever tell you that story of how he lost his rifle even though it was tied to him?"

Syd gave Steele an impish smile of her own. "Yes, he did. He also said you took the fall for him when he paid Smithy back."

Jack went stiff and turned a bit gruff. "I don't know nothing about that. I didn't do nothing." It was obvious he wasn't big on thank-yous, but she could tell that he'd done it all right.

There was something incredibly endearing about Jack. He was like an overgrown kid and a crazy uncle all mixed together. No wonder Steele liked him.

"Hey," Jack said to Steele, "is it just me, or does she really look like that actress, Angelina Jolie?"

Syd cringed. "I do not look like her — she looks like me. Only I'm shorter and fatter."

Jack made a rude noise. "I don't know about the shorter part, but the weight looks good to me. What'cha think, Steele?"

He gave her a hot once-over. "I couldn't agree more, Jack. But watch it. The lady doesn't like being told that."

Jack snorted. "What woman don't like to hear she's pretty? She's not one of them feminists, is she?"

Syd arched a brow. "Is there something wrong with feminists?"

"No, I suppose not. But they're the only kind of women I can think of what wouldn't want to hear they look good. Unless you're just weird or something. You're not weird, are you?"

This coming out of the mouth of Jack? Yeah . . .

"Not particularly, no."

"Well, good. I got enough weirdness for the lot of us. Don't want to share it." He winked at her.

Laughing, Syd headed for the trunk to pull the suitcase out before Steele could get it.

"I've got it," Steele said sharply.

She gave him a droll stare. "You're shot. *I've* got it."

"Shot?" Jack asked, his brow creased in concern as he walked over to them. "Where'd they get you?"

"Shoulder."

"Nah," he said irritably, "where were you when they shot you?"

"A hotel."

Jack shook his head and tsked. "I taught you better than that, Slim. What were you thinking by trying to hide out there?"

Steele pointed to her. "I told her it was a bad idea, but it's hard to argue with a woman while you're bleeding."

Jack snorted. "Hard to argue with a woman, period. Only time a man wins with one of them is when the woman is either on TV or dead. I don't supposed you'd want to kill her?"

"Not at the moment."

"Figures." Jack limped over toward her and pulled the suitcase out of her hand. He reached into the trunk for the other suitcase. "Follow me down before anyone else gets shot. Especially before I get shot, 'cause that would just ruin an otherwise nice day."

Syd opened the car door to retrieve Steele's weapon case.

"What have you gotten me into?" she asked Steele under her breath as they followed after Jack.

"Nirvana. With Jack we have a way to ID the hired gun and set up a place to take his ass down."

She hoped so. They needed to get this assignment under way, and the best way was to neutralize the unknown variable.

Jack tossed the suitcases into the trapdoor, where they landed with a solid thud before he crawled into the darkness after them. Syd gave Steele a sheepish look before she followed suit. The trapdoor led to a small elevator-type car. Roughly four feet by four feet, it held the three of them fairly easily. But even so, she felt a bit claustro-phobic.

A damp, earthen scent clung to the car, along with what seemed to be wet dog. How weird was that?

"Are you sure about this?" she asked Steele.

"I trust him."

But she noted that his face had its own pallor as Jack flipped a switch that closed the trapdoor above them. Lights came on an instant before they fell downward about six feet. Then they moved sideways for a few minutes before descending again.

"Where are we going?" she asked Jack.

"My house. I had it built about three years ago down in these old mining shafts."

Syd was aghast at his mindset. "Aren't you afraid of a cave in?"

"Ah, we all die eventually. At least this way no one has to go to the trouble of burying me." He grinned at her.

She looked up at Steele. "I don't find him funny. Do you?"

Steele laughed. "Relax. If I know Jack, he has more ways to escape out of here than Harry Houdini."

"Yeah, see, and that proves my point. What killed Houdini? A stupid accident. But for one moment of stupidity, he'd have grown old with his Bess and been happy as a pig in shit. Notice I ain't young, and if I die, old Cletus would kick my ass for leaving him all alone down here."

"So your friend lives with you?" Syd asked.

"Of course," he said as if offended by her question. "Where else would I put my dog? See, Cletus has this thing for cheese, but since he has no thumbs he has to have me to give him his cheese on his food every night. If I die, no one else knows about Cletus and the cheese, and poor old Cletus would lose his mind. So I can't die until he does. See how that works?"

Heaven forbid the dog go without cheese. "And how old is Cletus?"

"Two years. So you got at least a decade before you have to worry about me turning suicidal or croaking down here from a cave-in."

She looked over to Steele again. "Does this rationale make sense to you?"

"That's Jack-Logic. It makes total sense."

Well, then, who was she to argue? If it worked for them, it worked for her.

Y-e-a-h . . .

After what seemed like miles, the car came to a stop. Instead of the roof opening like it'd done on the surface, the side slid open to show her a huge, open room that had to be at least two thousand square feet . . . of NORAD and considering the fact that she had been to the military underground installation . . .

"Afraid of nukes?" she asked as she glanced around the computers, which were eerily state-of-the-art.

Jack shook his head. He took the suitcases over to a beat-up brown leather sofa and sat them on it. "Nukes don't scare me. The spooks do. You know they know everything about us now. Where we live, how we shop. Everything. They're going to be bar-coding our clothes soon."

He tapped twice on his head. "Imbedding them RFID chips in our brains so that as we walk around they can have our entire lives at their fingertips. Did you know you can't make a phone call that half a dozen people don't hear first, and you don't even know it?"

Steele gave her an amused look. "Yeah, those spies are *everywhere.*"

Jack snorted. "I know everyone thinks I'm crazy. But I'm telling you, I spent way too many years of my career at the Pentagon. People would die if they knew what I did, and that was years and years ago. I don't want no one to know that much about me.

Which is why I left the Pentagon and went back into special ops training. I'd much rather be left out in the dark with nothing but my rifle to protect me. But not even that's enough for them. Hell, no. They still call and bug me with stuff, and that after I retired a year ago." He shook his head. "They never really let you go."

"Yeah, I know," Steele said as he headed for one of the twelve computers Jack had up and running on three long buffet tables. "So what all are you hooked into?"

Jack headed back toward him. "Everthing. Who you want to spy on?"

"Need to search police personnel records."

"What state?"

Moving to stand behind the men, Syd cringed at the hopelessness of what they were attempting. How could they find one man out of thousands? "Can we search all?"

"Done." Jack took a seat and pulled his hat off.

Syd arched a brow as she saw the tinfoil that lined it. *Oh, don't tell me he's one of those weirdos who wears tinfoil on his head to keep the aliens from reading his mind.* "So if you're so paranoid about the Feds, Jack, why do you live this close to D.C.?"

He cast her an offended look. "I'm not one of those psychos who lives out in the woods of Montana, thinking there's some government conspiracy against them. Some of them are just plain weird."

Uh-huh. . . . She had to force herself not to smile at his indignation.

"Now, I know you think I'm off my rocker, but trust me, I ain't. I like being here so that I can talk to my buddies who keep me tied into the hotbed of everything."

"Such as?"

"Well, shadow agencies and such. There's this one in particular that I like to follow. I got curious about six months ago when I was reviewing the government budget. There was this insurance agency that had a huge budget that just didn't make sense to me. So I did some checking, and sure enough, it was a cover group. Bureau of American Defense." He gave her a penetrating stare. "You ever heard of 'em?"

She didn't answer.

"Yeah. Thought so." By his tone she knew he knew she was one of them.

"I think Joe needs to hire someone else," she said to Steele.

Jack blew air out of his mouth. "He ain't

got nothing I want, but that Tee woman . . . I might be persuaded. I've noticed she spends a lot of money on them high-end dog biscuits. Cletus would probably like some of them too. And that special padded dog bed she bought . . . well, it could work."

Syd gaped. She wasn't sure if she should be angry at his snooping or impressed. Steele had been right. This guy was a god-send, and they really did need to put him on payroll.

"So," Jack said, changing the subject, "I take it you're looking for someone in particular."

Steele nodded. "But we have no name."

"All right, give me the description."

Syd filled him in on the details while Steele went over to sit in a leather recliner. He looked tired, but still handsome, as he adjusted his seat. She couldn't imagine how much pain he must be in, and yet he said nothing at all about it.

If they weren't being chased, she'd make him go to bed and rest. But what good was that, when he might be forced to get up in just a few minutes to confront who knew what evils would leap out at them?

He lifted a remote and turned on the wall of monitors that showed different angles of the topsoil. Their BMW and the old Chevy were plainly visible on one screen. The highway where they'd entered was on another one, and other areas of Jack's land were equally covered.

"How many acres do you have?" Syd asked Jack while he typed in the information she had given him.

"About a hundred, give or take a few."

Steele laughed as he flipped the monitors from one scene of the property to the next. "Nice setup, Jack."

"Oh, yeah, hit number four on the remote."

Steele did. The center monitor lit up with CNN.

Jack made a frisky sound with his teeth. "You hit eight, and you get the Playboy Channel."

Shaking his head, Steele cast a sideways glance toward Syd. "I better not go there, huh?"

She gave him a hot stare. "Not if you want to keep all parts attached."

Jack made another odd noise — he seemed to enjoy that. "You his woman?"

"No."

"Why not?" he asked as if the thought shocked him.

"She finds me irritating."

Jack scratched his head as he digested that bit of news. "Then why's she here?"

"I've been asking myself that every minute since I met her."

Syd let out a disgusted breath. "I'm his spotter."

Jack looked impressed. "Really? *Dayam*, boy, my spotter never looked like this. They always picked men to help me line up my sniper coordinates. Who knew they'd be training women one day? Maybe I got out of the Army too soon, huh?"

She met Steele's less than agreeable stare. "I'm sure Steele is thinking he didn't get out soon enough."

Steele didn't comment as Jack continued the search. After a few minutes, several thousand files came up.

"Oh, this is hopeless," Syd breathed as she surveyed the results. It would take days to skim them all. "It's worse than finding a needle in a haystack."

"Hey, Jack? Can you cross-reference those results with a cop who has sniper training who was discharged from duty? One who now resides in the D.C. area?"

"Sure. You know a car make and model? I can cross reference with vehicle records too."

Syd actually got a tingle at that. Could it be that easy? "Black Escalade. 2005."

"Three of them," Jack said a few seconds later. He pulled them up on his monitor.

The first two were African-Americans who were still working for the police force, but the third . . .

He'd been discharged two years before for a weapons violation. "Steele? You might want to come see this."

Before he could get up out of the chair, Jack sent the picture to the center monitor. "That what you looking for, Slim?"

Steele grinned at the sight of the dark-haired man they'd seen in the hotel. "Hell, yes. Gator, you're a genius."

"Tell me something I don't know."

Syd ignored them while she read the man's dossier. He had been accused of drug trafficking, two assaults on his ex-wife, and shooting an unarmed college student. The last was what had finally gotten him thrown off the Baltimore police force.

But it was the last bit that had her smiling every bit as much as Steele. "It says he's currently employed by our favorite security agency."

"That's our bastard," Steele said in a voice reminiscent of a proud father. "Can you find his current location, Jack?"

"Give me about ten minutes."

Syd watched as he pushed her aside and

pulled up enough private records on the man to make Andre proud. But it was his cell phone that ultimately nailed him.

"God love the hot GPS and Nextel," Jack said. "Your friend is in a car about fourteen miles from here, heading this way."

Steele shook his head. "The guy's not that stupid. Everyone knows about GPS trace on a Nextel."

"Yeah," Jack said in an equally sarcastic tone. "And his boss ain't that trusting. Think about it. You have hired killers out there working for you, are you going to leave them alone or are you going to monitor them?"

Syd concurred with that. "He has a point."

Steele snorted. "Yeah, and it sits on his head . . . covered in tinfoil."

Syd had to cough to disguise her laughter.

Jack was completely offended by his words. "Well, get off your fat, lazy ass, boy, and come see for yourself. I have the ugly bugger right here."

Steele leaned his head back and sighed heavily. "You know, I'm tired, I hurt, and well, I'm not even going to go into the other. But the fact is that I don't want to get up from this chair. All I want is an hour of peace."

"You want me to kill him for you?" Jack offered almost gleefully.

"Not your fight, Jack."

He blew a raspberry at Steele. "That never stopped me before. Uncle Sam never cared if I had an issue with someone or not before they had me take their head off."

Syd frowned as she watched the constantly updating data on the computer that kept up with their "friend" while the men argued over his future. Honestly, she didn't care for their scenarios regarding him. "I don't think we should kill him."

Both men gave her a stunned look.

"We can use him," Syd explained. "You know, get information about APS out of him. I'm sure he knows some of their other contractors and how the company works. If he's dead, he's useless."

Jack shrugged. "Useless works for me. They can't shoot you in the back if they're dead."

Steele nodded emphatically. "Being the one with the bullet wound, I tend to agree with Jack on this. Dead definitely works for me."

She rolled her eyes. "You two are terrible. You can't just kill someone for no reason."

Jack frowned. "Does she not know what you did in the Army, Slim?"

Steele didn't answer as his luscious brown eyes bore into her. "Again, being the only one here with a festering shot wound, I think I have a good reason for wanting this asshole dead."

Syd crossed her arms over her chest as she insisted on getting her way in this matter. "And I have a better one for wanting him alive. He can help us get inside APS."

Steele let out an irritated sound.

"Well," Jack said slowly. "You two need to be making up your mind real soon, 'cause he's just about here."

Steele stared at Syd as he thought of how much aggravation this guy could cost them. Not to mention destruction. "If he escapes, we're screwed."

Her brow knitted as she considered that.

"He'd blow a hole straight in all your plans," Steele pressed, making her completely aware of what could go wrong. "They expect me to kill him, Syd. What if they want proof?"

She didn't answer that question. Instead, she turned to Jack. "Can we hide him here?"

Jack scratched his chin thoughtfully. "I got some handcuffs and stuff. I guess we could keep him here for a bit, long as he's housebroke and he doesn't snore. I can't stand people who snore."

She heard a dog barking before it came running from a tunnel on her left. A beautiful tawny brown with gorgeous gold eyes, Cletus came up to her knees.

"I know, Cletus," Jack said as he scratched the German shepherd's head. "It's company."

Steele got up, mumbling under his breath about unreasonable women, as he headed for the case with his rifle in it. He hesitated. "You know, it dawns on me that going up there with a loaded rifle when I can't kill the SOB is like being on guard duty with rubber bullets. A total waste of time. Jack, you got any tranks?"

"Sure." Jack ambled over to a trunk underneath a table. He opened it up to show several different kinds. "You want one to bring down an elephant?"

"Personally, I want the most painful thing you got." He glanced over to Syd. As he spoke, he enunciated each word carefully. "That won't kill him."

"Thank you," she said kindly.

Steele growled in the back of his throat as her words echoed in his head. *Thank you.* Yeah, thanks. The least she could do was thank him with something a little more tangible than words.

A nice kiss . . .

A little grope . . .

Nope, instead she was sending him out there to get his ass shot again. Why had he ever left jail?

Jack scratched his chest before he pulled out a rifle and loaded it. "This'll burn like acid." He handed Steele additional ammo. "Not that you're going to need this, right?"

"Right, but just in case."

As Steele started for the elevator car, Jack stopped him. "He'll hear you and have time to prepare his position." Jack handed him a Bluetooth earpiece. He put one on at the same time Steele did.

"Can you hear me?"

"You're right in front of me, Jack."

Jack gave him an unamused glare.

"Yes, Jack. You're in my ear."

"Good, 'cause cutie-pie and I are going to monitor you from here." Jack patted his leg and made noises for his dog. "Cletus, fetch your fuzzy."

The dog took off.

Jack motioned toward the area where Cletus had vanished. "Follow the dog. He'll take you straight to the chute that goes up the service area without the mechanical crap. You'll come up behind the assassin, silent and quick. Now go."

Steele still wasn't happy about this, but off he went after Cletus.

He could hear Jack and Syd talking as he followed the shepherd down a long, narrow tunnel. There were dim lights every few feet that kept it just light enough for him to find his way, but not so much that he could get a full visual of what was ahead of him. "You need a new generator, Jack."

"Nah, I like it dark."

"There's only one thing I like to do in the dark."

Syd made a disgusted noise. "You're such a pig!"

"Sleep!" Steele said defensively. "I meant sleep. I personally hate sex in the dark. I want to —" He broke that thought off as Cletus lowered his head and growled low and viciously. His ears were laid back, and every hair on his back was standing up.

"On your right," Jack said in his ear, "there's a lever. Press it and it releases the spring. Cletus'll show you the way up."

Steele did as he said. Another trapdoor snapped up. He climbed up the earthen ladder, half expecting the hired gun to be waiting there when he arrived.

"Don't worry," Jack whispered in his ear. "He's still creeping around your Beamer. Looks like he wants to make sure you're not in it. . . . You're a quarter click south of his position."

Steele went into military mode as he crept through the dense brush in a crouch with his weapon held at ready. Like his sniper rifle, it was bolt-action, with a scope on it that should allow him easy sights on the bastard.

Completely silent, Cletus led him forward like a bird dog after prey.

"What'cha been hunting for with this dog, Jack?" Steele whispered. "He's just a little too well trained."

"Trespassers mostly. Trust me, he knows how to track and not give away your position."

Yes, he did. Cletus was one hell of a pet.

Steele made his way along the edge of the woods until he came upon the clearing where the cars were. The assassin had moved on to search out the overgrown cabin. He didn't see the Escalade, but that didn't mean anything. No doubt the man had parked it a ways back to make sure they wouldn't hear or see him coming.

Disregarding his throbbing shoulder, Steele crouched low as he took position on the ground and prepared his rifle for the coming shot. Like him, Cletus dropped to the ground, and making a strange, snake-like profile, he edged his way through the foliage.

That was the oddest animal he'd ever seen. But Cletus was perfectly suited for Jack.

Steele tested the wind and listened as Jack went into spotter mode and gave him a few coordinates for his shot. Of course there was only so much Jack could give, since he was underground. And as Steele lined up for the shot, memories tore through him.

An image of Brian laughing went through his head, followed by the image of his friend lying dead barely a foot away from him, a bullet wound in his head.

He flinched involuntarily.

That action cost him as he scraped the ground with his foot.

The assassin snapped his head around and looked straight at his position, which wouldn't have been bad had he been wearing a ghillie suit. But in jeans and a sweatshirt . . .

Damn! Grinding his teeth, he held perfectly still while he watched the assassin pull his weapon out.

Maybe he hadn't seen him . . .

That thought died an instant later when the assassin started straight for his position.

Before Steele could move, Cletus lunged. The assassin took a shot at the dog. Thankfully, Cletus moved out of the way before the bullet struck him.

Cursing under his breath, Steele took his shot. It caught the man in the leg, but still he didn't fall. He kept moving forward.

Angry, the assassin took another aim at the dog.

Steele shot him again.

Cletus launched himself at the hired killer an instant later. The dog knocked him off his feet as he bit the hand that held the weapon.

"Sic him, boy," Steele said gleefully. "Tear his arm off."

By the time he reached them, the assassin was down and out from the trank.

Steele stood over him, contemplating what they should do. "You really ought to let me put a bullet right between his eyes, Syd," he said into his earpiece.

Syd's soft voice reminded him of something that was easy to forget. "We're the good guys, Steele. 'He who fights too long against dragons becomes a dragon himself; and if you gaze too long into the abyss, the abyss will gaze into you.' "

He spat on the ground in disgust. "What the hell is that? Nietzsche?"

"Very good," she said, her voice filled with awe.

Steele curled his lip. Being good sucked, and he ought to know. What had it ever gotten him in his life? Being good cost Brian his life.

And being bad cost you yours . . .

He sighed irritably. There was something to be said for that. In one heartbeat, he'd gone from decorated soldier to despised convict.

Cletus took off running toward the woods.

"Wait there, Slim," Jack said in his ear. "We're coming up, and you don't need to be moving him while you're wounded. Let us help you."

Help . . . you . . .

The words went through Steele's head two seconds before he realized something.

The assassin wasn't alone.

"Shit!" he snarled as someone opened fire on him.

Twelve

Steele dodged for the trees.

How stupid could he be? He'd been there at the hardware store with Syd when they'd seen the guy's backup, watching them. How could he have forgotten that little nugget so easily?

Moron!

Luckily, whoever was helping the assassin was panicking. He was spraying the whole area with bullets, not taking time to aim.

"What's happening?" Jack asked in his earpiece.

"Obviously, I'm being shot at."

"By who? I thought the assassin was neutralized."

"He is. But apparently he brought along a playmate." Steele dodged behind a tree an instant before a hail of bullets shattered the bark. He felt the stitches in his shoulder give way as pain tore through his arm again.

"Sit tight," Jack ordered. "The cavalry's coming."

"The cavalry better move its ass," Steele muttered under his breath as he reloaded the trank gun. The trank jammed. Steele cursed as he struggled to clear the trank's frayed end in the chamber. He placed the second round between his teeth as he tugged at the first one.

The bullets stopped.

Steele leaned back against the tree and willed his heart to slow its rapid pounding so that he could hear what the other guy was up to.

He heard the faint sound of feet stealthily approaching him.

Move damn it, move, he snarled at the jammed trank.

But it was useless. The trank wasn't interested in making his life any easier.

The backup assassin was coming closer . . .

Closer.

Steele pressed himself against the tree as he turned his head so that he could watch the man's shadow near him.

He heard the distinct sound of the man exchanging the magazine. Seizing the moment, Steele stepped away from the tree and swung his rifle at him, catching him upside his head with the stock.

Dazed, the man stumbled back.

Holding the rifle barrel with one hand,

Steele grabbed the trank from his teeth and sank it deep into the assassin's arm.

The man let out a curse as he rushed him. Unbalanced, Steele fell back and stumbled. He hit the ground hard, the assassin on top of him. The man pulled a hunting knife out from his belt. Steele let go of his rifle to catch the man's forearm in his hands.

The man clawed at his face as he pressed forward.

Steele ground his teeth as he prayed for the tranquilizer to permeate the man's system. The man delivered two more blows to his head before he was pulled free. The knife sliced into Steele's arm as the assassin was lifted off his chest and flung to the ground.

Sucking his breath in at the pain, Steele covered the new wound with his hand as he watched Jack kick the man repeatedly.

Two seconds later, a gunshot rang out, echoing in the trees around them.

The assassin's helper went limp.

"Jack!" Syd said, placing herself between him and his victim. "What did you do?"

"That bastard shot at my dog!" He moved her out of his way as he went for the dead man.

"Jack! Steele needs attention."

Jack was about to stomp the body when

her words finally penetrated his anger. He turned to look at Steele, who was still lying on the ground.

Syd felt her heart sink as she saw the bleeding wound on Steele's arm. She ran toward him and fell down by his side. She felt terrible about his newest injury.

"See what happens when you don't kill them," Steele said, his dark eyes accusing her.

"All right, you win. Next time, kill the bastards."

Those dark eyes of his narrowed accusingly. "You're not funny."

"I know," she said honestly.

Jack helped him to his feet. "We need to get that taken care of." He indicated Steele's wound with a tilt of his head.

Then he looked at the hired killer, who was still lying motionless. By the glint in his eye it was obvious he wanted to kill the assassin too.

Syd sighed. "We need to secure the killer first."

"You take Steele, and I'll handle him."

She gave Jack a suspicious look. "Can you handle him, or will he have an unfortunate accident too?"

Jack grumbled under his breath. "I'll hogtie him without any more harm. Unless he wakes up and tries to escape. Then what I do to him while trying to reapprehend him isn't my fault."

Syd let out an exasperated breath. But there was nothing she could really do with Jack. He was a man with his own mind. The best she could do was get Steele to safety and hope that Jack didn't play too rough with their captive.

As she looked at Steele and saw the heavy stain of red seeping through his sweatshirt, all thoughts of the assassin fled. "Oh, my God, are you okay?"

"You ever nick yourself while shaving?"

Completely confused by his question, she nodded. "Yeah."

"You know the burn you get that hurts like hell?"

"Yeah."

"This is nothing like that. It's a lot worse."

She rolled her eyes at his misbegotten humor.

"I'm just a little lightheaded," Steele said as he stumbled. "You can help Jack. I can make it back to —"

"No. It sounds like you're one step away from passing out from blood loss."

"I don't pass out."

She had to smile at his bravado. "It's okay not to be Superman, Steele. Here's the thing. I know you're human, and I like you that way."

His face softened as he placed his arm around her shoulders. "Good, 'cause I feel like shit, and all I really want to do is sit down and find some serious pain meds. You still got the bottle the doctor gave you?"

"Yes."

"Then find me a bed and let me sleep."

His voice reminded her of a little boy. And those words more than anything else told her just how badly he was hurt. "Okay. You got it."

She wrapped her arm around his waist and held his hand, which was still draped over her shoulders. It wasn't a lover's embrace, and yet it made her strangely hot. She really did like this man, for all his sarcasm and venom.

And she hated that about herself. Syd prided herself on being above the shortcomings of an "emotional" woman. She could be just as detached and businesslike as any man. Her mother had been a very gentle and sweet woman who had given up a great career in the business world to marry her father and raise them.

It was an unfortunate curse that two people couldn't pursue two high-profile jobs simultaneously and raise a family.

Someone had to give, and she didn't want it to be her. She wanted to be the successful professional her mother hadn't been able to be. Not to mention, she had a calling.

She'd sworn on Chad's grave that she would never allow another child to die so needlessly if she could help it.

But Steele made it easy to forget that harder side of herself. Something inside her felt giddy around him. Soft.

And Syd Vicious was anything but soft.

She didn't speak as she helped him back into the mine shaft and led him to Jack's command center. Steele had just sat down on the couch when Cletus came running into the room after them.

The dog launched himself at Steele, who sucked his breath in sharply.

"Easy, old fellow."

The dog licked his chin before bounding off again.

Syd went to her bag, only to remember that in the confusion of leaving the hotel, she'd left his meds after all.

"Uh-oh."

"What?"

She gave him a sheepish look. "I didn't get them. Sorry."

Disappointment flashed across his face, but he quickly recovered. "It's okay."

"Maybe Jack has some." But Syd felt awful as she went back to him and held a make-shift bandage to his savaged arm. She could feel the well-developed muscles flexing under her hand. "You need to hold still."

Steele leaned back on the couch and closed his eyes. She watched him with a foreign tenderness in her breast while he rested.

It amazed her that he trusted her enough to close his eyes and let his vulnerability show. This man didn't trust many people, and she was now one of the small handful that he did.

A smile of satisfaction hovered at the edges of her lips.

At least, until she heard Jack returning. Sobering, she turned her head to see him dragging the unconscious assassin inside. He really had hog-tied the man. Jack shoved him roughly against the wall.

Then, he moved to a small Army locker under the center table.

Frowning, she watched Jack rummage in it a few minutes before he brought what appeared to be an Army ammunition box to her. He flipped it open to show her bandages, alcohol, salve, and medical tape.

"If you root around in there, I have some Tylox too. That should help with the pain."

"Is it safe?"

Jack nodded. "We're about the same size. It was given to me six months ago when I had a tooth pulled. It should ease him some."

"Thanks, Jack," Steele said gratefully.

"No problem." Jack motioned for Syd to get up. "I have a guest room you might want to put him in."

Both of Steele's eyes flew open. "You're a god, Jack."

"I know. Now get your lazy ass up before you bleed on my sofa."

"I'll bleed on you, you old coot." Steele pushed himself up with a grimace.

As soon as Steele was on his feet, Jack led them to what Syd had thought was a wall. He pulled what appeared to be a stalactite in the ceiling. Two seconds later, the wall shifted to reveal a hidden hallway.

"I never sleep out in the open," Jack said with a wink. "You never know who might drop in on you."

She shook her head at him as he walked inside, then flipped a wall switch. Lights came on to illuminate the narrow hallway. "It's the second door on the left. The bathroom is right across from it. You get him situated, and I'll go see about making sure no one can find us."

"Thanks, Jack."

He inclined his head before he left them.

Holding the medical supplies, Syd led the way down to the bedroom, which was surprisingly hospitable. It had a queen-sized sleigh bed along with a dresser and nightstand. Like the rest of the place, there were no windows, but the lights were bright enough that she didn't really need one.

Steele headed straight for the bed while she set her supplies down on the nightstand.

She moved to help Steele take his shirt off, and cringed at the sight of his bleeding shoulder. "That looks painful."

"For once looks aren't deceiving. It hurts like hell."

She could just imagine. As soon as he was lying down, she set about cleaning and bandaging his injuries. The one in his shoulder looked incredibly angry. It was red and puffy, probably already infected. "You really need to rest this."

"That's what I wanted to do, but someone" — he glared meaningfully at her — "made me get up and go assassin hunting."

"Okay, I'm sorry. Happy now?"

"Not really."

Shaking her head at him, she left him long enough to go to the bathroom. Just as she'd hoped, she found a small stack of Dixie Cups. She grabbed one and filled it up before she returned to Steele. She handed him the cup, then dug out the meds from the Army container.

"Bless you," Steele said as he reached for it.

As soon as he washed it down with the water, she took the cup back and set it on the nightstand. She tucked him into bed, then brushed the hair back from his damp brow. He had a slight fever already.

"Don't get ill on me, Steele." She grabbed the box and dug out the supplies she needed to tend to his slashed forearm.

He opened one eye to pin her with a piercing look. "Don't worry. I'll be well enough to go confront your assassin leader tomorrow."

"That's not what I meant."

"No?"

She shook her head. "No. You're a good guy, Steele. I would hate to see you taken out over this."

He opened his other eye. "What? Are you actually softening up?"

"Just a little, but don't tell anyone. This is just between you and me, okay?"

One corner of his mouth quirked up. He reached his uninjured arm out to her so that he could cup her cheek in his hand. His rough palm scraped her skin. He lightly stroked her lips with his thumb. "It's our secret. Promise."

It took all her self-restraint not to turn her face in his palm and kiss his hand. It'd been way too long since she'd had such an intimate moment, and she had to say that she cherished the novelty of it.

She could hear Jack down the hallway.

Steele let his hand fall away as he closed his eyes again. The absence of his warmth brought an ache to her chest.

Good grief, Syd. What is wrong with you?

But then she knew. She was lonely. No matter how much she wanted to stand on her own two feet and have no emotional attachments, the truth was that she was human. And all humans wanted someone they could depend on. Someone they could call their own.

She'd never really had a man like that. One who openly acknowledged her. For some reason, she only seemed to pick guys who were afraid that by being open, they would lose some kind of respect or prestige. Guys who didn't believe in any kind of public displays of affection.

But she'd been raised on movies like *Ca-*

sablanca and *Gone with the Wind.* Movies of a woman being swept off her feet by a guy who didn't care what other people thought of him.

Oh, what a stupid thought!

She had much more important things to think about than long-buried high school fantasies.

She fought the urge to reach out and stroke Steele as she got up. He was delectable, lying there at her mercy. But she had an assassin to interrogate and a lunatic out there who might maim or kill him just for looking askance at his dog.

Syd hastened her steps as she went back to the command center. True to her fears, Jack had the assassin tied so tightly that his limbs were turning blue.

"Jack?"

Grumbling, he immediately set about loosening the ropes. "You know, that's the whole problem with this country. Too many bleeding hearts. What about my bleeding heart? They could have killed Cletus."

He tightened the rope again.

"Jack! If he hurts Cletus, then I'll let you kill him. As it was, all he did was *try* to hurt him."

"Trying is as good as doing in my book." Even so, he loosened the ropes so that the assassin's limbs began turning back to their original color.

"Thank you."

Jack made a rude noise as he ambled away. Shaking her head, Syd double-checked to make sure the assassin was still alive and secure, but not in danger.

"How long will he be out?"

She swore she heard him mumble, "I hope for eternity." In a louder tone he said, "I don't know. A couple of hours, probably."

Syd grimaced at that. So much for interrogation tonight. Damn.

Jack gave her a sympathetic look. "You hungry, angel?"

Syd nodded as she remembered the fact that it was dinnertime, and she hadn't eaten since breakfast. "Starving actually."

"So what appeals to you? And please don't tell old Jack that you're one of those cabbage eaters."

Smiling, Syd shook her head. "I like cabbage. You know, roughage is good for you."

"Yeah, well, I don't got none of it here."

"And I like corned beef too."

He actually looked relieved. "I got steaks and potatoes."

"That sounds great. You want me to help?"

"Nah, that's all right. You keep an eye on our friend, and I'll go fire up the grill."

She widened her eyes at that thought. "You've got a grill down here?"

"No, that'd be stupid. There's a difference between crazy and stupid, woman. And I'm the former, not the latter."

Syd held her hands up in surrender. Steele had been right, Jack-Logic was unique. Far be it from her to question it. "Do you mind if I tinker with your computer while you're gone?"

He scratched his chest as he thought it over. "You can use Roberta. I don't think there's anything you can screw up on her."

"Gee, thanks."

He winked at her as he went over to the computer next to the one he'd used to track their hired gun. He moved the mouse to bring it out of sleep mode. He turned toward her and handed her another earpiece. "You need anything, just holler."

"Will do. Thanks."

He inclined his head to her before he took off.

As soon as she was alone, Syd sat down and pulled up information about the Uhbukistanis. The president wasn't here yet, but the clock was ticking.

She considered contacting Andre, until

she glanced over at the assassin behind her. Given the weirdness of Steele's job interview, it might be better to go this alone. The last thing she wanted was to put Andre in any danger. Granted, he could handle himself, but then so could she.

Her heart stopped as she realized something. "The assassin's phone . . ." They could trace him right to their door.

She didn't realize that she'd spoken aloud until she heard Jack in her ear. "Relax, cookie. Jack already took care of it."

"How?"

"There's a steel box at your feet. You see it?"

She looked down. "Yes."

"It's plated so that nothing inside it can carry a signal. I stuck both their phones in there while you were tending J.D. Not to mention, you're far enough underground that it's unlikely even without the box that a signal would carry out to a tower. I just don't believe in taking chances."

"You ever think about working for the government again, Jack?"

"Time to time it crosses my mind. Then I go have lunch with friends at Langley, and that instantly kills all thoughts of it. I like my life, such as it is. What about you?"

"I liked it better when I didn't look like Angelina Jolie."

He laughed at that. "Don't feel so bad, Syd. I personally think you're a lot prettier."

In spite of herself, his words warmed her. "You're an old charmer, Jack. You keep talking like that, and you might get into trouble."

"Nah, I've seen the way J.D. looks at you. I've never been the kind of man to trespass on another one's territory."

She scoffed. "The only thing Steele wants is to toss my butt out of his life."

Jack became so silent that for a minute she thought she'd lost their connection.

"Jack?"

"You're an agent, Syd. Don't tell me you're not more observant of people than that."

Now it was her turn to be quiet. "I, uh . . . I've got work to do."

"And I've got steaks to burn."

She heard a click, as if he'd cut communication with her. Taking the earpiece off, she flipped the monitor off and went to check on Steele. She wasn't sure why she felt the sudden urge to look in on him, but she did.

She found him sound asleep, lying on his side. There was something about him that was sexier than hell, even while he was unconscious. Or maybe it was because when he was unconscious, he wasn't giving her that probing stare or making a smart-ass comment. But she had to admit that she actually liked his bizarre, often irreverent humor.

Then again, she really liked him. Period.

The bad thing was, she didn't even know why. He was so not the type who should attract her, and yet he did.

Shaking her head, she brushed his hair back from his face. Then she trailed her finger over the stubble on his cheek. There was something about a man's face late in the day . . . the ruggedness of his shadow coming in . . .

She bit her lip as she remembered the way he'd felt holding her while they stroked each other.

You are dangerous to me, Steele. To her sanity and her convictions.

And still she wanted another taste of him.

"You keep doing that, Westbrook, and I'm going to pull you into this bed with me."

Syd jumped back at the deep, rugged sound of Steele's voice. "I thought you were asleep and drugged."

"I was, but I'd have to be dead not to wake up with a woman groping me." He opened one teasing eye to stare up at her. "Interested in some *undercover* work?"

She tsked at him. "And to think, I was actually having a tender thought about you. Do yourself a favor, Steele . . . become mute."

He laughed, then ended with a hiss of pain.

"You okay?"

"Yeah, but you know it's bad when you're on painkillers and you can still feel the bite when you move."

He was right. "Thank you, Steele."

Scowling, he stopped moving. "For what?"

"Seeing this through."

"It's what I was hired to do, right?"

"Yeah, but still . . . thanks."

"You're welcome." He reached out and captured her hand. His eyes burning into hers, he lifted it so that he could lay a tender kiss on her knuckles.

The woman inside her melted under that tender assault.

Steele gently pulled her closer to him and the bed. Syd wasn't sure why she went, but she did. And when she was just above him, he lifted up to capture her lips with his.

Syd closed her eyes and savored the taste of him. There for a moment, she allowed herself to wonder what it would be like to be on the inside with this man. What would a relationship with him be like?

Never dull.

She laughed at the thought.

Steele pulled back with a scowl. "What was that?"

She bit her lip as she continued to smile. "I was just thinking that life with you is never boring."

His scowl melted beneath a dazzling smile. "I'd say the same of you, Syd Vicious."

Even though she knew she should step away from him, she traced his bottom lip with her thumb. "Jack is cooking. Are you hungry?"

"I'm sure what I want isn't on the menu." His gaze dropped down to her breasts.

She knew she should be offended by that, but for once she wasn't. "You are so stereotypical."

"And you're not?"

"No."

He shook his head as he pulled her close again. "Sleep with me tonight, Syd. I want to hold you."

"Why?"

"Because you set me on fire." He pulled her hand down to cup the bulge in his jeans so that she could feel how hard he was for her. "Have mercy on me, Syd."

"And how many people will you tell about it?"

"Not a soul. No one will ever know about it from my lips. I swear it."

He was so tempting. . . .

Syd licked her lips as she debated. "Shouldn't you rest?"

"I'll rest a lot better with your scent on my skin." He kissed her gently. "C'mon, Syd. I promise you, you won't regret it."

She wished she was so confident, but as he gently licked and teased her lips, her resistance fell. Honestly, it would be great to be held again in the late hours.

"One night, Steele."

He pulled back with a stunned look. "What?"

"You heard me."

Joy spread across his face.

"But you need to get some rest now." She gently pushed him back. "I'll be back with food in a little while."

His joy turned to a look of deep, dark suspicion. "You're not just stringing me along, are you?"

"No. Trust me, this isn't something I would ever tease about. You have one night, Steele. One."

Steele couldn't breathe as he tried not to show just how thrilled he was. Syd bent down and gave him a quick kiss before she pulled away and headed for the door.

He wanted to follow after her, but he was too dizzy from the medicine. She was right, he needed to rest for a little while and let his body recoup. Because he fully intended to give her a night she wouldn't forget. One that, when it was over, would have her coming back for more and more.

Thirteen

Syd finished up her steak, which was as burnt as Jack had promised. But she ate it without complaint as she watched their "friend," who was still unconscious, on the couch. She didn't know what was in store for them tomorrow. Most likely more of the same — mischief, mayhem, bloodshed. Heck, Steele would probably get shot again, the way his luck was working.

Sighing at the thought, she scooted off the stool. "Where should I —"

"Just leave it on the table there, and I'll take care of it," Jack said as he handed a piece of steak to Cletus, who greedily snatched it from him and chewed it.

Syd took Steele's plate and grabbed a can of soda before she headed back to his room. She veered off to the bathroom to grab a few supplies before she went across the hallway.

She pushed the door open to find Steele asleep. She smiled at the sight of him stretched across the bed — at least, until she saw the blood on the sheets from where he'd started bleeding again. She cringed at the sight. Poor guy. It amazed her that he was able to sustain such injuries and not complain about them. Most of the guys in BAD tended to whine like babies whenever they were hurt.

Moving to the nightstand, she placed the plate and soda there before she sat on the edge of the mattress. "Steele?" she said, shaking him gently.

"Syd?" His voice was deep and ragged, and he whispered her name as if in a dream.

"It's me."

"You got your gun?"

She frowned at his odd question. "Yes."

"Then put me out of my misery."

"Ahhh," she said as she cuddled up behind him. So much for him not complaining, but then she supposed he had every right to. "Poor baby. You've had a really crappy day."

He rolled over to look at her. "Yes, I have. And I hope you're here to make it better."

She smiled as he pouted. Good grief, the man was delectable. It was all she could do not to lean forward and suck that lip between hers for a long, hot kiss.

She brushed her hand against his taut arm as her heart started pounding. "How's the knife wound?"

"I'm relatively sure I'll live, barring infection or a new knife wound to my heart."

She cocked her head as she watched him watch her. "I brought you steak and mashed potatoes." She reached over to it and pulled it across the nightstand until she could pick it up and hand it to him.

Steele pushed himself up with a grimace.

"Here," she said, taking the knife and fork away from him. "You rest your arm, and I'll cut it for you."

She saw the relief on his face. "Thanks."

She cut the steak up, then offered him the fork. He captured her hand with his before he placed a sweet kiss over her knuckles.

"Why do you do that?" she asked.

"Do what?"

"Kiss my hand so much."

His eyes scorched her with heat. "I like the way your skin smells. You use some kind of scented lotion."

"Rose milk."

He nodded. "It makes me want to take a bite out of you."

But instead, he took a bite of the steak and then found out what she had . . . Jack couldn't cook.

Making a face at the charred taste, he chewed for several minutes before he swallowed.

Syd passed the soda over to him.

"I think I lost a tooth," he said before he took a drink.

She laughed. "He means well."

Steele looked skeptically at the plate before he tasted the potatoes.

"Betty Crocker," she told him with a smile.

"Oh, thank God."

Syd bit back her laughter this time. "Yeah, it's hard to mess those up." She watched him eat for a few minutes as she thought about their crusty host. "So why do you call Jack 'Gator' sometimes?"

Steele took a second to clear his throat before he answered. "When he was in the Army, he once got dropped into a pool of them by mistake. The Army was sure he was completely eaten, but they did a reconnaissance, and when they found him, he was surrounded by the body of ten gators he'd shot while waiting for them to remember where they'd put him. As a lark they started calling him Gator King, which later got shortened to just Gator."

"Ew!" she said, cringing at the thought of finding herself in a pond of gators. Even Jack had to have been terrified of such a thing. But it made her wonder about Steele. "What about you? Did they ever nickname you?"

"Steele pretty much says it all."

Yes, it did. It was extremely apropos.

"But," he said as he continued, "my code name was Azrael."

"Azrael?"

"The angel of death."

And that was probably even more fitting.

"So what about you?" Steele asked before he took another bite of potatoes. "Do you have a spook name?"

"Cobra."

He gave her an arched look. "Any special significance to that?"

"Quick and deadly, and I like to lie low until I have the perfect moment to strike."

He toyed with her hand, stroking her fingers with his. "We have a lot in common."

Funny, now that she thought about it, he was right. They did have a lot in common. Sarcasm, professionalism, and the innate need to protect those around them. Not to mention a few other less desirable traits, such as the tendency to keep everyone else at a distance.

"Did you ever think about doing something other than the military?" she asked.

He braved another bite of the steak. "When I was a kid, I used to think about being a race car driver."

She could see him doing something like

that. It was yet another profession that would take a lot of guts, and nerves of . . . steel. "Why didn't you pursue it?"

He snorted. "Are you kidding? My father was one bad-ass sniper. You didn't argue with a man who was trained to kill. When I told him I wanted to go to college, I thought he was going to snap an aneurism. We compromised only if I agreed to take ROTC and do my service afterward." He shook his head. "Then when my sister tried to sign up, he went wild on her."

"Why?"

"In his mind, women shouldn't be in the military. Her job was to look pretty, get married, and have kids. Not exactly Tina's goals in life."

What a throwback his dad must be. "I'll bet Tina didn't take that well."

"Not at all. Her and my father were really close until she hit puberty and he pretty much stopped talking to her except to correct her behavior. When we were little, I think he forgot the fact that she wasn't a boy. He used to take her hunting and fishing with us, but the minute it became obvious she was female, he started leaving her home for our trips."

Syd cringed in sympathetic pain for his sister. "My dad was always great. He wanted one of us to follow him into finance so badly that he actually bought me an adding machine for my fifth birthday."

Steele laughed. "Did he really?"

"Yes, he did. He was so upset when all of us kids went into different fields."

"Such as?"

Syd felt a wave of love wash through her as she thought about her family. They weren't perfect, but she had to admit that she'd been very lucky to have such a great group of people to share blood with. "My sister owns a small boutique in Boston, and my brother is a high school coach. My dad's still proud of us, but every time we go home, he brings out the *Fortune* magazine and starts trying to get us interested in investing."

"What about your mom?"

"She's great too. She works as his office manager. I think she kind of got lost once we were all grown and out of the house."

He cocked his head as he watched her. "You're afraid of that." It was a statement, not a question.

Syd swallowed at his perceptiveness. "In a way. I mean, don't get me wrong. I love the fact that I had a stay-at-home mom, but I remember the way she was once we were grown. There for a time it was like she couldn't remember what to do with her own life. It was kind of scary. I never want to give my whole self up to other people." Old fears and uncertainties swelled inside her, and she couldn't believe she was confiding this to him. It wasn't something she ever talked about, yet Steele seemed so easy to talk to. "Is that selfish?"

He brushed the hair back from her face. "No, babe. It's not selfish to want to be true to yourself. You're a great woman with a lot to offer the world."

No one had ever said anything kinder to her. Some hot, foreign emotion swept through her as she offered him a smile. She squeezed his hand before she kissed it.

He moved his hand away so that he could continue eating.

"What about you, Steele?" she asked, "Were you planning on staying in the Army?"

He shook he head. "I'm not my father. I didn't mind serving, but I didn't want to be like him — so distant from my emotions that I barely qualify as a human being."

"Was he really that bad?"

Those dark eyes burned her with sincerity. "You have no idea. My dad never said, 'Get me a glass of tea.' It was more like, 'Boy! Get a glass from the cabinet. Set it on the counter. Get some ice. Shut the door.

Put the ice in the cup. Pour the tea over the ice. Now bring it to me. Now. Now. Now!' "

She had to give him credit, he had the drill instructor rhythm down pat.

"He spent so much time out in the field that he lost his ability to relate to anything but that damned rifle that he used to spend hours at night polishing. I swear he held it more than he ever held my mother. Jeez, the man actually bought both Tina and me shotguns for our seventh birthdays. Then he sold Tina's when she turned twelve, and he spent the next few years teaching me every trick he ever knew."

His dark brown eyes were filled with pain as he met her gaze. "I'm not my father, Syd. This afternoon when I tried to shoot our friendly hitman, I choked."

"No, you didn't."

"Yes, I did, and I wasn't even carrying a loaded rifle. Instead of taking the shot when I should have, I saw Brian again." He clenched his eyes shut, as if his spotter's ghost was haunting him even now. "I don't think I can kill anymore, Syd. I can't."

Her heart ached for him. And as she thought about it, she realized that he hadn't taken a single shot the entire time they'd been on the run. She had . . . but he hadn't.

"What happened with you and Brian?"

Even more agony creased his brow. She'd never seen anyone look so tormented. "We followed orders. What we didn't know was that the captain didn't have clearance to send us out. More than that, the bastard had shoddy intelligence information. Our target wasn't where he was supposed to be. So being the good schmucks the Army had trained us to be, Brian and I moved closer until we could complete our assignment. I knew in my gut that we should leave. That it was a setup. But Brian shook his head and refused to abort. To him, the objective was everything. So we lay there for a full ten hours until I had the target in my sights. I took my shot, and all hell broke loose. Our target was a decoy meant to draw us in. As soon as I took the shot, they used it to pinpoint our location."

"They killed Brian."

He nodded. "Suddenly, I wasn't a soldier anymore, I was a scared eleven-year-old again, laying in my backyard with my father screaming at me. He used to force me to lie still while he marched over my body. He told me then that the training he was giving me would one day save my life. The sonofabitch was right. I lay there, unable to breathe or think. And I'm sure that alone is why I'm still here and not lying in a grave next to Brian."

Syd wanted desperately to soothe him, but she had no idea how. What he'd been through . . . it was scarring, and no amount of words would ever be able to heal that wound.

It would take time, and she knew it. She just wished she could move time forward so that it wouldn't be so raw for him now.

His eyes were filled with horror. "They captured Brian's body and actually stepped right on top of mine without knowing it."

"How did they not find you?"

"I had a thermal disguise in my ghillie suit, so they couldn't pick up my body temp. And I literally didn't move for a full day. They sprayed the area with bullets, and I took one in my leg and arm without flinching. Finally, the largest part of the group left. There were three who were left behind to search for me." His eyes burned her. "I killed them, and then I made my way back to rendezvous."

And now she was asking him to kill again. "Why did you shoot at your CO?"

Steele fell silent, as if he were reliving that moment in his mind. "The simplest reason was that he threatened me, and I was too angry to take it. He wanted to send me out with another spotter, on another assignment that I didn't think we had clearance for. He'd told the higher-ups that Brian and I had lost our way, and as I watched him walk away as if nothing had happened, I couldn't take it. He'd told me that accidents happen and that if I wasn't careful, one could happen to me. So I decided to show him an accident myself." He let out a long, tired breath. "I really fucked up."

Syd brushed his hair back from his face as he took another bite of his steak. She didn't know what to say to him. She couldn't imagine going through what he described. He must have been terrified. Alone. No one to pull him out or help him.

He really was tailor-made for BAD.

His eyes burned into her. "So do I go back to jail now?"

She frowned at his words. "Why?"

"I told you. I can't do it. I can't set my sights on another living person and pull the trigger anymore. If you send me after this assassin, there's no guarantee that I'll be able to do what you ask."

"Steele —"

"Don't, Syd," he said, cutting her off. "There's no argument you can make that'll sway me."

"You would really rather spend the rest

of your life locked up than put down a rabid dog?"

"That rabid dog could have a son. A best friend. A mother who'll miss him."

"And that rabid dog might unleash a nuclear bomb on my parents' house. That's what keeps me up at night. Doesn't it you?"

He looked away from her.

"C'mon, Steele. You're the only shot we have. APS won't let anyone else near them. You pull the name of the contractor they have assigned to the president for me, and I'll take care of the rest."

The disbelief in his eyes scorched her. This was a man who was well used to betrayal, and she knew it. "Will you?"

"Yes," she said emphatically.

And still those intense eyes watched her. "Tell me something, Syd. Have you ever killed anyone?"

It was her turn to look away.

"You haven't, have you?"

"No, but —"

"There's no buts in this, Sydney. Killing someone changes you forever. When you close your eyes, you know what haunts you? Their faces. That look they have when they realize that they're dead and that all the things they wanted to do with their lives are over. There aren't any more second chances for them. And with every kill, more of your soul dies. It's what turned my father into a heartless bastard."

She heard what he was saying, but it changed nothing. "It's a risk I'm willing to take."

"You're playing a game that you don't even understand."

"Well, then, what do you want me to do?" she asked, her voice tinged with anger. "Sit by and watch our country get blamed for an assassination we had nothing to do with? Watch a power-hungry kid hold an auction so that some other power-hungry person can get his hands on a nuclear arsenal to intimidate the rest of the world? I don't know about you, but I never could stand a bully."

Steele fell silent as he thought about that. She was right, he'd never been the kind of person to stomach a bully either. "I will get you inside APS, but that's all I can promise. I'm sorry."

Syd nodded. "You know something, Steele?"

"What?"

"I trust you to do what's right." She couldn't believe those words had left her mouth. After all these years, Joe was finally wearing off on her. "I know you won't let us down."

The look in his dark eyes said he didn't agree, but for the first time in her life, she meant that. She didn't know where her faith came from. But inside, she knew he wouldn't disappoint her.

Steele finished his food in silence while she checked his injuries. The bullet wound looked a little better than it had earlier. It wasn't quite so angry. But it still had to be extremely painful for him.

As she ran her hand over his skin to smooth the bandage, she realized Steele had his eyes closed, as if savoring her touch. She paused to smile at the peaceful expression on his face. He opened those dark eyes to look up at her with a tenderness that made her stomach flutter.

"You have the gentlest touch."

"Hunter would disagree with you."

He smiled as he reached a hand out to cup her face.

"How are you feeling now?" she said, and then realized why she asked that so often. She loved hearing his innovative and often sarcastic comebacks.

"Like I could make love to you all night."

Her body warmed at the thought. "You really should rest."

"I'll sleep better with the smell of you on

my skin," he said before he captured her lips with his.

Syd sighed at the taste of him. Honestly, he was better than chocolate.

He turned to pull her against him as he leaned her back against the bed. Oh, it felt good to be held like this. Too good. There was just something about the hardness of a man's body lying next to hers that defied description. And Steele in particular felt like heaven.

Steele couldn't really think as he worked the buttons on her blouse. He wanted to rip it open, but he didn't want to scare her with how badly he needed to be inside her. The softness of her skin was like a song that whispered through his very soul. He didn't know why, but something about her soothed him in an unbelievable way.

He should be angry at her for pulling him into this mess, and yet he couldn't. How could he be angry at a woman who had not only given him his life back, but set him on fire like this?

He popped the catch on her bra and hissed as her large breasts sprang free. He loved the fact that she wasn't skinny. Her lush curves set him on fire and made him so hard that it should be illegal.

Pulling back from her lips, he cupped her

right breast in his hand as he savored the feel of her taut nipple teasing his palm. He blew a cold breath across the tip, watching as it puckered even more. Oh, yeah, that's what he wanted. Syd warm and pliant in his arms.

At least with her, he knew she wasn't hopping into bed with whatever guy she picked up in a bar. He didn't know why, but he felt oddly special being with her.

His heart hammering, he squeezed her breast gently before he took the nipple into his mouth to taste it.

Syd arched her back as her stomach fluttered with every lick of Steele's tongue against her sensitive flesh. She felt so strangely vulnerable to this man.

It's only sex, Syd.

And yet she felt herself opening up to him. Trusting him. And if he betrayed her . . .

She didn't know what she would do. Kill him, most likely. And not regret it.

But those thoughts scattered as she ran her hand over the planes of his back and felt his muscles flex. She leaned her cheek down against the softness of his dark hair as he played with her. She sank her hands in the silken strands, letting them wrap around her fingers.

Why was she breaking her strict no-touch

rule for this man? She had no idea, other than the fact that he made her burn in a way no man ever had before.

She cupped his face in her hands and pulled him away from her breast so that she could kiss him soundly. She moaned at the taste of him, at the sensation of his tongue spiking through her mouth. Every hormone in her body fired as her emotions swept her away.

Steele trembled as Syd breathed in his ear. Chills shot all over his body. He laid himself over her, feeling her soft, warm body pressed against his.

He moved away from her only long enough to remove her pants and shoes. All he wanted was to be skin to skin with her. To feel her breath on his naked skin. It'd been way too long since he'd made love to a woman. He didn't count what they'd done earlier. That had been scratching an itch.

This was different. He wanted to claim her, which was a completely bizarre thought. But he did. He wanted to feel her wrapped around him as he came inside her. Wanted to hear her cries of pleasure in his ear and feel her nails scoring his back.

Syd wrapped her body around his before she rolled over with him in her arms and pinned him to the mattress.

Then she pulled away.

Had she changed her mind? Steele frowned until he saw her reach over to the nightstand and grab a small foiled pouch. It was a condom.

Damn, the woman really was prepared for anything. "Where'd you get that?"

"They were in the bathroom."

He laughed. "Jack, you sly dog."

"Yeah, but you should be lucky that every dog has his day. Otherwise you'd be waiting until we had time to find a drugstore."

He swept a hot glance over her lush, naked body that beckoned him in the worst sort of way. "Believe me, I am grateful as all get-out to him."

Steele watched as she opened the condom, then slid it over him. His heart was racing at the thought of having her.

Syd thrilled at the sight of Steele lying on the bed, at her mercy. All that tanned, masculine flesh begged her to taste every inch of him. She toyed with his hard cock as he sucked his breath in sharply between his teeth. Smiling at him, she ran her hand down to his sac, where she took her time stroking and teasing him. Unable to stand it, she bent down to gently lick and tease that most sensitive spot.

She felt him tense around her as he groaned. That sound made her even hotter. She didn't know why, but she loved giving this man pleasure.

She pulled back to look at him. "Tell me what you like, Steele."

His eyes were dark and heated as he watched her. "I'd like for you to call me Josh."

Those words shattered something inside her. This man hated intimacy as much as she did. Yet he was giving her a name she knew he didn't allow anyone else to use. In that moment, she felt closer to him than she'd ever felt to anyone.

"What else would you like, Josh?"

"To be inside you, Sydney."

Syd locked gazes with him before she slid herself onto him. The look of ecstasy on his face thrilled her, as did the thick fullness of him finally inside her. She hissed as he drove himself in so deep that it pierced her with pleasure.

Oh yeah, this was what she'd been craving too. She ran her hands over the hard strength of his chest.

Syd leaned forward so that she could take him in even more. Deeper. It'd been so long that she'd almost forgotten just how good a man felt like this, and honestly, she couldn't remember anyone filling her better than Steele did.

Steele pulled her hand to his lips so that he could nibble her sensitive fingertips as he watched her ride him slow and easy. Nothing had ever been sexier to her. She began to move faster against him as she felt her pleasure building. Steele lowered his hand so that he could thrust against her, driving her even closer to the edge.

When she came, she bit her lip to keep from crying out in relief.

Steele cupped her cheek in his hands as he watched the pleasure on her face. The sight of her combined with the spasms of her body around his succeeded in pushing him over the edge too.

He growled deep in his throat as he exploded inside her. Fully spent, he didn't want to leave her. She was beautiful straddling him. He could feel the short, crisp hairs of her body tickling his skin, while her breasts were still puckered from their play.

Their bodies still joined, Syd leaned forward to cover him. Truly there was nothing better than the sensation of her bare breasts resting on his chest. All the pain of his injuries was completely forgotten.

But more than that, the pain of his past

seemed to be dulled too, and that made no sense whatsoever to him.

Steele held her quietly as he simply enjoyed the sensation of her body covering his. Of her silken limbs entwined around him. It was one of the most peaceful moments of his life. He never wanted to get up and leave this bed.

Syd had never been more satisfied in her life. Completely sated, she was suddenly terribly tired. She closed her eyes to rest, and before she knew it, she was sound asleep.

Steele smiled at the soft little snore. Well, that was a first. He'd never had a woman do that with him before. Usually they bitched when he fell asleep on them.

But then they'd had a long day, and she, unlike him, hadn't had a nap.

As gently as he could without waking her or hurting his arm or shoulder, he wiggled out from under her. She sighed sleepily before she readjusted herself on the mattress. Her naked body was flushed from their play, her lips swollen from his kisses.

Steele took a minute to lie there beside her and just watch her. An unexpected tenderness flooded him as some foreign part wondered what it would be like to spend the rest of his life like this. Syd was a unique kind of woman.

Closing his eyes, he buried his face in her silken black hair and inhaled the sweet fragrance.

He was lying there lost in thought when all of a sudden he heart a sharp, unmistakable pop.

It was a gunshot.

Fourteen

Steele grabbed his pants from the floor and hurriedly dressed. He glanced at Syd, who was still asleep. Damn, she really *was* tired. Maybe he'd been mistaken about the sound and what had caused it. It hadn't been particularly loud.

Still . . .

He reached for his handgun before he opened the door and made his way down the hallway, toward the command center.

With his weapon held out before him, he crept forward, ready for anything. He pressed the lever at the end of the hallway and waited expectantly as the door opened.

Steele's jaw went slack at the sight that greeted him.

Jack was in the process of cleaning blood off the floor. "You smart-ass bastard," he grumbled. "You couldn't just sit there, could you? Oh, no, you had to go and make a mess for me to clean up. I ought to shoot you in the head again, just for good measure."

"Jack?"

His expression completely irritated, he looked up. "I know you're there, kid. I'm not deaf or stupid."

Steele relaxed as he moved forward and saw the body on the other side of the couch. "What happened?"

He made a disgusted sound in the back of his throat. "Syd had me loosen the ties on him 'cause she was afraid I was going to hurt him, and he was pretending to sleep. I was getting ready for bed when the bastard lunged at me. He thought the little old doddering man couldn't hold his own. Well, I showed him. Now I'm sure Syd'll have my head for breakfast. But it wasn't my fault. What was I supposed to do? Let him kill me?"

No doubt, Syd would be pissed. Jack really had made a mess of the guy. "Yeah, she did want to question him."

Jack paused to look up at him. "Do you really think he would have told her anything useful?"

"Not in a million years."

"Exactly."

After putting his gun away, Steele helped him clean up the mess, even though his shoulder protested greatly. As Jack bent to drag the body away, an awful thought went through his head.

"Hey, Jack?"

He paused to look up at him. "Yeah?"

"I'm having a bad Soylent Green moment."

Jack frowned. "Soylent Green? What the hell's that?"

"You know the cheesy science fiction Charlton Heston movie where they have a new food source for an overpopulated planet, and no one knows what's in it? And at the end when he finds out what it is, he screams, 'Soylent Green is people.' Please tell me the steak I ate wasn't the other guy you killed earlier."

Jack grew silent.

Too silent.

Steele's stomach turned. "Jack, you didn't . . ."

Jack's solemn expression ended in a smile. "Nah, I didn't think that fast, but you know . . . not a bad thought, except I don't like the taste of people. Too gamey."

Steele wanted to think he was still toying with him, but with Jack you couldn't be too sure.

"Cletus is the one with the taste for human."

Steele looked over to the dog, who was on the floor, gnawing a bone. Yeah . . .

Unlike Petey, Cletus didn't look particularly vicious. But then you never knew.

"So what did you do with the other body?"

Jack shrugged. "I got it stashed in the freezer where I keep deer meat in the winter."

Thank God for small favors. "What are you going to do with the bodies?"

Jack paused as he thought about it. "I got a backhoe and a hundred acres. Guess I'll bury them out near the road."

Steele didn't know what was worse, the freezer or the ground. "Leave them in the freezer for the time being. I'll call Andre tomorrow and see if they have a way of hiding this mess and turning the bodies over to the authorities."

Jack scoffed. "Take all the fun out of this, why don't you? You know, in my day, you just ground them up in a wood chipper, and you got the bonus of fertilizer for your lawn. Made it really green in the spring."

"Yeah, but I don't want you to go to jail for something I caused."

Jack harrumphed as he seized the body and started hauling it toward the hallway that Steele had used earlier to go up to the surface.

He moved to help him.

"Don't even think about it," Jack snapped

at him. "You're shot. Go on back to bed and let me take care of this."

"Okay. Um, there's just one problem."

"And that is?"

"I gave Syd my bed."

Jack gave him an irritated grimace. "Fine, my bed's —"

"I'll take the couch," he said, interrupting him. There was just something gross about taking a man's bed away from him, especially if the sheets hadn't been changed.

"You sure?"

"Yeah. Where are the extra blankets?"

"Bathroom closet."

"Thanks, Jack."

Steele headed for the bathroom, but before he entered, he couldn't keep himself from checking on Syd again. She was still asleep, right where he'd left her.

Jack was right, he should just crawl in beside her, but she was so paranoid about anyone knowing they'd been together that he thought it best they keep up the appearance of not sleeping together.

You are such an ass.

Yep. He wouldn't argue that. Stupid and Steele went hand in hand. If he had a single brain cell, he'd curl up right beside that beautiful naked body and wrap himself around it. God, he couldn't imagine anything better than waking up with her in his arms.

Sighing, he left her and went to get his blanket to make a miserable night on the sofa.

Syd woke up with a start as she tried to remember where she was. Then suddenly her memories rushed forward, and she remembered falling asleep in Steele's arms.

She glanced around her bed to find herself alone. A strange sense of sadness filled her. As she sat up in bed, her gaze fell on a small note that was folded on the nightstand.

Frowning, she picked it up and opened it.

Morning, Angel,
    Don't worry, no one knows about us. Jack either. It's just a sweet memory for the two of us alone.
                                        Josh

Syd bit her lip at his note as she literally choked up. It was a pithy, stupid note, and yet it touched her deeply.

But even more significant than the words was how he'd signed it. Josh.

"I hate you," she breathed. Because with that one simple gesture, he had shattered the part of her that wanted to keep him at a distance.

The man was evil incarnate. Aggravated at him, she gathered her clothes and went to the bathroom to take a quick shower before she changed into a pair of jeans and a top.

As soon as she was dressed, she headed for the command center, where Jack was busy working at one of the keyboards.

He looked up as she entered and motioned for her to be quiet. It wasn't until she drew even with the couch that she understood why.

Steele was asleep.

Syd crossed the room to reach Jack. "Why's he on the couch?" she whispered.

"He said he gave you the bed, and he refused to take mine."

She felt terrible about that, especially since the man was wounded. "I didn't mean to kick him out of the bed."

"Yeah, well, that's what he gets for being an ass."

"How so?"

He winked at her. "If I'd have been him, I'd have made you share."

She blushed, until she realized something. "Where's the guy we captured yesterday?"

Jack looked suddenly sheepish.

"Jack?"

"He's dead."

She turned at Steele's groggy voice to see him watching her. "Dead?"

"He tried to kill me," Jack said defensively. "It was total self-defense."

She looked at him doubtfully.

"It was," Steele corroborated. "And you should learn to wake up when you hear a gunshot, Agent Westbrook. I shudder to think what could have happened to you had Jack and I not been here."

Now that was ludicrous. "I *did not* sleep through a gunshot. There's no way."

"Yes, you did," the men said in unison.

She actually felt the blood drain from her face. There was no way she was *that* tired. Was there? "Are you serious?"

By their faces she could tell that they were. She felt her face drop at least another three shades. "I can't believe it."

"Believe it," Jack said. "I did what I had to. I make no apologies."

Syd believed him, but she still couldn't believe that she hadn't heard a gunshot. "I know you did, Jack." She returned to the couch. "How you feeling this morning?"

"You know the pain doesn't really set in until the next day, right?"

"True."

"Then you can imagine how I feel. But

I'm more than ready to go face Randy and kick his ass."

Problem was, she wasn't so sure about that. The last thing she wanted was to see him hurt any more.

"What time is it?" she asked.

"Ten past ten," Jack answered.

She let out a slow breath. "We don't have much time."

"No," Steele agreed, "we don't."

Syd looked up at him. "So what's our game plan?"

He looked stunned by her question. "You're actually asking me this time?"

"Yes, but don't tell anyone, okay?"

Steele didn't know what surprised him most, her words or the fact that right after she said them, she walked over to him, leaned close enough to press her cheek to his and whispered, "Thank you, Josh." Chills spread over him, especially since she pressed her lips to his cheek before she withdrew.

And that just made him hard all over again. Damn, what was it with this woman and his hormones? He hadn't been this out of control since his teen years.

And what fond memories those years weren't.

He pushed himself up from the couch and tried not to groan too loudly. "Let me go shower, and we'll talk about it when I get out."

Syd grimaced at the pained way Steele was moving. "Jack?" she said after he'd left them alone. "Is there some other way you can think to get inside APS without using Steele?"

"Why you asking?"

"He needs to rest, and the last thing I want is to see him shot or stabbed again."

Jack scratched his chin as he thought about it. After a few minutes of silence, he shook his head. "As paranoid as those bastards are, no. I can't see any other way in either."

She supposed a miracle was too much to ask. Oh, well, it was worth a try. Hoping for a better day than yesterday, she went to the suitcases, pulled out a change of clothes for Steele, and went to the bedroom where she'd spent the night.

She was laying them on the bed when he entered the bedroom behind her.

Her breath caught in her throat at the sight of him wet and dripping with nothing but a blue towel covering him. The light glistened against the sleekness of his shoulders as he brushed a hand through his wet hair.

His bandages were gone, leaving his red, puckered skin all too obvious. But even so, he was gorgeous.

It was all she could do not to cross the

room and rip the towel from him and lick every inch of that divinely masculine body.

"You keep looking at me like that, Syd, and we're not leaving this room today."

Heat crept over her face, especially since she could see proof of his desire.

"Sorry. You should have warned me you were heading in here."

Smiling, he sidled up to her and pulled her into his arms. She could feel his hard cock against the center of her body, and it made her ache for him even more. "I like catching you unawares."

She closed her eyes as he nuzzled her neck, and chills went over her. "You have to stop doing this, Steele."

"Josh," he murmured.

"Josh," she repeated, savoring the fact that he let her use it.

He cupped her rump and pressed her hips to his so that she could feel the large bulge of him even more. "If I live through today, promise me that I get a taste of you again as a reward."

Syd slid her hands down until she pushed his towel to the floor. She cupped him gently in her hand before she slid her hand to the tip of his cock so that she could coat her fingertips in his moisture. Steele hissed in response.

She fingered the wet tip of him before she brought it up to her lips to taste it. "You live through today, and tonight, I'll get a taste of you."

He actually whimpered at that. "You are cruel, Agent Westbrook."

She smiled wickedly. "I know, but it's a great incentive not to get yourself killed today, isn't it?"

"Yes, it is."

She rose up on her tiptoes and gave him a sizzling kiss as she rubbed herself against his erection.

Pulling away from her was the hardest thing Steele had ever done. But unfortunately, they didn't have any more time to waste. They had an all-too-pressing engagement with a lunatic.

M Street was still crowded, but at least this time a car pulled out a few feet from the front door of APS. Syd deftly slid their BMW into it.

She glanced over at Steele with a worried brow. "I still wish you'd wear a wire."

He just gave her a droll stare. "It didn't help us yesterday."

"I know." And she did, but still she hated to send him in alone.

He leaned over and kissed her. "Keep the

engine running, just in case." He reached around her back and pulled her gun out. He tucked it in beside her thigh.

She frowned at him. "Paranoid?"

"No, I just want to make sure nothing happens to you."

His concern warmed her. "Don't worry. I can handle myself."

Steele nodded before he got out of the car. He sauntered down the street as if he owned it. In the event he was being watched, he wanted Wallace to know that he had no fear of the cheap-ass punk.

He opened the door to the office and narrowed his eyes on the receptionist. "Hi, Agnes. Buzz Wallace and tell him his three-thirty appointment is here."

She looked a bit surprised to see him, which played into his thoughts about her yesterday. She must know what it was that they really did for a living.

Before she could press the button, Wallace's voice sounded over the intercom. "Buzz him in, Agnes."

Steele looked up at the camera and gave it a mean, shit-eating grin before he headed toward the door. As expected, the bruiser was there again, waiting for him.

"Don't even look at me, asshole. In the mood I'm in, I'll break your neck in half."

Bruce didn't say anything as he escorted him from the hallway up to Wallace's office.

Just like the day before, the prick sat at his desk with a stony look on his ugly, chubby face. "Still alive?"

"No. I'm a walking corpse. Can't you tell?"

Wallace snorted. "You know, just because you're here proves nothing. For all I know you just ran away from my contractor."

Steele gave him an equally deadpan expression. "You didn't tell me I had to prove anything other than to be here today."

Wallace glared at him as he reached for his phone and picked up the receiver. Steele crossed his arms over his chest as he watched him dial it.

Two seconds later, the cell phone in his pocket vibrated. Steele pulled it out and flipped it open. "Lee Perry can't come to the phone right now, since he's unfortunately suffering from a fatal dose of lead poisoning. If you would like to leave a message for him, I suggest you see a priest or a psychic."

He hung the phone up and tossed it to Wallace, who actually paled. "You satisfied?"

He nodded glumly.

"So do I have a job or not?"

★ ★ ★

Syd couldn't stand not knowing what was going on. Her nerves were completely racked. She didn't like being out of touch with Andre, and she really hated being out of touch with Steele.

She kept glancing at the clock, then the door, then the clock again. What was going on in there?

Finally, after what seemed like forever but was really only fifteen minutes, Steele headed out of the offices with a grim look on his face.

Syd popped the lock on the car door as he reached it. He jerked it open and got inside. "Well?"

"We're in."

Joy tore through her. "Really?"

"Yeah, but before you get overly excited, don't." He handed her a small Vaio laptop.

Her heart pounded even faster. "Is their information in there?"

He shook his head. "Nothing is in there. It's specially coded so that whenever Wallace has a hit he wants me to make, I either come here to pick up a flash card or he e-mails me the files that only this computer can read. I open the files and get my target."

Syd cursed in frustration. "This leaves us no better off than when we started."

"You? I'm worse off. When this started, I didn't have a bullet and knife wound."

She cringed at his reminder. "I know. I'm sorry." She sighed. They'd been trumped once more by the bad guys. "He's not assigning you anyone to show you the ropes or anything, is he?"

He shook his head. "I've already been initiated. But . . ."

"But what?"

"I'm thinking that all files are sent from Wallace's office. From his own personal computer."

She understood where he was going. "We can break in after he leaves tonight and steal it."

"No."

Frustrated, she glared at him. "What do you mean no?"

"Asshole has a laptop. It sits on his desk on a stand. I'm sure it goes wherever he goes. He's a particularly OCD sonofabitch."

"Then what do you propose we do?"

A slow grin spread across his face. "We watch him, and when we have our chance, we steal it straight out of his hands."

"I don't know. I think I have an even better idea."

"What?"

She answered him with a wide grin.

Fifteen

Syd and Steele drove around the block and parked in the public lot again. Steele headed out onto the street to keep Wallace's office under surveillance while she contacted Andre.

What Wallace didn't know was that Steele had picked up a couple of toys from Jack before they'd left his bunker. Steele's intent had been to tag Wallace, but the paranoid bastard hadn't allowed him close enough to plant the bug on his body.

Failing that, Steele had placed a small, innocuous mic in the cushion of the chair he'd sat in. Now, with Jack's PDA and its receiver, Steele was able to listen in to what Wallace was doing.

At the moment, though, the prick wasn't saying anything much. At least ten minutes went by before Steele finally heard the intercom buzz.

"You have a phone call on line one, Mr. Wallace. It's from President Kaskamanov."

President? Steele frowned at Agnes's

words. She meant the kid, right?

Steele pressed the earpiece in deeper and turned up the volume so as not to miss anything.

He heard Wallace pick up the phone. "Hello, Mr. President. It's good to hear from you. Yes, yes, we have everything arranged. I have my best contractor for your case. Stalin has been briefed and will be standing by to ensure your safety. Yes, sir. Very good. The wire transfer for the balance is to take place within three hours after our services are rendered. Yes, sir. We'll see you in two days. Have a nice flight."

Steele stood there as he listened to Wallace hang up the phone. Then everything was quiet again.

Now that was just sick — the company was telling the president that they were going to protect him while they were secretly taking money from the son to kill him? He had to give them credit. It took balls to give the president the name of the man who had most likely been assigned to kill him.

But at least now they had a name to search out — Stalin, which was most likely an alias. All they needed was to cross-reference it with whatever files Wallace used to keep track of his contract workers, and they'd have their sniper.

Steele turned the volume down as Syd rejoined him, beaming like a cat that had gotten locked in an aviary.

"What?" he asked.

"We don't have to tail him."

He arched a brow at that. "How so?"

"Give Andre twenty minutes."

"And?"

She pulled out a stick of gum and slowly unwrapped it before she put it in her mouth and chewed it like a happy schoolgirl with a crush. "You'll see. C'mon." She indicated a building across the street, with a small café on the bottom floor. "Let's go get us a good seat for this." She offered him some gum, but he declined.

"Syd? What's up with this?"

She didn't respond as she headed for the restaurant.

"Syd!"

He had to give her credit, the woman could keep a secret, and it was starting to piss him off. He followed her into the restaurant, where she grabbed a table by the window that looked out onto the APS offices outside.

No matter what he tried, she refused to answer any of his questions about what they were waiting for. It was extremely annoying to be around someone who could remain so tight-lipped.

But his aggravation ended a short time later, when he saw a plain black sedan with government plates pull up. A few seconds later, it was followed by several squad cars and a black van that blocked the street.

Steele choked on his coffee as he saw Carlos and Andre get out of the sedan. Dressed in black suits and dark sunglasses, they reminded him of Will Smith and Tommy Lee Jones in the movie *MIB.* Both of them were also dressed in black FBI windbreakers.

The two of them walked side-by-side in federal agent formation, looking tough as they entered the building while directing the police into action.

He turned the volume up on the PDA to listen in.

It took several minutes before he heard Wallace let loose a string of expletives. "What is this?" he demanded.

It was Carlos who answered in a deadpan voice. "Here's your warrant, Mr. Wallace. It appears that several members of your staff were arrested this morning in a pornography sting." He tsked. "We have traced their IP's and have learned that they were using many of the computers here in this office for illegal purposes."

"Bullshit! Bullshit! Bullshit!" There was no way to miss the belligerent anger in Wallace's tone. "That has nothing to do with me!"

Andre spoke next. "Yes, sir, it does. We're here to pull all the computers from your offices as evidence in our case."

"Your people have been very naughty, Mr. Wallace," Carlos said in a thick Spanish accent. Then his voice leveled out to his normal cadence, which only held a tiny trace of his accent. "We're from the FBI and your computers are being seized even as we speak. Oh, and let us not forget this one here —"

"Don't you dare touch it!"

"We're the FBI, Mr. Wallace," Andre chimed in. "We dare anything. Your staff has been under surveillance for the last six months, and now all of them are busted."

"Eeh!" Carlos snapped. "Step away from the laptop, Mr. Wallace. That is now property of the U.S. government."

"This is bullshit! No one has touched my laptop but me."

Andre tsked. "If it's in this office, they had access to it, which means it comes with us. But don't worry. Here's your receipt. The address is on the back. If there's nothing on it pertaining to our case, you'll be able to pick it up once we're through with it. Otherwise, we'll see you in court."

"I'm calling my attorney."

"You do that, Mr. Wallace," Andre said in a low, lethal tone.

"Don't touch that!"

"We're the government, Mr. Wallace. You can't stop us. Have a nice day, sir."

More expletives followed at such an ear-splitting level that Steele had to pull the earpiece out to keep from losing his hearing. He looked over at Syd, who was still grinning ear to ear.

"You people are sick."

She laughed evilly. "Aren't we, though? You gotta love Carlos and Andre. Now you know what Andre did in the FBI. He's good, isn't he?"

"And what if Wallace calls the FBI?"

"They won't tell him anything. He has a case number on the paperwork and warrant that will route him to Tee in Nashville, who gives the runaround so good that by the time you hang up, you forgot why you called."

She tossed a few dollars on the table for the waitress. "C'mon, it's rendezvous time."

Steele took one last sip of his coffee before

he got up and followed her to the car. She drove him over to the Mall in front of the old Smithsonian building, where he saw Andre and Carlos eating a hot dog while sitting on a bench. Carlos had ditched his tie and coat and wore his white shirt with the collar unbuttoned and the hem untucked.

Andre still looked impeccable sans the FBI windbreaker.

They parked the car, then went over to them.

"Hot dog?" Carlos offered as they drew near.

"Computer," Syd said without hesitation.

Carlos took a sip of his soda. "You didn't say please."

"Please, Carlos, let me have the computer."

"Simon didn't say —"

Andre let out a disgusted breath. "Oh, for God's sake, give her the damn computer, boy."

Carlos was completely unruffled. "You need to learn to zen, Andre. Ohm . . . ohm . . ."

"I'm going to ohm your ass. Now hand it over."

"Impatient gringos." He reached down between his legs and opened the briefcase between his feet. He pulled out Wallace's laptop. "We also seized the secretary's hard drive and the payroll computer."

Steele shook his head. "You do realize you just stole computers from a man who kills people for a living, right?"

Carlos swallowed a bite of his chili dog. "Let him take a number. Believe me, I have much better men than him wanting me dead."

Syd pushed Carlos over so that she could sit down as she booted up the laptop. After a few seconds, she cursed. "It's password-encrypted."

Steele gave her a droll stare. "You think?"

She glared up at Steele before she handed it off to Andre. "Get us in."

"No problem. Give me a few minutes in the van." Andre crumpled up his hot-dog wrapper, then got up and headed for the black van across the street.

"So when did you get in?" Syd asked Carlos.

He wiped his mouth with a napkin. "Joe sent me in yesterday after Steele was shot. He thought you guys might need a little backup."

Syd smiled, and a weird jealous twinge went through Steele. "Well, we're glad to have you."

Carlos gave her a wicked grin. "And I'd be glad to be had by you, Syd."

Steele had to force himself not to leap at Carlos's throat.

"Careful, Carlos," Syd said. "You'll be limping."

"Ah, don't tease me, Syd. I dream of being so frisky with you that it leaves me limping afterward."

Syd frogged his arm.

"Ow!" Carlos said as he rubbed his biceps. "Anyone ever tell you you hit like a man?"

"Just Hunter."

Carlos slid farther down the bench, away from her.

Syd looked up, and he must have had a grim expression on his face, because she immediately frowned at him. Steele didn't say anything for fear it might end in his choking Carlos.

Or shooting him.

At any rate, he was hoping the man would choke on his chili dog.

After a few minutes, the horn beeped from the van. The three of them headed across the street and climbed into the back.

"Well?" Syd asked.

Andre sighed. "I'm not sure how much we can use. Gotta give the man credit, he is paranoid. Everything is key-coded. No e-mails are kept, but I know his server info, so I've already called Marc, who is doing a scan of outgoing mail for that service. It'll probably take a few hours, or even a couple of days."

Syd shook her head. "We don't have a couple of days, Andre."

"It's the best I can do, Syd."

Syd leaned her head back as she felt completely defeated. She was beyond frustrated and tired. Every time they took a step forward, it seemed like they took ten back.

"We'll get them," Steele assured her.

"How?"

"Have faith."

"No offense," she scoffed, "but I'm all out."

Steele gave her a wickedly charming smile. "Well, that's because you're not thinking right."

Now that offended her. "How so?"

"Pretend for a minute that you are the owner of a ring of assassins and mercenaries. The government just came in and swiped your computer. What would you be doing right now?"

"Freaking out," Carlos said as he moved over toward one of the panels. "You'd be

377

contacting your people like a motherfucker, trying to warn them."

Steele nodded.

He was right. Syd watched as Carlos started running a trace on Wallace's phones while Steele pulled the PDA out of his pocket and listened.

But as they listened to the telephone calls, Syd's hope quickly dwindled again. Wallace used so much doublespeak and so many vague references that he might as well be speaking ancient Greek.

Time dragged by as they listened to phone call after phone call without much progress.

"Stalin? This is Wallace. Our security data has been a bit compromised."

"This is it, Carlos," Steele said, poking him on the shoulder. "Trace it and record it."

Carlos frowned at him.

"Trust me."

Carlos did as he said. But Syd was with Carlos. What on earth made Steele think that this was the right call?

Steele took his earpiece out as Carlos turned the speaker up inside the van for them to listen to the whole conversation.

"What do you mean, compromised?" The voice was thick and deep, and tinged with a southern drawl. There was some kind of distortion on it, probably to make it sound a few octaves deeper. But with a little cleanup, Andre might be able to decipher it for a voice match.

Syd watched as Steele's face turned to stone.

"Don't panic," Wallace said. "I doubt they can find anything. I'm not that stupid."

"Everyone's that stupid, Wallace. Mission is compromised, breached, and over."

"No! Listen, I don't have time to assign another contractor to the case. Finish it, and I'll give you a twenty-thousand-dollar bonus."

"I don't know —"

"C'mon, Stalin. We need you on this one."

"Fifty thousand."

Steele's eyes narrowed even more.

"Fuck you," Wallace snarled. He paused briefly before he added, "Twenty-five."

"Fifty-five thousand."

Wallace growled low in his throat. "You're supposed to go the other way in negotiations, dickhead."

"Sixty thousand," the distorted voice insisted.

"Fifty."

There was silence.

"You still there?" Wallace asked.

"As I said, fifty, wired to my usual account after I complete the assignment."

"Deal." Wallace hung up.

Syd looked up at Steele. "Now what makes you think that that is the right call? With the exception of the bonus, it sounds like everything else we've heard."

"I overheard a conversation in Wallace's office earlier. It's the right person."

"What conversation?"

Steele didn't feel like answering that question at the moment. He was feeling ill at what he'd just heard.

He couldn't believe it. He just couldn't.

"What time was the conversation?" Andre asked. "We can pull it out of the recordings."

Steele shook his head. "You don't need to."

Syd opened her mouth to argue, but he cut her off. "I know who they've hired."

"This is great!" she said, her eyes filled with joy.

Funny, he didn't feel that way. He was actually sick to his stomach.

Unaware of his turmoil, Syd continued making plans. "All we have to do now is keep an eye on this guy, and when the time comes, we arrest him."

"It's not that simple, Syd," Steele said, his throat tight.

"Of course it is."

"No, it's not."

Nonplussed, she frowned at him.

"Did you ever study Russian history in school?" he asked her.

"Of course."

"Do you remember what the name Stalin means?"

Her frown deepened. "Why is that important?"

"It means 'steel,' " Carlos said.

Steele nodded slowly. "Yeah. That contractor on the phone . . . he's my father."

Sixteen

Syd felt her jaw drop as Steele headed for the door and left the van. She glanced to Carlos, who whistled low.

"Man, that's harsh," he said quietly.

Andre nodded. He looked up at Syd. "I think we should replace Steele. I don't see how he can complete the mission when he's this emotionally involved."

She agreed. Emotions and their kind of work had no place together. In fact, to tangle the two was most often a death sentence.

Her heart heavy for Steele, she left the van to follow him.

He was steadily making his way across the lawn, toward the natural science portion of the Smith. She quickened her steps to catch up to him.

"Josh?" she said, pulling him to a stop. "You okay?"

A tic started in his jaw as he stood there. Instead of looking at her, he was looking at the museum. "You know, my dad brought me here when I was thirteen. All I wanted was to look at the dinosaur bones, but he dragged me up the hill to the Vietnam War memorial and showed me the name of his older brother, who'd died over there."

He looked at her, and those dark eyes scorched her with their pain. "He made me read every single name on that wall and told me that God, country, and duty were all that mattered in life. You do your duty, and you never betray your honor. To break that code dishonors every name on the monument, and it spits in their faces and on their memories. God damn it, Syd, how could he do this now? How could that man become a contract killer?"

Syd ached for him as she pulled him into her arms and held him. "Maybe it wasn't him."

His arms held her close as he lay his head on her shoulder. "I know the sound of his voice, Syd. Even when it's distorted. He's my father. It was him. Those were his words. It was his cadence and method. He always loved Stalin and the man's methods. If he had to choose a code name, that would be it."

She squeezed him tight, wanting to ease the agony she heard in his voice. But she didn't know how. Honestly, she didn't think anything could ever ease the pain of this moment. Dear Lord, how would she feel if she were in his shoes?

"Don't worry, Josh. It's over for you. We'll take it from here."

He shook his head as he pulled back to stare down at her. "No. God. Country. Duty. I signed on for this, and I will see it through."

"But —"

"No buts, Syd. You can't arrest him until he makes his move on the president."

"You can tell us how to catch him."

"No," he said emphatically. "I want to see this through."

"Are you sure?"

He nodded. "Don't worry. I'm your ace in the hole. There's no one on this planet who knows that man better than me. I know every tactic, every move."

She supposed he did. And that broke her heart. But in that moment, she gained a respect for him unlike anything she'd ever had for any other person.

Lifting his hand, she placed a kiss on the callused palm, then held it to her cheek. If she lived a thousand years, she would never understand the strength of this man.

Steele melted at the sensation of her soft lips on his skin. The sunlight highlighted the reddish streaks in her black hair. God, she was beautiful.

And for a moment, he was lost in those green eyes. He'd never felt like this about anyone else. He was hot, yet chills spread over him.

"I won't let you down, Syd. I promise."

A slow smile spread over her face before she pulled him into her arms again for a quick hug. "I know."

She let go and pulled back. He felt the sudden emptiness of his arms, and it went through him like a knife.

She took his hand and led him back toward the van. But what amazed him most was the fact that even though she let go of his hand to climb back inside, she took it right back.

Andre arched a brow as he saw their joined hands, but he didn't mention it.

The fact that Syd would do something like that when he knew how much she hated the thought of anyone knowing they'd been together warmed him.

"Okay," Syd said as she looked back at Steele. "What do we need to do?"

Steele rubbed his chin as he went into sniper mode. "We need the president's agenda."

Carlos turned around to look at him. "We don't have the route from the airport."

385

"We don't need it. My father won't hit him in a motorcade. You can't see through the darkened windows to your target. I need to know what he's planning to do while he's here."

"There's a reception to be held day after tomorrow at the embassy, and then there's the meeting with our president and a few other dignitaries the day after that."

Steele's mind whirred. "That's it. The embassy reception. It's big and public, with lots of people to panic and shield him as he gets away. Do you have a layout for the grounds?"

Carlos turned around to pull it up.

"We'll also need the caterer's schedule," Steele said.

All three of them turned to stare at him.

"Why?" Syd asked.

"Because they will know when and where the president will be sitting. They'll know at what point he will enter the room, since they will want to make sure that they don't have any waiters or food there. Best of all, none of their information will be secret. All you have to do is tell them you're with the florist and ask, and they will hand it over."

Andre shook his head. "That's a scary thought."

Syd agreed, but it made sense. "It's always the one thing you overlook that gets you in the end. No one would ever think to look at the catering company as an opening. It's brilliant, Josh."

Carlos handed him a printout of the embassy floor plan, then went to procure the catering schedule.

Steele sat down with the maps so that he could get a good feel for the area. It was a fairly large embassy with a large terrace and good-sized courtyard at the back.

Within a few minutes, Carlos had the additional information. "Dayam. You were right. They didn't even hesitate. We have ten tents that will be set up."

Steele studied the layout carefully. "This is a pain in the ass."

"How so?" Syd asked.

"Too much overhang. You have a balcony, trees . . . linens and decorations. It's going to be hard to line up a shot."

But there had to be one he could take. There was always some overlooked weakness that could be exploited.

He looked back at the schedule. There wasn't a speech prepared. The president would be led from his office through a narrow corridor, then out to a table in the northernmost tent to eat lunch with the bigwigs.

This was tricky, but as he examined it, he

realized that one place should give a good vantage point.

"What's right here?" He pointed to the building behind the embassy.

Syd looked over his shoulder. "It's a fancy bed and breakfast."

Steele shook his head. It figured. "That's it, then. He'll be taking the shot from one of those rooms."

Andre immediately grabbed the phone and dialed the bed and breakfast.

Steele took the phone from him. "Hi," he said to the clerk after she answered. "This is Joseph Dzhugashvili, and I have misplaced my confirmation number. I was supposed to check in day after tomorrow . . ."

Syd was amazed by his calm facade. Damn, the man was a natural at this.

But as she watched him, she realized that he wasn't happy.

"Are you sure? I should be booked. My assistant made the reservation. Could you check to see if it's under the name of either Steele or Stalin? Yes, Steele with an e."

He met her gaze and she could see that it wasn't going down the way he'd hoped.

"Hmm, very well. Thank you for your help." He hung up.

"No reservation?" she asked.

"None."

Andre shrugged. "Maybe he used another name."

"No, he wouldn't have." Steele went back to the layout and studied it again. But the longer he looked at it, the more he was convinced that something was wrong. "The president isn't the target."

Syd rolled her eyes. "Yes, he is."

"No. He's not. He can't be. Not with this itinerary. Someone has their facts wrong."

Now that made her angry. "I don't make those kinds of mistakes."

"And as my father said, we all make those kinds of mistakes, Syd. Trusting intelligence is how Brian ended up with a bullet in his head."

She folded her arms over her chest and narrowed her eyes at him. "Fine. Let's say for one second that you're right, and I'm wrong. Who would the other target be?"

Steele didn't know. His mind was whirring with everything as he tried to sort through this. "Andre? Didn't you say you could pull the conversation I overheard earlier?"

He nodded. "I just need the time the call was made."

"About two hours ago, from Wallace's cell phone."

While Andre moved to work on it, Steele returned to the sheets.

Syd leaned against his back to read over his shoulder. "Are you sure he couldn't have used another name to make the reservation?"

"No," he said in a distracted tone. "I know my father. Believe me, when it comes to stuff like this, he isn't that creative."

Even so, Syd wasn't so sure he wasn't mistaken. She believed in her facts. "What about here?" she said, pointing to the building next door to the B and B. "Couldn't he use that one?"

Steele shook his head as he reached for the caterer's sheet. "There'll be a portable cocktail cart there."

"But they'll be moving it."

"Not when the president is announced. They'll wait until he's seated. You don't take a shot when someone could sneeze the instant you pull the trigger and get their head blown off by mistake. Remember, one shot, one kill."

"Hey," Andre said. "I think I have it. . . . Is this the conversation?"

Syd looked up as it started playing.

"Hello, Mr. President. It's good to hear from you."

"Greetings, Mr. Wallace. I just wanted to verify that everything is as we dis-

cussed earlier with the party. It is to be a grand affair, is it not?"

"Yes, yes, we have everything arranged. I have my best contractor for your case. Stalin has been briefed and will be standing by to ensure your safety."

"And you are sure he understands what his duty is?"

"Yes, sir."

"That is good. You know, in my country, Stalin was a hero. He was a god. He did what was necessary to protect his people, no? Let us hope that this man lives up to his name. I have been assured that the amount we have agreed upon will be wired into the account after the event. I sent the second deposit in this morning, as you requested."

"Very good," Wallace said. "The wire transfer for the balance is to take place within three hours after our services are rendered."

"Excellent. I have to say that you have indeed lived up to your company's reputation. I now know why you have been so highly recommended to me. It is sad that in this world such things are needed. That we must hire people such *as Stalin to protect us. I wish that one day the world would be a peaceful place for all. Don't you agree?"*

"Yes, sir. We'll see you in two days. Have a nice flight."

Steele snorted. "Sounds innocuous enough, doesn't it? God, I hate this business."

Syd rolled her eyes at him.

"Andre," he said, raising his voice. "Play the Stalin part again."

Syd listened carefully. "Why would he be hiring APS to protect him when his son has hired them to kill him?"

Steele went ramrod stiff. "Do you have any calls from the son to APS?"

"Yes."

"Syd," he said slowly. "Think about this. Are you sure you have data coming from the son to APS? Or were you just told that he had contacted them, and you have data showing a call from their capitol to the APS offices?"

Suddenly, she wasn't so sure. "What are you thinking?"

"There's no shot for the president at this event. And you guys know the doublespeak. Listen to that call again."

Once more Andre piped it through.

Syd listened carefully once more. "Okay, I know it's them playing nice, nice, but what are you hearing that I don't?"

Steele's expression was hard and cold. "What I'm hearing isn't the son hiring APS to kill his father. What I hear is the father hiring them to kill his son."

Seventeen

Syd shook her head at Steele's words. No . . . surely not. "It's not possible. What kind of father would ruthlessly set his own son up to be executed on foreign soil?"

He snorted. "Stalin. Remember? His son was captured and held during World War II. The Germans tried to exchange him, and Stalin refused. He sacrificed his son for the greater good of his people and was thought to be a hero." He glanced to Andre. "Play that last bit one more time for the lady."

She listened as the president spoke. . . .

"Excellent. I have to say that you have indeed lived up to your company's reputation. I now know why you have been so highly recommended. It is sad that in this world such things are needed. That we must hire people such as Stalin to protect us. I wish that one day the world would be a peaceful place for all. Don't you agree?"

She cursed under her breath. Steele was right, and she had missed it. Man, the president was cold-blooded. But then, in the world of politics, she had seen far harsher things than this, so why it surprised her, she didn't know.

"Where would they shoot for the son?" she asked Steele.

"I don't know. His schedule isn't here for the caterers."

Carlos scratched his chin. "We know the son smokes, right?"

Syd nodded.

"Where would he go for a cigarette?" Carlos and Steele said simultaneously.

Steele grabbed the layout again. "You would head out a side door, away from the party, so that Daddy wouldn't get mad at you."

"But there are multiple doors," Syd said, looking over his shoulder. "How do you know which one?"

"We guess."

Suddenly, she didn't like his humor anymore. "I was being serious."

"So am I. He could head out of any of them. The only way I know to stop it is to follow him and keep him from leaving the building or nearing a window."

"You know," Andre said, "he's probably

right. I doubt Steele's father would shoot him." His gaze went meaningfully to Steele, who laughed.

"You don't know my father. Trust me, he wouldn't hesitate to put a bullet in my head if I got in his way."

Syd would like to think he was kidding, but the tone of his voice said he meant every word of it. She reached out and lightly stroked his arm. "I'll go in and follow the son."

Steele shook his head. "You hired me to do this. At the end of the day, I'm a Steele, and we see our missions through."

She had to admire him for that. She wasn't sure how she would be feeling right now if she knew she was going in to set up her father. But he was holding up with re-markably grace.

"Then let's set up for it," Andre said. "I'll get to work on the forged invitations. Syd, you two need some wardrobe."

"What about you two?" Syd asked.

"We'll be there," Carlos said. "I'll go in as Secret Service."

Andre arched both brows. "I don't think so. It's your turn to go in as a waiter, and my turn to be Secret Service."

"You were Secret Service last time."

"No, I wasn't. Remember? You went in, and I was the bartender."

Carlos opened his mouth to argue then paused. "Oh, wait. You're right, I was the Secret Service agent last time. Damn. Okay, you be the SS and I'll be the waiter."

Andre crossed his arms over his chest and beamed.

Steele laughed. "You people seriously scare me."

"We scare each other too," Carlos said with a laugh.

That was certainly true enough. Syd pulled at Steele's arm. "C'mon, we have a lot of stuff to take care of. You two get busy, and we'll meet up for dinner."

"You got it," Andre said as he sat down at a laptop.

It wasn't until they were outside the van that Steele pulled her to a stop. "You do realize how many times you've grabbed my hand today, don't you?"

She looked down to see their hands joined.

"For someone who doesn't want anyone to know about us, you're not exactly hiding anything."

Syd cocked her head at that as she continued to stare at her hand tucked inside his much larger one. Steele hadn't said anything to anyone about their being together either time. In fact, he'd gone out of his way to keep them a secret.

Maybe she should learn to trust again, after all. It was hard after being burned, and yet, as she looked up at him, she didn't see a snake waiting to hurt her. She saw a man who had already walked through the fires of hell, and done it with honor and dignity.

Surely such a person wouldn't betray her.

For the first time in a long time, she wanted to trust again. Before she could stop herself, she lifted up on her tiptoes and placed a hot kiss on that delectable mouth.

Steele closed his eyes as he savored the taste of Syd. Her tongue danced with his as he inhaled the sweet fragrance of her hair and breath. She was the most beautiful woman in the world to him, and the heated passion of this kiss set fire to his body.

Reluctantly, he pulled back from her kiss and pressed his forehead to hers. "You know Andre and Carlos can see us, right?"

She smiled a smile that hit him like a fist in his gut. "Let them."

He returned her smile before he pulled her even closer and kissed her again. Honestly, he'd never been the kind of man to be public with a kiss, but at the moment, he didn't care. All that seemed to matter was Syd.

But unfortunately, they had way too much to do to neck like two horny kids in the mall. Hissing in regret, he forced himself to leave that tempting mouth.

"We've got a party to attend, young miss."

"I know," she said before she gave him one last quick, scorching kiss. She sighed as she stepped away. "What will you need?"

"Nothing but a suit."

She nodded. "I can pick up a dress and shoes. It shouldn't take too long, and then . . ." She dropped her gaze meaning-fully to the bulge in his pants.

Steele felt his cock jerk as a rush of excite-ment went through him. "Don't tease me, Syd."

She bit her bottom lip playfully. "Haven't you learned yet that I don't tease?"

God, he was beginning to seriously adore this woman. "How long does it take a woman to buy a dress, anyway?"

She laughed evilly as she started back to-ward their car.

Steele learned a few things that afternoon. The first was that women took an excruciat-ingly long time to find clothes and shoes.

The second was the fact that Syd thought her ass was the size of a movie screen, but honestly, he loved the extra weight on her. He thought her lush curves were sexy as hell, and every time she turned around to give him her back and stick her butt out to ask if the dress made her fat, he thought he'd die from the pain of his erection.

The third was to always say she looked edible, no matter what she tried on, and she'd reward him with a kiss, then fuss at him for lying.

And the fourth was the most important of all . . .

"Josh?" Syd called in a loud whisper as she edged the dressing room door open an inch. "I need help."

He pushed himself away from the rack to move closer to her. "What?"

"The zipper's broken. I think. I can't get the dress off."

Those words almost made him drool. "Okay. Turn around, and I'll unzip it."

She glared at him. "Not out here in public. I don't have a bra on under this, and I don't want anyone to see me." She stepped back into the room.

The no-bra comment put an image in his head that was absolutely cruel, to his way of thinking.

Steele looked around to make sure there weren't any other women in the area before he stepped inside and shut the door. The room was a lot nicer than most of the men's dressing rooms he'd been in. It had a nice padded chair and two mirrors that reflected the two of them.

Syd turned around to give him her back. Steele paused at the sight of her standing in front of him. He had a perfect view of her backside as he took the small zipper in his hands and wrestled with it.

At first it was a stubborn bugger, but he finally got the cloth out from under it. He yanked the zipper down, baring the whole of Syd's back.

That was a mistake.

The minute he saw the pale skin, all he could think about was tasting it.

Syd couldn't breathe as she saw the fire in Steele's gaze. Every hormone in her body fired. All she could do was watch as he gently ran his hand from the small of her back, up to her shoulder. Chills erupted in the wake of his hot touch.

His gaze met hers in the mirror before he pushed the dress off her shoulders and bared her to his hungry stare. It was so strangely erotic to stand naked in front of him with her nipples puckered, her breasts heavy.

He pulled her against him before he slid the dress over her hips. It fell to her feet with a rush as her body throbbed with sudden need. There was something about Steele that always made her hot.

Steele dipped his head down to bury his firm lips against her neck. Syd leaned back with a hiss as his arms came around her to cup her breasts and tease them until she was weak with hunger. She sank her hand in his thick hair while those large, dark hands soothed and teased her.

She'd never done anything like this before, and for some reason she couldn't fathom, she didn't want to stop. She liked being naughty with him. His lips burned her flesh as he kissed his way up and down her neck. He breathed into her ear a second before he ran his tongue over the sensitive flesh there.

She was completely done for, and she knew it. Her body was too revved up to stop him now. All she wanted was a taste of this man.

She turned her head to capture his lips an instant before he lowered his left hand down over her stomach.

Syd ached with expectation as he teased and tormented her with an excruciatingly slow path toward the part of her that was craving his touch. And when he finally cupped her between her legs, it was all she could do not to cry out in relief.

Steele knew what he was doing was completely inappropriate. Hell, he'd never done anything like this before. Someone could come upon them any second, and that knowledge only added excitement to the moment.

His breathing ragged, he moved his hand up enough so that he could sink it beneath her pink satin panties. She trembled in his arms as he brushed his hand through the short, crisp hairs until he could touch the most sensitive part of her.

He drew a sharp breath between his teeth as he felt how wet she was. Oh yeah, this was what he wanted. Pulling back, he watched her face in the mirror in front of them as he sank two fingers deep inside her.

Her grip tightened in his hair as she spread her legs wider for him. His heart raced wildly while she bit her lip seductively and slowly rode his fingers. He loved it when she did that. She wasn't coy or embarrassed. She was a woman who knew what she wanted.

He rubbed his swollen groin against her hip. "I want inside you so badly I can taste it, Syd," he whispered against her ear. But he knew that he couldn't. They didn't have a condom.

So instead he pacified himself with pleasuring her.

Syd couldn't think straight with Steele's hands and lips on her body. All she could do was watch him in the mirrors as he worked magic. Those fingers stroked and pleased until she couldn't stand it anymore.

She had to force herself not to scream as her orgasm claimed her. Steele captured her lips with his while her body spasmed. Still he didn't pull back. He tormented her until every last tremor had been milked from her body. It was only after she collapsed against him that he pulled his hand away.

He smiled tenderly as he cupped her with his hand. "Now that's what I like to see . . . my Syd well sated and purring."

His Syd. Those words should make her angry, but instead there was a strange sense of pleasure inside her. And in truth she was purring. How could she not be?

But then turnabout was fair play. . . .

Licking her lips, she turned around to face him.

Steele had a moment of panic as he saw the determined look in her eyes. That feeling only heightened as she reached for his fly.

"What are you —"

She interrupted his words with a scorching kiss before she unzipped his pants and pushed them down enough that his hardened cock was free. Steele growled deep in his throat as she cupped him in her hand.

She pushed him back against the chair. He stumbled, then landed on it. Before he could recover, Syd pulled his pants down even more on his legs. Licking her lips, she eyed his cock with a seductive intent that had him hotter than he'd ever been before.

He didn't dare breathe as she spread his thighs wide and placed her body between his knees. He'd never seen anything sexier than that in his life.

She yanked his shirt up high on his chest, then ran her hands over him, teasing him. Her breath fell against his erection as she dipped her head to tease his nipple with her tongue.

He could swear he saw stars as intense pleasure went through him.

Syd wanted to laugh in triumph at the sexiness of Steele at her mercy. She inhaled the musky scent of him as she trailed her lips down his chest toward his navel.

He arched his back as he watched her carefully.

She glanced up at him and reveled in the look of pleasure on his face. He was always so kind, so careful to make sure she had her pleasure first. He really was a gentleman — in every sense of the word.

Wanting to make him happy too, she smiled at him an instant before she lowered her head and took him into her mouth. Syd moaned at the salty taste of him as she gently teased him with her tongue.

Steele sank his hand into her hair as he watched her in the mirror. He could see every nuance of her pleasuring him. She was naked except for the panties that he hadn't removed.

Why hadn't he removed those?

Even so, it was the most incredible moment of his life. Nothing had ever felt better than her mouth on him. Her hand massaged his sac as her tongue worked magic on his body.

And when he came, he ground his teeth to keep from making a sound. But it was hard . . . damn hard.

Syd didn't pull away as he shuddered around her. Instead, she took her time, making sure to give him just as much satisfaction as he had given her.

When she finally pulled back, the little smile on his face warmed her completely.

She licked the taste of him from her lips as an awful jealous thought sought to ruin this. Steele's earlier words came back to haunt her with a vengeance.

Steele frowned at her as if he sensed her sudden mood change. "What?"

Don't say it. . . . But it was out before she

could stop it. "Am I better than your fiancée was?"

He looked a bit dazed. "Huh?"

She pulled back. "I know it was stupid. I was just wondering how I rated. Never mind. Forget it."

As she stared to move back, he stopped her. Those dark eyes scorched her with sincere heat. "Baby, you're the best I've ever had."

Those words thrilled her. "Thank you, Josh."

He inclined his head to her an instant before he kissed her. He pulled back with a grin. "Of course, I might have to have another go-round just to make sure that I was right."

She shook her head at him. "You are so bad."

"Yeah, but you love that about me."

And in that moment, she realized something. He was right. She did love that about him.

They didn't say much that night as they prepared for the president's arrival. They checked and double-checked every bit of data, and the more they looked at it, the more she was convinced that Steele was right about who the real target was.

How could they have mistaken the fact that the contract was for the son and not the father?

But the recriminations died as the afternoon of the party arrived.

They arrived as a couple to find Andre already in place as an agent. Steele looked impeccable in his black suit with a red silk tie, while she wore a simple black dress with pearls and conservative heels . . . just in case she needed to run after someone.

"Remember," Syd said in Steele's ear as she straightened his tie. "They're from Uhbukistan, not Ooga-Booga Land."

"King Oompa-Loompa, gotcha."

She rolled her eyes at him before she stepped back. Neither the president nor his son were there yet.

Where could they be?

"President's in the study with his son," Carlos said in a very low tone as he came up behind her with a tray of wineglasses. "Kid didn't look happy to be there."

"I wonder if he found out," Syd said without moving her lips as she reached for a glass.

Steele cleared his throat. "Can Andre get in to check on them?"

"No," Carlos said under his breath before he moved on.

Steele let out a sigh. "Well, that ended that idea." He glanced toward the door that separated the banquet area from the offices, then handed Syd his wineglass. "I feel a sudden need to get lost."

Syd wanted to follow after him, but she knew better. She was already garnering way too much attention as heads came together trying to figure out if she was Angelina Jolie or not — and that was with her hair down. If it wasn't for the fact that she might have to run and shoot, she would've worn her glasses.

Honestly, she felt like having the words *Not Angelina* tattooed on her forehead. But that would only make her stand out more.

So instead of joining him, she stayed back and tried to be inconspicuous as he wandered over to the double doors of the president's office.

Steele walked into the room without preamble. The president, his son, and the guards all looked up at him.

"I take it this isn't the restroom," Steele said jovially. "My apologies, gentlemen."

The son was a short man with dark brown hair and a smarmy look to him. Eurotrash. He'd always hated that term, but it was strangely fitting for this man.

"I feel the need to go relieve myself too,"

he said with a sneer to his father. "Follow me, American, and I will show you the way."

Steele didn't miss the way the president's eyes narrowed on the much younger man. Oh, yeah, no love lost between those two, even though they both shared the same hawkish features.

The son pressed past him and didn't look back as he jerked open the door to the hallway.

Steele excused himself from the president before he followed after him. The son was mumbling in Uhbukistani as he led the way down a narrow hallway toward the bathroom.

"Tell me, American, you have a father?"

"Haven't met anyone yet who didn't."

The younger man laughed. "I like that. I shall have to remember it." He sobered. "Do you like your father?"

This was a little too personal for strangers, and it made Steele damn uncomfortable. "He's all right."

"All right . . . *pricca*. You are lucky, American. My father . . . I have tried to please him, and all he can see are my faults. He thinks the worst of me no matter what I do or say. I give up."

Steele decided to be a little bolder with the conversation. "Well, you know how fathers can be. They want their sons to walk in their footsteps."

"And I have tried repeatedly. But some things, I just can't agree on."

"Such as?"

"His weapons policies. I am hoping that your president will help him understand why it is our country needs to disarm the old Soviet weapons. They are nothing but a magnet to other countries who wish to steal them or buy them so that they can use them against their neighbors. The last thing I want to see is a nuclear bomb detonated in my backyard or anyone else's. I don't know about you, but bullies sicken me."

Steele nodded as he realized just how wrong Syd's information was. This kid had been set up, and the poor bastard didn't even realize it.

This wasn't a man who wanted to sell nukes. This was a man who had his head on straight.

He sighed heavily before he extended his hand out to Steele. "I am Viktor, by the way."

Steele shook his proffered hand. "J.D."

"Nice to meet you, Jaydee. Come. The bathroom is over here."

Steele followed him into the room as he kept watch for anything odd . . . like his father kicking in the door to gun them down. Or something a little more subtle, such as his father entering the room and knifing Viktor in the ribs.

But nothing was setting off his alarms.

They went about their business and didn't speak again until they were leaving the room.

Viktor hesitated in the doorway as he made a little noise of excitement. "Is that the actress who is Lara Croft? You know, Angelina Jolie?"

Steele watched as Syd chatted with a group of women while her gaze casually but thoroughly kept tabs on the other people in the room.

"No. That's my woman," he said, grateful Syd couldn't hear him. No doubt it would piss her off. But honestly, he would love nothing more than to be able to really lay claim to her.

"You're a lucky man, Jaydee," Viktor said before he excused himself and headed off for a small group in the center of the room.

Yes, I am. In more ways than one.

Syd sidled up to him and returned his drink to him. "Learn anything?"

"The kid doesn't want to sell the weapons."

Syd actually choked on her wine. "What?"

"You heard me. I'm beginning to seriously doubt your intelligence, Syd."

"Thank you," she snapped in an angry tone.

Steele cringed as he realized what had just leapt out of his mouth. "I meant your reports, not your brains."

"Uh-huh. Sure you did." But he could hear the amusement in her tone.

She moved to the other side of him. "Any sign of your father?" she asked behind her wineglass before she took a sip.

"Nada." And that concerned him. Where could the old man be? There wasn't really any place for him to set up the shot, which meant he'd have to be in the building somewhere.

But where?

Steele had started to turn around when someone bumped into his injured arm and sent the wine sloshing onto his clothes. He bit back a curse as the Greek ambassador apologized to him.

He glanced over to Syd as his arm burned as if it were on fire. "I have to go back to the bathroom. I'll be right back."

She inclined her head to him. "I'll keep an eye on our guy."

Syd didn't move as Steele wandered off. She watched as Viktor made his way around the room, from small group to small group. He seemed rather personable for a terrorist.

Maybe her intelligence was off.

She rolled her eyes at the bad pun. As Viktor drew near another group, a tall blond woman walked in. Syd felt an instant dislike for the thin, gorgeous creature, who oozed sophistication. She glanced down at her black dress and felt completely hideous in comparison.

What was it with women like the blonde who always made her feel so damn inadequate?

Suddenly, she was glad Steele wasn't here to see this. If he gaped at that woman, she'd have to hurt him.

The blonde took a glass from Carlos before she made her way straight toward Viktor, who had his back to her.

Every male eye in the place followed the woman as she paused behind him and tapped him on his shoulder.

Viktor's eyes widened the instant he turned and saw the stunning creature who had disturbed him. The woman extended her hand and whispered something in his ear that caused him to smile and laugh.

Syd took a deep draught of her wine as she tried not to be ill at the sight of them.

Refusing to watch the mating ritual of the posh and loaded, she glanced around the room for signs of Steele's father.

Steele rubbed at the wine stain on his pants. Of all the times for such a thing to happen, this wasn't it. He let out a disgusted breath as he tossed the towel into the garbage can. He couldn't spend any more time on this.

Still pissed, he left the bathroom and headed back to the party.

He saw Syd the instant he returned. She was a hard one to miss, especially since the sight of her always warmed him. But as he glanced around the room, he didn't see Viktor.

He crossed the room to Syd's side. "Where's our guy?"

She pointed to a corner with her thumb. "Making time with Cameron Diaz over there."

Steele started to give the man kudos until he realized something.

He knew that woman.

Syd frowned as she saw the color fade from Steele's face an instant before he made his way straight toward the tall blond woman.

What the hell was that?

But at least it wasn't attraction. She knew exactly what Steele looked like when something turned him on.

Curious as to what had caused him to look sick to his stomach, she followed after him. As he drew near, the blonde looked up. Her face paled just the same way as Steele's had an instant before she looked about as if she'd been caught in the middle of . . . well, what they'd done yesterday in the dressing room.

The woman rushed for the hallway.

Steele ran after her, with Syd right on his heels. Once they were out of the reception room, Steele stopped in the hall and glared after the woman.

"Tina!" Steele barked in the most commanding tone she'd ever heard. "Don't you dare run from me."

Tina? The name went through Syd like a knife. Tina as in sister Tina?

The woman paused before she turned back toward them. "What are you doing here, J.D.? You're supposed to be in jail."

"And you're supposed to be at UVA in class." He moved to stand just in front of her.

Tina shrugged as if she were trying to pull off nonchalance, but it wasn't working. The girl was nervous. Too nervous. "I was invited to a party. But that doesn't explain how you got here. I thought you were on the run."

Suddenly they heard shouts from the reception area. Someone was calling for an ambulance.

Steele was torn as he heard the panicked cries from the reception area. Damn it! It was a hell of a time for his father to make his . . .

He looked back at Tina as a really bad feeling came over him. She was edging toward the door.

"Oh, God, no," he breathed. "Tina, please tell me you didn't do it?"

Her face blanched again as she ran for the door.

Steele bolted after her. He grabbed her before she could make her exit, and her purse slammed into his arm. Snatching it from her, he opened it to find a small empty glass tube snuggled in with her lipstick, wallet, and compact.

Tina shoved him away and tried to run again, but he caught her.

"Don't make me hurt you, Tina."

Her hazel eyes were filled with panic. "I won't go to jail, J.D. I won't."

Syd swallowed as she realized what was happening. "She's the assassin APS sent?"

Steele nodded as he stared into the face not of a woman, but of the girl he'd spent so much of his life adoring and protecting. Tina had always meant the world to him. "Why, peanut? Why would you do this?"

Anger darkened her eyes as she stared up at him. "Why do you think? I wanted to join the Army like you did, like Dad did. But they wouldn't take me as anything more than a clerk or a truck driver. Daddy trained me just as he trained you, and I'm every bit as good at this as you are."

Her eyes narrowed on him. "Even better, in fact. It wasn't fair that you got to be a sniper while I was relegated to some office somewhere, doing paperwork. I was born to do this."

"Apparently not," Syd said snidely, "since you got busted."

She cut a nasty look at Steele. "It must run in our family."

Steele's face was stoic as he handed the vial to Syd. He was torn between wanting to spank Tina and wanting to protect her from what she'd done. "I don't know what's wrong with Viktor, but my money says this is what's causing him to be sick. Get it to the medics."

"What about Tina?"

He didn't know how to answer that. She

was his sister, and she'd done something so wrong that he wasn't even sure if he should protect her. What was the right thing to do?

But then he knew.

"She's under arrest."

Tears welled in Tina's eyes. "You wouldn't do that to me. You can't."

God. Duty. Country. He didn't have any choice. Sick over that fact, he pulled the handcuffs out of his pocket and snapped them around her tiny wrists. "I never tried to kill anyone, Tina."

"No? You have sixteen confirmed kills on your record, big brother. There's no difference between you and me and what we do."

"You're wrong about that, little girl," he snarled in her ear. But even as he said the words, Syd could see the indecision in his eyes.

"Keep her out of sight," she said before she dashed off with the vial.

She made her way back to the reception area, where Viktor was lying on the floor, writhing in pain. She went to Andre, who was standing over two men trying to help the younger man as the ambulance sirens blared from outside. She pressed the vial into his hand and saw the recognition in his eyes.

The ambulance was just arriving as she

rushed back to Steele to find him and Tina still arguing.

Honestly, she felt like tossing water on the two of them to calm them down.

"Hey, Steele? Enough. If we don't get her out of here, we're all going to have some serious explaining to do. Right now they think Viktor's sick, but it won't be long before they realize it's poison."

Inclining his head to her, Steele looked less than amused as he grabbed Tina's arm and hauled her down a back hallway that led to a side entrance reserved for the help. It wasn't until they were out of the building that he finally slowed his long, angry strides.

"Get her in the van," Syd said, "before someone sees the cuffs."

"I'd rather beat her."

"Beat her later."

He glared at Syd before he complied. He placed Tina down roughly on one of the seats. Tina sat stiffly, her entire body rigid as she glared at her brother.

"I can't believe you'd do this to Mom and Dad," he said between clenched teeth. "How could you?"

"Me?" she snapped. "What about you? Dad won't even go near a military post because of you. He's so embarrassed that he's terrified of running into one of his Army buddies who knows what you did."

Steele clenched his fist as if he'd like to backhand her. "Why would you throw away your entire life for something so stupid?"

Her eyes narrowed on him. "Why did you?"

"I was angry."

"So was I. It's not fair that I can't do what you do because I wasn't born with a dick."

"You watch your mouth."

"Fuck you."

Syd stepped between them. "Okay, children. Stop fighting, or I'm going to put you both in your rooms."

"Who the hell are you?" Tina snapped.

"You don't talk to her like that, Tina. I mean it."

Syd appreciated his defense of her, but she didn't need it. "Don't worry, Josh, I can hold my own. If she wants to tangle with me, I'll be more than happy to kick her skinny little ass."

Tina jerked herself upright. "Try it." But even as she said the words, there was no denying the shame in her eyes.

Steele met Syd's gaze, and she saw the pain inside him. "How many people have you killed, Tina?" he asked quietly.

She looked away from her brother.

But Steele wouldn't let her. He took her chin in his hand and forced her to look at him. "Answer me."

"More than you, less than Dad."

He cursed. "Why?"

"Why did you do it?"

"Because the Army told me to. I was doing my job."

"So was I, J.D. So was I. They were all political targets. None of them were innocent. What I did, I did for God, country, and duty."

"How do you know that?"

She didn't flinch as she stared at him. "How do you? What's the difference between Wallace telling me who my target is and a captain telling you?"

Damn her for her blindness. "Did it never occur to you that Wallace might be lying to you? I talked to Viktor earlier, Tina. He's the one who wants to disarm his country. Not his father. He's the only thing standing in the way of keeping us safe."

To his relief, she actually paled. "What?"

"You heard me."

"No," she breathed. "You're lying. My intelligence showed that Viktor was ready to sell his country out. He was going to kill his father if I didn't kill him."

"Excuse me?" Syd asked.

"His father contacted us to kill him after his father had learned that Viktor had contracted with a group of mercenaries out of Europe to assassinate him at home. The president had sent in a group of soldiers to arrest them, and then he decided an eye for an eye."

Steele exchanged a stunned look with Syd. Were no one's hands clean in this?

"That must have been what Yuri was trying to tell us," Syd breathed, "when he got killed. Damn it!"

Before he could comment, the back door to the van swung open. Syd turned to see Carlos climbing in. He paused as he saw Tina in handcuffs. "Is she our man?"

Steele nodded. "How's Viktor?"

"They don't know yet. But he stands a good chance of surviving, since they can test the vial and see what ails him."

Steele wanted to weep at what his sister had done. And he was angry at her for putting him in this position. How could he live with himself if he put her in jail, when the very mission that would condemn her was the one that had set him free? "Damn you, Tina."

She looked away from him.

"You know her?" Carlos asked.

"She's my baby sister."

Carlos snorted at that. "Hell of a family you got there, Steele. And I thought mine was bad. Anyone in your family not a killer?"

Steele felt his jaw out of joint, but he couldn't blame Carlos for asking. "I don't know. After this, I'm beginning to wonder if I don't have a serial mom."

Tina curled her lip at him. "I wish. She should have beaten you to death with a turkey leg."

Syd had had enough. "Carlos, watch Blondie. I'm taking Steele outside to cool down."

"Gotcha."

Syd literally had to shove Steele out of the van. He paced around outside it like a caged lion. She truly felt for the man and the pain he must be feeling. "Look on the bright side. At least it wasn't your father."

"That's not a bright side, Syd," he said sullenly. "I'd much rather have faced my dad than turn my sister over to the authorities." The torment in his eyes made her ache for him. "You have no idea how horrifying prison is. What it does to you. How can I do that to her?" He raked a tormented hand through his hair. "I'm her brother, Syd. My job is to protect her."

"And you have always done your job, Josh. With dignity and honor."

Funny, he didn't feel that way right now. All he could think of was what this would do to his poor mother. It would kill her.

"I want to know who her targets were."

Syd nodded. "We can find out."

Maybe he could find some solace if Tina wasn't lying to him about who they'd assigned to her.

Syd pulled him into her arms and held him. "It'll be all right."

"How, Syd?"

Syd paused at his question. Odd how a few days ago she hadn't believed in people, or in miracles. But Steele had taught her a few things.

Most of all, he'd taught her to believe in him.

"How, I don't know, Josh. But I have faith."

Steele closed his eyes as he let Syd's embrace ease the fury and pain inside him. It was strange how such a simple act could make him feel better.

He would do what was right by his sister.

But most of all, he intended to do what was right by Syd.

Epilogue

Six months later

Steele sighed as he rolled over with a very naked and well-sated Syd in his arms. His body was sore from their marathon, but he loved the feeling of it almost as much as he loved the woman draped over him.

Joe wasn't happy about the fact that the two of them were living together, but he didn't give a damn what Joe thought.

All that mattered was having beautiful days like this, where he got to wake up to Syd's sweet face.

And better yet, her hot body.

She pressed her cheek to his chest as she traced idle circles over and around his nipple. "That was a nice wake-up call," she said with a laugh.

"Yep. Hard to be irritated on a Monday after that."

She laughed at him before she placed a kiss on his chest, then pushed herself away.

Steele actually whimpered. "Where are you going?"

"Terrorism waits for no one, Josh. We have work to do."

He made a face at her. "Work, work, work. It's all you think about."

She raked a heated look over his body. "Of all people, you know better than that."

Yes, he did.

Thrilled at how much he knew the truth, he followed her into the shower.

Syd didn't speak much as she bathed Steele. They had fallen into an easy relationship that still amazed her. She wasn't a doormat with him. They were partners. Never in her life had she expected to find someone like him . . . and definitely not where she'd found him.

Who knew men like him could be real?

No sooner had they left the shower than she heard a knock on the door. Out of habit, she grabbed her gun and tucked it in the back of her pants before she answered it.

No one was there.

Irritated, Syd shut the door and started away from it. She'd only taken four steps when the knock came again.

She pulled the door open to find a small bouquet of roses on the porch. "What on earth?"

She looked around the yard, but saw no

one. Frowning, she bent down to pick up the roses.

There was no card.

Weird. She closed the door and started away again. And yet again, she'd only gone a few steps when the knocking sounded.

Totally agitated by it now, she snatched the door open to find a small box right where the flowers had been. As she bent over to pick it up, she sensed Steele coming up behind her.

"What'cha got there?" he asked.

She shrugged. As she stared at the box, she realized it looked like a box of chocolates that had already been opened. "I don't know. Maybe I should call a bomb squad or something."

"Hmmm . . ." Steele stepped past her and reached for the lid.

Before she could stop him, he pulled it open.

Syd's heart stopped as she saw a beautiful solitaire diamond ring resting in the center of the chocolates.

"It's definitely for you."

Tears welled in her eyes as she stared at it.

Steele pulled the ring out before he knelt down on the porch in front of her. "Sydney —"

"Yes! I will!" she screamed as she launched herself at him.

He laughed. "I didn't ask the question."

She felt heat creep over her face. "I'm sorry."

He cleared his throat as he took her hand into his and stared up at her with those beautiful dark eyes. "I love you, Sydney, and I don't want to live the rest of my life without you in it. Will you marry me?"

"Hell, yes!"

He laughed as he slid the ring on her finger, then kissed it.

She bent to kiss him when the knocking started again . . . only this time it was from the back door. Cursing in frustration, she marched over to it and ripped the door open to find Tina standing outside in the back-yard.

"Did you accept?"

She held her hand up to show her soon to be sister-in-law. Now she'd just have to think of some way to break it to Steele's father and mother, who were still a little cool toward the two of them.

Neither of his parents really believed that his case had been overturned in the courts. But they were so grateful to have their son listed as an honorable discharge that they didn't question it . . . much.

Tina did a two-thumbs-up before she opened the door wider. "Good, 'cause now you're both late to work. *Huch, huch.* Time's a-wasting, and Joe's going to be mad enough at you two as it is."

Syd laughed at Tina's reference to Joe's memo about agents not fraternizing. "That's okay. If he says anything, I know where we can get some good strychnine."

Tina grimaced at the reminder. But she couldn't really be angry. As Steele had asked, they had looked into her prior contracts and learned that Tina really had chosen her targets with care. She hadn't gone after anyone BAD wouldn't have targeted.

God love the woman, she was a compatriot. That alone was what had made Joe offer her a job.

Syd held her hand up to stare at the beautiful diamond that sparkled on her finger.

"What are you thinking, Syd?" Steele asked as he wrapped his arms around her and pulled her back against him.

"How much I love you."

He kissed her gently on the cheek. "Good. 'Cause however much you think it is, it's nothing compared to what I feel for you. And if you want, you don't have to wear the ring at the office. I know how much you hate that." He started to pull it off her hand.

Syd balled her hand into a fist, trapping his fingers between hers. "You take that ring off, and you'll be limping, Josh Steele. There's nothing about you or us that I would ever want to hide. In fact, I want the world to know exactly how much you mean to me."

Because in the end, she knew he would never hurt her. And that meant more to her than anything else.

The employees of Thorndike Press hope you have enjoyed this Large Print book. All our Thorndike and Wheeler Large Print titles are designed for easy reading, and all our books are made to last. Other Thorndike Press Large Print books are available at your library, through selected bookstores, or directly from us.

For information about titles, please call:

(800) 223-1244

or visit our Web site at:

www.gale.com/thorndike
www.gale.com/wheeler

To share your comments, please write:

Publisher
Thorndike Press
295 Kennedy Memorial Drive
Waterville, ME 04901